BRIGHT SHINING WORLD

BRIGHT SHINING WORLD

JOSH SWILLER

ALFRED A. KNOPF
NEW YORK

THIS IS A BORZOI BOOK PUBLISHED BY ALFRED A. KNOPF

This is a work of fiction. Names, characters, places, and incidents either are the product of the author's imagination or are used fictitiously. Any resemblance to actual persons, living or dead, events, or locales is entirely coincidental.

All rights reserved. Published in the United States by Alfred A. Knopf, an imprint of Random House Children's Books, a division of Penguin Random House LLC, New York.

Knopf, Borzoi Books, and the colophon are registered trademarks of Penguin Random House LLC.

Visit us on the Web! GetUnderlined.com

Educators and librarians, for a variety of teaching tools, visit us at RHTeachersLibrarians.com

Library of Congress Cataloging-in-Publication Data is available upon request.
ISBN 978-0-593-11957-0 (trade) — ISBN 978-0-593-11958-7 (lib. bdg.) —
ISBN 978-0-593-11959-4 (ebook)

Interior design by Ken Crossland

Printed in the United States of America
November 2020
10 9 8 7 6 5 4 3 2 1

First Edition

For Leah

Perhaps the wilderness we fear is the pause
between our own heartbeats, the silent space
that says we live only by grace.

—Terry Tempest Williams

The lamps are different,
But the Light is the same.

—Rumi

PART I

ONE

"RISE AND SHINE, Wallace."

My father woke me with that hard, open-handed push on the face he liked. I blinked awake.

He said, "We're leaving."

I'd been having a dream about trees that could communicate with each other by flying box kites. They discussed the wind. They waved to clouds. Then a pack of aphids, falcons, and men with knives descended on them, and they screamed.

Again.

Why couldn't I just dream about sex?

"It's still dark out," I said.

Dad flicked on the lamp. "Get your stuff together. We've got a long drive."

We were living in a two-bedroom rental with walls made out of stale crackers. None of the overhead lights worked. In the kitchen, duct tape held together two cabinets, three windows, and four drawers. I couldn't tell you if the decrepit white

3

stove was gas or electric, or if it even worked—we'd never turned it on.

"I already packed up the kitchen," Dad said.

That meant he'd grabbed his bottle opener.

"Where we going?" I asked.

"New York."

Shoot. That was a thousand miles away. "I'm presenting my science project third period tomorrow," I protested. "Or today. Whenever it is. With Nicole."

With nods and single-eyebrow raises, my father had approved of Nicole. Maybe mentioning her now would change his mind about leaving and we could stay in Kentucky a little longer. Until the weekend, say, when Nicole and I might go camping along the Cumberland River. Or if not until then, maybe we could stay just one more day, just one, because there was no question in my mind the announcement to Nicole of my sudden departure would lead to emotional last glances, a ride out on the dirt road behind Bueller's pasture to that whispery grove, unbuttoned clothing, breathless quivers, breathful quivers, all different kinds of quivers, and—

"That's not happening," my father said. "The science project."

"You can't wait a day?"

"Let's go."

I sat up. "We're going to present on local pollution. We worked hard on it all afternoon"—actually, we had mostly been fooling around in Nicole's hand-me-down Civic—"about Jackduke and how it's poisoning the river. Did you know not a single black-throated blue warbler has been seen in this county since the plant had that accident? The one right before we got here?"

Dad paused checking through a closet. "Black-throated blue warbler?"

"Black-throated blue warbler. It's like a regular blue warbler but with more black. On the throat part."

I liked Nicole. She was all-county in swimming, had chlorine-bleached hair and lats for days. Sometimes she spoke so fast she lost track of what she was saying, and kissing her felt a bit like an X-wing starfighter diving into the canal in the Death Star—her braces were that stupendous. Yes, she did get a bit weirded out whenever I shared my deep thoughts, and she made her own herbal teas that had pieces of grass floating in them and tasted like butt—but! These kinds of things can be forgiven, and we were almost past the "We shouldn't be doing this" phase of hooking up.

And the next phase of hooking up? The "Let's do this" phase? I'd only been there once, and that was by accident.

"I'm falling in love," I said.

Dad snorted. "You've known her four weeks, Wallace. It's not love."

"It might be."

"You don't even know what love is."

"Well, how can I when you rip it out of my hands?"

Dad was quiet at that. He was filling a trash bag with my clothes. Or perhaps trash—both tended to smell and to collect on the floor of my room. My life: a moldy pile in a Febreze commercial; a garbage bag thrown in the back of a truck; love, crushed by fate.

It was hopeless. I had one thing left to hit him with.

"This is not what Ma would want," I said.

"You're wrong," he countered. "This is exactly what she'd want."

"She'd want me to be alone?"

"She'd want me to do my job."

That's it? Dad hated when I brought up Ma. It was a direct circuit to the pain center of his brain. I'd say to him: "Hey, I had a dream about Ma on a midnight ferryboat," and Dad would grab his head like spiders were laying eggs in there. Then he'd give me a twenty to disappear.

But not this time.

I felt a sudden gust of fear. What the hell was happening in New York?

"AC is cranked," Dad said. "Beef jerky is bought—that gross honey-mustard kind you like. You can sleep in the truck."

It was hard to sleep in the truck. The thumping and jostling of buckled midwestern pavement did not lend itself to sleep. The thoughts of where we were going and what I was leaving behind did not lend themselves to sleep, either. Before my iPhone died somewhere in Indiana, I tried out a few texts to Nicole, explaining my sudden departure: witness protection, a fatal illness from a secret space wormhole mission, vengeful Congolese warlords, leprosy (non-contagious, don't worry), a retaliatory raid on the Westboro Baptist Church. But I didn't send any of them. I'd learned from previous experiences of leaving towns abruptly (thanks, Dad) that continuing communication after a sudden departure just made things messy.

I knew that regardless of what I wrote, I would never hold Nicole again. A quiet exit was a clean exit.

Cool.

I looked out the window at the truck headlights slicing across bleached-out billboards. *Our Happy Meals come with apple slices! Our lawyers sue with a smile! You've never seen antiques like these antiques! You will never know love, Wallace!*

Cool, cool, cool.

Across the cab, my father smoked like a busted piston. As we crossed the state line into Ohio, I leaned my head against the window and watched the curtain lower forever on a short, reasonably happy, and sexually promising chapter of my life.

"No!"

I jerked awake to Dad talking on his phone. To the moment when everything began.

"How long ago? What was the last measurement?"

I looked over. Dad sat hunched against the driver's-side door, phone pressed against his face.

"Sorry, sir. I didn't mean to shout. That's not what I would have—"

I carefully lowered my head back to the window.

"Yes, sir," he said, his voice quieter, strained. "You're right. You have been patient. We are close. A full-strength test could—"

I coughed involuntarily from the air's carbon monoxide

content, and Dad whipped his head around to look. I rubbed my nose, kept my eyes shut, pretended to be asleep—not easy with my nerves on edge.

"Good idea. It would be nice to have Marguerite there," Dad said. "Just to head off any issues."

Pause.

"Right, sir. There won't be issues. Right. Thank you."

He snapped his phone shut, hit the steering wheel, opened his lighter, lit a cigarette, dropped the lighter, grabbed the lighter, dropped the cigarette, hit the steering wheel again.

Then to himself he whispered: "Shit. He's going for it."

Now would be a good time to explain exactly what my father does for a living. Except that I can't. Ronald Cole works for Jackduke Energy, and far as I can tell, he's like a superstar engineer who parachutes in for emergency repairs when all the locals are out of their league. Like one of those wild-eyed movie geniuses who fix spaceships orbiting Mars from their bedroom.

Except he's not an engineer. So it's more like he's a business-consultant genius who parachutes in when there's an administrative breakdown. Like Steve Jobs saving Apple, both times. Except my father knows squat about running a business. He doesn't even own a laptop. His ATM code is *1234.* And he definitely doesn't own a parachute.

What I can say is that Lawrence Hoch, Jackduke's CEO—a man who oversees a workforce of tens of thousands and, according to websites that obsess over such things, has the kind of wealth that buys Caribbean islands and moves them if they're not exactly where he wants them to be—this man calls my father direct when he has a problem at a power plant. And my father goes and fixes it.

How does he fix it? Somehow. That's how.

This sounds vague and sinister, but that's only because it is vague and sinister.

Alternate theory: My father doesn't actually do much at the power plants. He's a temp, an interim coach, the guy who comes in for a few weeks and keeps everyone from melting down while the fired coach slinks off and the CEO negotiates to get the hotshot new coach hired, the one with the Zen management techniques and walking desks and motivational videos clipped from action movies.

Except my father has never, far as I can tell, said kind and meltdown-preventing words. It's not his thing. And he doesn't own a suit.

Are you starting to get the picture? There is no picture. The man is one of those subatomic particles that disappear when you look directly at them.

He's also my only family.

And if you're wondering why I, a curious lad with time on his hands, didn't just ask my father directly what he does, well, I have, many times. He didn't answer.

Here's an example, from somewhere in southern Ohio, an hour after that phone call.

Q (this is me, I'm the *Q*): Soooo, so tired. Just waking up here. Whew, what a nap. . . . So, New York, eh? What's happening there?

A (Dad, obvs): Work.

Q: Ever thought of taking a break from work until the end of the school year? I'll be graduated then.

A: No.

Q: Working remotely? That's big now.

A: No.

Q: What about work is so important?

A: The work part.

Q: Care to elaborate?

A: No.

(Note that *A* has the warmth and eloquence of a fire door. Hence, the new and subtle approach *Q,* an adroit improviser and keen reader of emotional cues, takes below.)

Q: Father, do you hate me?

A: Come on, Wallace.

Q: Yes or no? It's a straightforward question.

A: It gives me a headache.

Q: Most people would say love involves care for the person being loved. Ergo, from your lack of same, one might deduce subconscious hatred.

A: Is that a question? Someday you'll understand. You know, this kind of talk is why principals are always on your ass.

(No answers, no girlfriend, all out of honey-mustard beef jerky, *Q* is now actively trying to give *A* a headache.)

Q: Here's a question: What's the point of my life?

A: Oh, God.

Q: Him? Surprising. Or her. They. I don't mean to assume.

A: That's not what I meant. We're going to stop soon. We'll rent a movie. I'm going to focus on driving now, okay?

Q: It's not that hard. The brake is on the right.

A: It's not— Okay, Wallace.

Don't drink and drive or these children will die! Sex leads to pregnancy! Free pretzels with a large sub! You'll die alone. Alone!

We stopped at a motel on the strip of Pennsylvania that nestles between Ohio and New York like a deflated penis. Our room smelled like it was shaken out of an ashtray. Dad reneged on a promise to rent a Keanu movie, and I fell asleep to him smoking and watching a news report about natural disasters. It had been an unprecedented fall everywhere: in Vermont, a flock of geese fell out of the sky, stone dead; in Florida, a pod of dolphins crawled onto a country-club fairway in a mass suicide. All of Siberia was on fire, apparently. This had never happened before and we're all going to die, but also a bear was walking around on its hind legs in suburban New Jersey. Just like a furry person!

I woke up sweating. We were back on the road by six. In New York State by seven. At nine, we switched off the interstate to a two-lane road and hit hill country, and as we drove through a light rain, we were often higher than the towns we passed through, and we looked down on gas stations and repair-shop roofs. I felt like a tornado, picking a target. I flung buildings down valleys and over ridges, and future people knew I had been there. Dad's truck was an old Ford with a duct-taped bench seat, and was so large it made regular-sized cars cower out of the passing lane and onto the rumble strip. Puddles sounded long *sheeeeeeits* as we drove through them much too fast. As we sped through western New York, Dad glowered and did that I'm-exhaling-out-the-side-of-my-mouth-into-this-sliver-of-a-window-opening-so-you-can't-blame-any-future-lung-troubles-on-me thing.

Our destination, he did share, was a small town in the Finger Lakes called North Homer. It had been named by classics professors, not Simpsons fans. Jackduke had a power plant two miles outside it.

"I read that Jackduke is the second-largest polluter in New York State," I said.

"It's worse in China," Dad countered.

"What does anything I just said have to do with China?"

"India is just as bad. Not a lot of people know that."

"The maple-sap harvest in the northeastern states has declined an average of eight percent a year since 2000."

"In Delhi, they throw their trash right in the street."

"You work for Satan."

"Wallace, for Christ's sake. I work for a company that provides a tangible, essential product for people. Light for their homes, heat to cook their meals. I'm not saying Jackduke is perfect. But there's worse."

The blur of trees by the road cleared for a moment and opened up into a broad field. It was October, but shirt-sleeve weather, and the fields were still bright green. The trees were, too. Even with the rain, it was warm.

We passed a sign saying we'd reached North Homer's town line. The speed limit dropped to thirty. Nothing else changed, no houses or stores, just more trees and rain, blurring into a green smudge.

"So, what's the issue with this plant?" I asked.

"I don't know yet," Dad answered.

I took a deep breath. "I heard you talking on the phone in Indiana. Was that Mr. Hoch?"

Dad stiffened like he'd been punched in the ribs. Bit his cigarette so hard it bent and touched the scruff on his chin. My legs started buzzing. I don't think I'd ever so directly caught him in a lie.

"You shouldn't eavesdrop on my conversations," he said.

"We're in a truck. It's kind of hard not to."

"It's just that the less you know, the better."

"Then, trust me," I said, "I'm in great shape."

Dad unrolled the window, spit out his chewed-up cigarette, lit another. "Okay. Okay. There's some things I can share. Listen closely."

"I was going to listen from a medium distance, if that's all right."

"Do you want to hear this?"

"Yes, go ahead."

He exhaled smoke. "Look, North Homer is a nice little town. Has a lake. Woods."

"A lake *and* trees? I don't believe you."

"Wallace. I need you to keep a low profile. Don't go around annoying people, getting in fights."

"Oh, I never do that."

Dad exhaled again, squeezing his forehead, trying to knead out a pain inside. "There's a situation here. An outbreak."

"An outbreak? What? Like measles?"

"Sort of." His voice was heavy, cornered.

"Sort of measles?"

He mumbled. "Hysterics."

"I'm sorry, what?"

"Hysterics. There's an outbreak of hysterics in North Homer. It's a very rare mental illness. Basically, people contract it in groups. They catch it from each other, like the flu. It was much more common in the old days. Though I suppose you could make the argument that it's just as common now, only contained online. Hell, now that I think about it, maybe there's more of it these days. The whole virtual world is rampant hysteria, you could say." He took a deep drag off his cigarette. "But the lake is supposed to be really pretty."

It took me a minute to get my mind around what he was saying. And actually it got only halfway around, and then it stalled out. Stalled out right on the train tracks.

"Wait, what? This town is a Twitter feud?"

"No. Nothing like that. Nothing that bad. It's hysteria. And it's not everyone. Just a few people. Actually, it's, uh, pretty much contained to the high school."

"But I'm going to the high school!"

"Yes," Dad said. "Four kids got it last week. It's not an ideal situation."

"You took me out of a nice high school with a nice girlfriend who I dearly and truly love to go to a school with hysterical people? Holy shit, that's *not* ideal."

He shrugged. "I didn't have a choice."

"There's always a choice."

"Not always. You'll learn that. And you weren't in love. There was nothing special about that relationship."

"Well, that makes me feel better," I said.

Dad slowed down for a traffic light, flicked his cigarette out the window. It was raining hard, so the view, our first of downtown North Homer, was of a gray smudge, as opposed to the previous green one. "When you get older, Wallace," he said, "you'll realize how insignificant all the romance stuff is. The quality of your life doesn't depend on love. It depends on one thing and one thing only."

"Emotional support in childhood?"

He turned to me. His eyes were burned out, dark, done talking. "Survival."

The light changed, and he accelerated through the intersection, cutting off a Prius. I sank down in my seat.

My life: a truck full of secondhand death, a gray smudge, a school full of hysterical people.

Brilliant.

TWO

DAD WAS AWOL that first night in North Homer. He was gone the next two nights also, which happened to be the weekend. He was gone when I woke up each morning and gone all day, reappearing around eight each evening to drop off a pizza before heading back to the plant. In the mornings, some kind of egg sandwich in a box was on the kitchen table. If he slept, I didn't know when or where. I wasn't surprised. This was his normal behavior when he was summoned to a new Jackduke plant.

I stayed in the small apartment that had been arranged for us. Mostly I stared at the ceiling. It was tin, covered in flaking yellow paint, water stains, and manic, disoriented ants that argued a lot. It was on the first floor of a duplex; the top floor was empty. The duplex was one in a row of about five; far as I could tell, all the others were empty as well. On the street, heavy old oaks dominated unkempt lawns and weed-filled sidewalks. Not a lot of cars passed, and the ones that did were outnumbered by pickups, three to one. Nobody was out walking.

Which brings me to the most important thing about the view from the apartment—I didn't see any hysterical people. True, I wasn't exactly sure what they would look like; I imagined something quick and lethal, like rabid squirrels or movie zombies, and not the staggering, can-barely-walk zombies but the ones who hurdle cars and climb on top of each other to dismember the brave families defending the walls. But nope. Didn't see any of those.

I did get bored. I didn't know anyone in the entire town or state and didn't have a working phone. Masturbation took heroic effort I wasn't up to. Well, once. Okay, twice. Okay, never mind. I rehearsed conversation starters to use if I met hysterical students at school but couldn't think of any besides "How many fingers am I holding up?" "Please don't bite off my face," and "Do you ever feel life is so pointless it drives you insane? Oh, I see."

Evenings, I lay in the bathtub and considered the state of my life, uncovering much evidence that it had missed its potential and become sad and toxic, like Texas.

To wit: I didn't have any friends. I was in a town full of an indeterminate type of zombie. I had two pairs of jeans and I once went three months without cleaning either, and nobody noticed. I had hair that looked unwashed no matter how much I washed it. I had a build you could describe, if you're feeling charitable, as going to fill out. (I do have a list of all the places I will be adding muscle. When I'm done, it'll be sweet.) The whole package has been described to me as decent but reckless-looking, like the guy in the teen movie who dies doing drugs in the first scene so that the main characters can learn important lessons about not doing drugs.

That's me, more or less. Doomed and in need of a shower.

And you know what? Who cares?

Why? Because the world is a fucking shitshow.

Where do you even start? Seabirds hatch on Pacific beaches and in the ecstasy of their chickatude eat the most colorful plastic they can find. Fad drugs too new to have names are swallowed by college students by the fistful, soupifying their brains. Deer gnaw off their legs to escape forgotten traps. Deep coronary arteries store undigested Happy Meals. That girl will drive into a semi while texting, "I'm on my way, can't wait ☺!" At the playground, a mother does not hear her baby crying, because she is too busy checking Facebook on her phone. Everyone has a happier life than her. They go on vacations to resorts that serve cocktails right in the pool! They take selfies behind waterfalls!

And men in suits swear to us they have identified the source of the shitshow and that carpet bombing said source will eliminate it, and so our missiles soar across the oceans on missions of peaceful shit-cleaning and explode in impoverished desert villages on the other side of the world. Our God says your God is a fake God, suckers! Eat this! But oh! The fake God does not agree! He goes to a shopping mall in Atlanta and blows himself up. Ball bearings in the perfume counter! Blown-off limbs in the jeans rack! The forests on fire!

Do you see it? How can anyone not see it at this point?

* * *

My father did emerge on Monday morning for a half hour to take me to North Homer High School for my first day there. He'd been working hard all weekend, and his dark eyes were ringed in black underneath his black company ball cap. He looked like a shadow that had gotten roughed up in an alley by other, darker shadows.

The school was a dead brick turtle in the bottom of a valley, hemmed in by hundred-year-old maple trees, untrimmed hedges, and incongruously pristine athletic fields. There were signs out front for the upcoming homecoming football game and a PTA meeting, as well as for spray foam insulation and less restrictive gun laws. At the front entrance, Dad fished a crumpled twenty out of his pocket.

"Make friends," he said.

"Good thinking," I said.

"Be nice to your teachers."

"Smart. You could write a book on parenting."

"Got it."

"That's what you could call it. *Got It: Parenting with Less,* by Ronald Cole."

"I'm late for work."

"That works, too. *I'm Late for Work.*"

"Enough, Wallace."

"*Enough.* Perfect. Bestseller!"

We'd stopped at a Dunkin' Donuts drive-thru on the way to the school, and he'd gotten us a couple of sausage-donut things that combine the least healthy parts of each. He'd also gotten himself a cup of coffee as long as his arm. He had to lift the cup in both hands to drink. Mentally he was already back at the plant—if he'd ever even left.

I got out of the truck.

"Hey," he said.

I turned back.

"Any strange behavior, you steer clear, okay?"

"Dad, you just defined high school."

He sighed deeply. "It's for your own good, Wallace."

Morning I spent in the principal's waiting room, waiting for the mean-eyed secretaries to put together my schedule. Lunch I passed alone in the cafeteria, eyeing the students for signs of zombie outbreak while gathering the courage to eat. I could not find the courage. The four ashy-colored piles on my tray reminded me of a recent documentary on pollution in West Virginia. In the documentary, dead fish floated down rivers past clumps of tires while white male politicians said the water was perfectly fine. It came out of the trailer-park faucets on fire. On the cafeteria walls, white-teethed kids with ironed jeans ate apples and said no to drugs. Next to the walls were round tables ringed with hard plastic chairs; in the center of the room were long rectangular tables. The round tables were where the cool students ate: the boys who could grow facial hair and had muscle definition and knew that punching each other on the arm as hard as they could was the height of comedy; the girls who threw themselves, laughing, into a friend's lap, imprinting their bra straps into various male and female spank accounts. Meanwhile, in the center of the room, flannel-wearing acne farmers mind-melded with their phones.

That's where I ate.

It was normal enough, same as any other high school cafeteria, save for a tension in the air, hard to put my finger on. When students looked around, it wasn't to see who was watching them but who needed to be watched. A lot of them had apparently decided that person was me—especially two boys sitting at the next table. Shoot. One was pale, skinny as a stop sign, with stringy blond hair and a Pac-Man T-shirt; the other, nearly a foot shorter, had a regular build, an aggressively unattractive starter mustache, and elaborate forearm tattoos.

"Yo," the skinny one said.

I ducked my head.

"Yo," he said again. "Yo."

I stayed down. You can't talk to just anyone on your first day.

Then: "You're new."

A sharp female voice. I looked up. A tall girl with an unbuttoned letter jacket, dark hair, knife-edge cheekbones, an arrowhead-straight nose. Her features looked like they had been assembled in a weapons lab to conduct clandestine missions in failed states with surgical precision. It was intimidating.

"Where are you from?" she asked. "Hello? Can you hear me?"

It took me a minute to gather myself. "I can," I said.

"I asked where you're from."

"Everywhere," I answered.

"Excuse me?"

"Like the wind, you could say. Where do you want me to be from? Name a state. Go ahead."

The tall girl didn't name a state. She blinked warily, like I was a mission target. "Do you want to be left alone?" she asked.

"No. Sorry," I said. "Have a seat. If you want."

Surprisingly, she sat. Beneath the red-and-black letter jacket with a tennis racket on one shoulder and a giant *C* on the other she wore a tight, expensive-looking gray top that scooped low on her chest. Beneath that everything appeared appropriately shaped and in place—I checked. She checked me out, and her look said there was not much to check. That was fair.

Her name was Megan Rose. I introduced myself.

"Want to buy a raffle ticket?" she asked. "Five dollars for one, three for ten."

So that's why she was talking to me. Of course. "Pass," I said.

"You can pay me later, if you need to."

"Those things are always rigged. The best friend of whoever's running it wins."

Her eyes narrowed. "I'm running it."

"Oh. Well. Good for you."

"The raffle's for prom."

"I'm not going to prom."

"Why aren't you going?"

"I won't be here."

"Where will you be?"

I swept my hand through the air. "Everywhere, as I said. Where the wind takes me."

Megan Rose grimaced. "Are you on drugs?"

"No. You offering?"

I cursed silently—I'd honestly been trying to not be aggravating. And I was failing hard, I could tell. It was unintentional. I was an unintentional aggravator. I blamed my father—pissing him off was often the only way to keep our conversations interesting.

I hastily explained that my father moved a lot for work and that I'd been to no fewer than fourteen different high schools. Had lived in twenty-two different states altogether, if you went further back.

"Twenty-two? For real?" asked Megan Rose.

I nodded. "A couple of them twice. And don't ask me about Texas."

"That sounds like a lonely life."

"Well. There are some benefits. You develop a refined palate for Egg McMuffins. You save money on sports jerseys, because you're never anywhere long enough to become a fan. You learn the actual names of interstates, not just their numbers. The Turquoise Trail. The Beartooth Highway. The Vince Lombardi Memorial Rest Stop. You see everything there is to see in this fine country. Nothing ever surprises you."

Megan Rose's eyes opened wide. "So you saw the trees?"

"The trees?"

"You saw them? What they've been doing?"

"I'm not sure I'm following you," I said. "What are the trees doing? Changing color?"

Megan Rose twisted her lips, disappointed but unsurprised. "You haven't seen everything. Not even close."

Not knowing what to say, I took a nervous glance around. A lot of students in the cafeteria were watching us. All of them, pretty much. When I turned back, Megan Rose was staring down at her lap. A long minute passed, during which she didn't look up once but appeared actually to have entered a place deep inside herself, a place too deep for conversation or even basic manners. It was like she was free-diving her mind.

That was a dangerous sport, I knew. Sometimes people didn't come back.

What the hell was this?

Lost in worries that I had stumbled onto a hysterical person, I put a spoonful of the food on my tray in my mouth. It tasted like a road puddle.

Just then, a squadron of ten students in school colors trooped into the cafeteria. One of them did that fingers-in-the-mouth, ear-drum-busting whistle, and conversation zipped right up. *"Fighting Poets!"* she yelled. *"Friday night is the homecoming game! We're playing Big Rival! We're gonna beat them like a drum! And know happiness! Meaning! And now we're going to buy raffle tickets!"*

They split up to work the room. Two determined-looking cheerleaders made a beeline for Megan Rose and me. Without saying hi, they detailed raffle-sales totals, quotas, and concerns to Megan Rose, who returned from her free dive, blinked several times, and responded. I had the sense, observing the way others looked at her and talked to her, that she was no less than the sun around which the North Homer student body revolved.

When one cheerleader spoke to her, the other shot me a look of pure disdain. I said hello to them, but they'd lost their hearing, the poor things.

One of them, a compact girl with bulging deltoids and a rebar-tight blond ponytail, started pulling Megan Rose's arm to leave.

Megan Rose put her hands on the table to stand. "It was nice to meet you, Wallace. I hope you enjoy your time here."

"Okay, you're good," I said. "I'm creeped out. I'll buy your tickets. How many for ten dollars?"

"I'm not trying to creep you out."

"Okay. So what are the trees doing?"

"I'm sorry you came here."

"Hey, I apologized. I promise I'm not always this annoying."

"No," said Megan Rose. Her features softened. "I mean, I'm sorry for you."

My breathing stopped. "Let's go, Megan Rose," said her impatient friend.

Megan Rose turned to leave, but then she turned back. "Three," she said to me.

"What?"

"Ten dollars gets you three tickets."

I dug in my pocket for the money. She leaned way over the table to reach for it and, softly, so no one else could hear, spoke into my ear. Her breath was warm. I felt it in every nerve.

"Watch the trees," she said.

THREE

LUNCH STILL HAD another ten minutes to go.

I looked around the cafeteria, more carefully this time. More than a few eyes glared back. It appeared to be the same clique-fest that constitutes every high school in America, including the schools that have been segregated by race, sex, or a belief in a God with a different, better shade than yours—geeks, jocks, stoners, America Firsters, etc., etc.—arbitrary tribalism is baked into teenage DNA right alongside phone addiction and body-shaming. Even the one-room schoolhouse outside Anchorage I passed some time in a couple of years back was as demarcated as Middle Eastern holy cities. It's such a stereotype, this splitting of students into stereotypes, and they were all represented in the North Homer lunchroom.

All of them seeming normal, non-hysterical, and non-tree-watching, so to speak.

What was Megan Rose talking about?

I left my tray and walked over to the hunger-strike-skinny kid who had waved to me earlier.

"Yo," I said in his preferred vernacular. "Yo. I'm new here. Can I ask you a few questions?"

He didn't look up. "You were ignoring me before," he said.

"Right. Yes. Sorry."

"Like you were too good for me."

"No. Not at all. I was . . . shy."

His name was Stuart. He really was epic pale and skinny: he looked like a regular skinny kid who'd been stretched out and printed on copy paper. He looked like one of those people who think they're going to live forever because they're eating only four apple seeds a day.

Despite his misgivings, he answered my questions about North Homer High. Megan Rose was indeed the school's organizing celestial body, its student-body president, its sun—or its black hole, from Stuart's perspective. I should avoid her and her warped gravitational pull, he counseled, and as long as we were on the subject, I should avoid the athletes: they were the worst. And I should especially avoid, if I wanted to survive North Homer in one piece, a football player named Brad Stone.

"But he'll find you," Stuart said. "He hates you already."

"He doesn't know me," I said. "I'm sure we'll get along."

Melvin, Stuart's grotesquely mustachioed and elaborately tattooed friend, was silent. He had taken out a pen and was adding to the ink on his left forearm, a rather disturbing rendering of a decapitating sword. I saw now that all of his tattoos were self-administered—not without skill and ambidexterity.

"You don't talk a lot, do you?" I said to him.

Melvin shrugged.

"He's got a lot on his mind," Stuart said. "You wouldn't understand."

"Like trees?" I asked.

"Like trees what?"

"Trees are on his mind?"

"What? What are you talking about?"

"I don't know," I admitted.

Stuart sneezed, vigorously rubbed his nose, and then, unprompted, shared the very core of his life philosophy.

"You're an oof," he said.

"Excuse me?" I said.

"An *Oof*. You are. A loser. Your T-shirt looks like you found it in a dumpster. Your hair looks like it was washed with a stick of butter. It's okay. I'm a loser, too. Cleaner, though."

"I'm not an oof."

"You're forgettable."

"Dude. Hey."

"Here's my point. Megan Rose is not like you and me. She's going places. Yacht places. Places with million-dollar membership fees and five-hundred-dollar meals that look like dirty water on a plate. They're waiting for her there, at these first-class places, her reservation's all ready. She's just killing time here for a few more months until she finishes the formal paperwork. Then she's gone. But we're not. We're not going anywhere. We're stuck here. Forever. Because we're losers."

The word landed like a sledgehammer at a carnival, harsh

and abrupt, with a ringing after. The weight behind it clearly had had time to build.

Stuart had spent many lunches thinking this philosophy through, I gathered.

"I don't think I'm a loser," I said.

"No one does," he said. "It's best to just accept it."

Sometimes people get so into their grievances they lose track of how disturbed they are. I've learned that it's best not to argue with such people online or to support their campaigns for higher office. I dropped my objections to Stuart's philosophy and changed the subject back to what I was hoping to discuss.

"What are the trees like in this town?" I asked.

"The trees?"

"Are they okay? Different from usual? Doing anything weird?"

Stuart looked at Melvin and then at me. "What is it with you and trees?"

"Forget it. The students who got the hysteria—what's up with them?"

"The students who got what?"

"Hysteria. Ungovernable emotional excess. That's the DSM definition. I looked it up."

"What's a DSM?"

"Doctors, um, Speak Medicine."

"Again, what the hell are you talking about?"

"The kids who got sick? Didn't students get sick last week?"

Stuart twitched, a quick, jerky movement of his neck. "They had stomach flu. Principal said they went to Syracuse."

"They didn't go hysterical?"

"No. To Syracuse."

Stuart wasn't playing dumb. He was truly bewildered and at least mildly freaked out by my questions. He'd never heard of hysterics. Which meant that those kids Dad told me about in the truck . . . someone wasn't telling the truth about what had happened to them.

Or was trying to hide it.

What the hell, indeed. A rod of ice stabbed down my spine.

"I don't think I like you," said Stuart.

Melvin caught my eye and nodded sorrowfully.

My first-day strangeness didn't end there. Not hardly.

The bell rang. Students gathered their bags and trays. Social studies, my next class, was at the other end of the school. I quickly got lost, too busy replaying my conversations to keep track of where I was going. Soon enough, the hallways were empty. Pictures of pumpkins and squash, pinecones and over-size turkeys in Pilgrim hats, were taped up on the walls; they felt out of season and creepy, even though it was mid-October. It was that warm.

And then I turned a corner and came face to face with pretty much the largest human being I'd ever seen in person.

Brad Stone blocked the hallway like a skin-covered toll-booth. He started at middle linebacker for the North Homer Fighting Poets and, according to Stuart, had a fondness for Skoal dip, protein powder with dubiously legal ingredients, Red Bull, tight shirts, Ayn Rand, free markets, and picking up students' cars by their bumpers and moving them a few feet so that getting out of parking spaces was impossible.

And also he hated new students.

In the middle of the hallway he uncrossed an arm, raised a water bottle, and spat a jet of dip into it.

"Why are you here?" he asked.

Brad Stone straight up asked me that. Though it's a question I often asked myself, in this context I didn't know what to say. To be fair, I'd never found a satisfactory answer.

He repeated the question.

Shit, this day.

"Are you asking me for money?" I said. "It would be easier if you just named your price, if that's the case. Then we could start negotiations."

"Negatory. We've got trouble." Brad tongued his dip from the left side of his mouth to the right. "We've got trouble in North Homer. Weakness. Psychological-type weakness. Weakness that is ripe for exploitation by outside forces. And what do you know? The American way to vanquish weakness and reclaim civic strength is to kick ass. The ass of outsiders who show up where they don't belong."

He spoke slowly and carefully, emphasizing every word. His breath smelled like bacon, Gatorade, and Skoal, like composting violence.

I took stock: an empty hallway, and a bully with deep-state hate and WWE muscles. I'd have to handle this delicately.

"Are you an asshole?" I asked.

Brad whipped a shoulder forward, and I jengaed right to the ground. I picked myself up.

"What's your name?" he asked.

"Dan," I answered.

"Dan what?"

"Gleeballs."

"Dan Gleeballs?"

"If it's not too cold."

Where Brad Stone's neck should have been, had he ordered one at the body-parts store, went bright red. He swung his shoulder out again.

"You're missing the point, newb," he said. "Do I have to explain it all over?"

"Please," I said, picking myself up again, buying time. "If you don't mind."

Normally, being a dick took bullies, so used to obsequious supplications (obsequious supplications!), by surprise. Then I'd make my exit, to their sputtering confusion. Unfortunately, being a dick doesn't work when there's a bigger dick right in your face. Not a situation I'd been in before, in any way, to be clear.

I'll spare you the lecture I received here, expanding on the role of faltering masculinity in the breakdown of societal order and the decline of American exceptionalism. It was somewhat repetitive. I zoned out. I'd never met a bully like this, a hate site crossbred with a thesaurus and biceps the size of cantaloupes. My own arms tended more toward overcooked pasta. Fruit, noodles . . . Lunch had been unsatisfying. I was still hungry.

When I zoned back in, Brad was talking again about weakness taking over the school.

Wait a second—was that the hysterics?

"Do the weak, like, become sick?" I interrupted.

"Are you listening?" Brad snarled. "Weakness is the illness. Strength is the cure."

"So, they are hysterical?"

"They're sick!"

"Right. But what's the sickness look like?"

"Weakness!"

"I got that! That's not helpful!"

Brad raised up his fists, put a knuckle to his nose, and cleared it against a locker. "Let's do this."

"Seriously?"

"Seriously."

Shoot, there were some troubled people in this school. Something was deeply off. Megan Rose was right—in twenty-two states, I hadn't seen anything like this before. At the moment, I was getting more than a little frustrated by it.

"For the record, you're wrong," I said to Brad. "Society's not based on strength and weakness. Society runs on one thing."

"What's that, newb?"

"Pain."

Brad wasn't expecting the punch, and it actually tagged his jaw pretty hard, judging by the jolt down my arm and into my spine—though maybe it wasn't all that impressive. My defeat was swift and total and included, free of charge, more brute-force philosophizing. Damn. I was going to have to handle Brad very carefully. But how? I closed my eyes and pondered it. Pondered Megan Rose, too—what she'd said about trees and the way her breath had felt on my ear when she said it (fluttering, pepperminty, damp). Pondered the fact that students were getting sick and nobody seemed to know what was happening to them. Pondered—might as well, Brad had stamina— the Siberian permafrost, the glacier melt in Greenland, and the president of Brazil trading the southern half of the Amazon jungle for a bright red Ferrari.

Just got to town and I had a lot to think about.

FOUR

THE NORTH HOMER High School principal's office was like the private sanctum of a Mafia boss. You passed through an outer office and then an inner office, and the principal was sequestered in another office past that. Assassins would have a hard time getting a clean shot, for sure. I had spent all morning in the outer office with the mean-eyed secretaries while they made up my schedule. They displayed no surprise at my quick return and responded to my greetings as if I had thrown them from a bucket of rotting vegetables.

Brad Stone was already parked a few seats down when I arrived, his giant frame spilling out of his chair. He gave me the finger without looking up from his phone. Still without a power cord to replace the one I'd left in Kentucky, I had nothing to do but picture ripping that finger off.

Which is how I spent the rest of the afternoon. Didn't make it to a single class, actually, but that was okay—I was grateful for the English teacher who had happened upon our hallway discussion, broken it up, and brought us here.

From time to time I could feel Brad Stone glaring at me.

"What?" I said.

"Understand, this is a temporary stay of the inevitable by an overly involved, overly redistributive authority."

He flexed his arms as he said this.

"You've got to have a small penis," I said.

"Your mom didn't think so."

I stared into the distance and listened to the capillaries in my temples exploding.

The office was busy all afternoon with phone calls, students coming in and out, teachers checking mailboxes, and UPS deliverymen in shorts waiting for signatures. When the last bell finally rang, the school emptied out in seconds and a fat man with a flattop and a whistle around his neck stuck his head in the door and said: "Stone, what the fuck-all you doing here?" And Brad Stone said, "He started it." And the coach said, "I don't care. Get your pads on. Now."

As he passed, Brad knocked my bag to the floor.

Then it was quiet. The secretaries were gone. After a while a janitor came in pushing a cart. He was tall and veiny thin and had the unkempt graying hair and beard of people who did too much acid back in the day. He emptied the wastebaskets one at a time into the big trash can on his cart, moving with no hurry at all, as if there were absolutely nothing troubling in the world, no hysterics or bullies or injustice anywhere, as if even the thin layer of dust covering the school were of no concern to him, though it was right there in his job description.

I had to admire that.

My father finally arrived, three whole hours after school had ended. I was the last student in the school—the sports teams had finished practice, and other kids in the yearbook office or the weight room or just smoking out in the parking lot, uneager to go to their homes, had in fact left for those homes. Even the unhurried janitor had finished and gone home. Dr. Rathschild, the principal, wasn't too happy to wait through dinner for my father, and in glimpses of her behind the desk in her inner office, I could see the thoughts she was having about what kind of influence I would be at her school.

Dad's hands materialized in front of me holding a cup of coffee and his keys. His jeans were streaked with oil and dirt. The smell of cigarettes was so strong I sneezed.

He picked my chin up in his rough fingers and turned it to the side so he could get a better look at my developing black eye. "Nice work," he said.

"Thank you," I said. "You should see the other guy."

"I don't see another guy. You get him worse?"

"No. He must be six-five, two-fifty. I mean that you should see him."

Dad snorted. "I'm glad you think this is funny. You know this is the worst time for me. Right after we get to a new place. Hoch is busting my ass, and it's not funny to me when I've got to leave work early and pick you up because you can't behave. On the very first day."

"Not really feeling the love and concern, Dad," I said.

"Do you feel the aggravation?"

"Yeah."

He dropped my chin. "Right next to it."

"That's the contempt, I thought."

"Wallace."

When he said my name that way it meant: Shut up, idiot.

"He insulted Ma," I said.

"So? Who cares?"

I didn't expect that. I thought he'd care about that. "So? So that's not right. He crossed a line."

He sighed. "The world is full of people and their lines. It gets to the point where that's all they can see. Lines all the way to the horizon. Don't be like that, Wallace. The best way to survive is to get rid of your lines."

"So Ma is just a line?"

"Everything is just a line."

I stared up at him. A wave of fear rippled through me.

Dr. Rathschild appeared in the doorway of her office. She was tall and wide. Her pantsuit was a study in shades of intestinal distress. Her haircut said: I have more important things than this haircut. Her face said: I should be home by now, ffs.

"Eleanor Rathschild," she said. She held out a hand to my father. "We spoke on the phone."

My father shook her hand and unlocked his face into something intended to resemble a smile.

"Ronald Cole. I am sorry I couldn't get off work until now. Busy times at the plant."

"Perhaps Mrs. Cole could have come for Wallace in that case?"

"She's dead."

This caught the principal up short. She blushed, pulled her hand back.

Yes, she's dead, Principal Who-Already-Thinks-I'm-a-Problem. How's that feel?

"I'm so sorry," Dr. Rathschild said. "I didn't know."

Dad said nothing. Loudly.

"Okay. Yes. Wallace's transcript hasn't arrived yet. I will make sure that it's faxed here first thing in the morning."

"Great," my father said. "We done?"

"Well, no. Your son's perfunctory disruptiveness concerns me."

Dad glared at me without looking at me. "He's sorry."

"It's not about being sorry. It's about being smart."

"It won't be an issue again."

"I don't like this any more than you do," Dr. Rathschild said. "I want to get home and see my children before they go to sleep. But your son started a dangerous altercation. His actions indicate a reckless self-disregard, which can be a symptom of deeper emotional issues. I'd like to understand this better. We should have a follow-up, just the two of us. Thursday? Is this time the earliest you can do? I can make plans to come back to the office to meet you, if that's the case."

"No."

"No, there are other times?"

"No, I can't meet you," Dad said, his eyes blank and expressionless.

Cold. Ice-cold. Thanks, Dad. For sure, this principal will love me now.

"Mr. Cole." Dr. Rathschild dropped all pretense of being pleasant. "I don't know how they do it where you're from, but here in my school, I find my students behave better when they care what happens to them. But it's hard for them to care if nobody else does. So let's just say you come in Thursday or you go down to the district and fill out the paperwork to take over Wallace's education full-time."

My father said nothing. Then he nodded once, the muscles in his jaw wrestling with each other, signaling he was pissed. Didn't she understand that he had to get to the plant? And more important, did I, Wallace Cole, understand that this whole mess was my fault? He would check later to make sure I did understand.

We drove to the apartment in silence. Night had fallen, clouds covered the stars, and in the darkness the roads of the town seemed, like the hallways of the school, deserted and vaguely haunted.

It was a quick five-minute drive, but my father managed to smoke three whole cigarettes while also radiating epic displeasure. I'd like to say that he was only like this when I had done something necessitating a trip to a principal's office, but truthfully he was always like this. Work consumed him, and the rest of the world was an annoyance. And by being part of the rest of the world, and a part that needed a tad more attention than most of it, I was a special annoyance.

I had learned not to take it personally.

By not taking it personally, I mean that I had learned how, when a feeling or body part ached like it wanted to burst, to shove the sensation way down. And I don't know if it was the day I'd just had or what I'd left in Kentucky or the cumulative injustices of the last seventeen years—but on that drive, I was feeling there was too much to push down.

In front of the apartment, Dad called for a pizza and handed me a twenty to pay for it. Then he said he had to get back to the plant.

I pointed to my swollen eye.

"There's ice in the freezer," he said.

"Does it bother you that I got hurt?"

"Very much. Walk away next time."

"What if I have reckless self-disregard?"

"You can still walk away."

"Parental neglect."

"Self-reliance."

"Abandonment."

"Survival." Dad popped the truck out of park. "Wallace, I really don't have time for this. You remember Arizona, the chemical fire that took us twenty-one days to put out? That was small potatoes compared to the situation I'm dealing with here."

I did remember Arizona. Of course I did. Ma'd been gone

for a couple of years by that point, left in a hillside graveyard in California during a thunderstorm, and Dad and I had been bouncing around the country, plant to plant, five, six months a pop, not that much time at each stop but enough for me to develop a semblance of a social life at whatever school I landed at—hell, long as we're on the topic, it was in Arizona that I lost my virginity. (A keg party on someone's porch, Christian rock going at jet-engine volume, the girl saying she wanted me to hear this song in her Jeep, the most amazing song, the song being a Britney Spears tune that just spoke to her, and then in the Jeep our shirts were off before the first chorus, our shorts were around our knees, there was the sensation of trying to dock a sailboat on a windy lake, and I experienced the ultimate in human pleasure. In case you were wondering.)

Point is, in Arizona Dad arrived home each night with strange burns on his arms and blank, hollowed-out eyes. Rather than coming home from a job each night, he seemed to be coming home from a war. A war that was going poorly.

As I've said, the man took his job seriously.

He nodded me out of the truck. I stepped down to the pavement but held the door open. He had to turn.

"What now?" he said.

"I met a girl today."

"Great."

"Thanks for asking how my first day went."

"Happy for you."

"I like her," I said.

"Great."

"She's pretty and smart. Is organizing the prom here, actually. Invited me to it. Maybe I'll go."

"Great, I—"

"I know. I know I won't be here."

"Wallace, I—"

"She said to understand what was happening in North Homer, I should watch the trees."

Dad didn't move a muscle for fifteen long seconds. Then he let out a deep exhale. He put the truck back in park, took his hands off the wheel, grabbed the pack of cigarettes off the dash, lit one. He took a drag so hard I thought he might just suck the thing right into his mouth and start chewing.

"What's she mean?" I asked. "You know, don't you?"

"Can't you leave it alone?" he asked.

"Dad? That's your answer?"

"We'll be gone soon. This town—there's nothing good here for us. Let me finish my job here, and then we'll go. Anywhere you want."

"Well, no," I said, my voice rising. "I'm not leaving it alone. Fuck that. I'm already alone. I'm always alone. You go and do your job, like always. Fine. But I'm going to find out what she means, if it's the only thing I do in this stupid town."

Dad gripped his forehead. He appeared about to respond several times, each time deciding that it was better not to.

"This won't end well," he finally said.

FIVE

MY FATHER DROVE off. It was quiet. Dark. No other cars or people on the street. I looked around in that way you do when you've finished a long day and you let the exhaustion sink in.

And I looked up at the sky, as you do in such moments.

There were three oak trees in front of the apartment. Their trunks were about fifteen feet apart, their branches filling the gaps between them. They were enormous, old, and so expansive that I felt like I was on their turf, not the other way around. Which is not the worst sensation, as trees are generally better turf owners than people. (The sun is the best turf owner of all but too much of an absentee landowner.)

They all still had their leaves—fall hadn't really hit yet, which was some kind of New York State record.

And then, as I watched them, the oaks, as I took in their distinct *treeness*, a single branch from the center tree, one of the lower ones, easy to see, rustled back and forth, back and forth.

In other words, it waved.

I'm telling you, the tree waved.

I ran inside.

SIX

I COULDN'T CATCH up to my brain that night. Eight hours straight, it raced, it zoomed, it zigged, it zagged, it Olympic-gold-medal slalomed. No wonder—it had a lot to cover: Megan Rose, Brad Stone's cement-fisted sociological theories, the principal's glare, Megan Rose, my father's grim prediction, and Megan Rose. Also, yes, the fact that an oak tree had waved to me.

Okay, last things first.

No.

Just no.

It couldn't have. I checked the tree out the window at dawn and again on leaving for school in the morning. It was, for sure, an impressive, I-am-old-and-behold-my-girthiness tree. It was definitely there. But it did not wave one time. So, no, come on now.

All right, then: Megan Rose.

What about her?

Well, there was the way she looked like the kind of person who could break hearts *and* bones. The way she wore a gray tank top. The way she'd dropped deep into herself in the middle of the cafeteria—what the hell was that?

The way her breath had felt against my ear.

Obviously, the thing to do next was to ask her to a private place where the two of us could talk. Just talk. But Megan Rose wasn't in any of my classes, I discovered. And Brad Stone and his football teammates, who all shared a "Look at me wrong and I'll break you in half" vibe, made it clear that I wasn't welcome in the cafeteria. Brad took it further, making sure with some hard shoves that I understood I wasn't welcome in the entire zip code.

I wasn't able to talk to Megan Rose a single time the entire week, actually. I did learn that in addition to student-body president she was captain of the tennis team, which only added to my frustration, because I was sure—well, almost sure . . . well, had a strong hunch—that if we did get the opportunity to talk, it might lead to her falling for me. Not because I was intentionally trying to make her do that. I wouldn't do that; just because, you know, beautiful and athletic student-body presidents falling for aggravating newcomers with no outstanding attributes—in the movies, it happens all the time.

I did see Megan Rose around the school but only from afar, save for once when I was at my locker and she passed a few feet from me. Four friends were with her then, however, protecting her like hired muscle and filling the hallway with so much conversation the air got thin. I wasn't even able to say her name.

So what, then? How was I going to find out what the hell was going on?

Friday at lunch, I got help from an unexpected source.

It had been another morning of cranky teachers chugging from gallon-sized coffee mugs, staring down over their clunky reading glasses, and assigning a month of makeup reading on top of the regular homework. ("It's not about brains, new kid," they said, "but effort. And, kid, it's early, but"—the quiz tossed through the air, plopping on my desk, the failing grade circled in red pen—"we're not seeing the effort.") I grabbed potato chips and Twix from the vending machine and ate them while sitting on the floor next to my locker, the safest place I could find. And as I finished off a third bag of Lay's and a sci-fi novel about young men and women trapped in a pointless space war that never ends, Stuart appeared. He arrived so suddenly, looking so broken, I thought for a second he'd fallen out of the ceiling.

He pointed at what remained of my five-day-old, Brad Stone–administered black eye. "That hurt?" he asked.

"Only when rude people stare at it," I said.

"Really?"

"God, it's throbbing."

"Okay," he said. "That hysteria stuff you were talking about. Is it for real?"

"I'm trying to find out."

He sat down like a collapsing stack of broomsticks. "Melvin's been acting strange the last few days. I know, save it—more strange than normal. He didn't come to school today. He isn't answering my texts. I'm getting worried."

"Maybe he doesn't like you," I said.

"He's been staring at trees all week."

A potato chip went down the wrong tube. I coughed.

Stuart nodded knowingly.

"That's it, isn't it?" he asked. "The hysteria. It's in the trees?"

"I don't know." I coughed again. "I think Megan Rose knows, but I haven't been able to get near her all week."

"I can help with that."

That surprised me. "You guys are friends? I thought she was going special places and we're losers."

"She will be," said Stuart. "For sure. Places that don't want us. But right now she lives across the street from me."

After the last bell, I jogged to the apartment, dropped my bag, and inhaled a cold pepperoni slice. It was another ridiculously warm fall day in a month full of them—instead of fall crispness, the air had the warm grittiness of car exhaust. The half-hour walk from the apartment to Stuart's house was straight uphill and got me sweating hard.

Now, I'm not sure what the Greek poet foresaw when he daydreamed about upstate New York municipalities being named in his honor, especially as he was blind. I figured most of Homer's daydreams were of Helen of Troy in the bath anyway. Or Achilles. I forget which was his preference. Regardless, you picture a town with broad boulevards and fountains of naked archers and houses fronted by majestic columns and maybe a flat-topped mountain in the distance, where the gods interview virgins for internships without triggering performance reviews. North Homer had no such things. It was jammed into a valley at the south end of a long lake, squeezed between two steep ridges left by retreating glaciers in the last Ice Age. It had rusted pickups, sidewalk weeds so high you had to step around them, abandoned houses next to prefab ones on cinder blocks. The tuition-free revolution and the Confederacy were running neck and neck in bumper stickers and lawn signs. There was an ongoing debate between the residents and the town about when garbage would be picked up. The streets appeared paved not for cars but to make a point about the relentless passage of time.

And hysterics?

I passed a woman in a tattered bathrobe walking a panting dog in a shiny new sweater, a bearded man unloading two-by-fours from one pickup and loading them into another, a middle school student texting while skateboarding downhill at high speed, and an ornery deer shitting pebbles in the middle of the street.

None of them were hysterical, it appeared. Still, how did you know for sure?

Stuart lived on what had to be one of the nicest roads in town. Large houses, lawns professionally cut, trees pruned of dead branches. His house was a cedar-shingled three-story with white trim and an elaborate bush game. Directly across the street was the only fenced-in property around. The home inside the fence was the color of a storm cloud and the shape of a brick, and had a single giant window.

I knocked on Stuart's front door, and he called from the

side of the house. I picked my way around some rhododendrons to a basement entrance.

"Megan Rose?" I pointed at the strange building across the street.

"Yep," he said.

"For real? It looks like a black-ops torture site."

"Could be. Her father is about as friendly."

Inside Stuart's basement, the walls were covered with wood panels and posters of pensive superheroes. In the fight against crime, they were on the verge of going too far. Midpunch, they paused, shocked at just how far they had gone. A massive brown couch ran the length of one wall, and above it was a shelf of books with titles like *How to Be Your Own Best Friend* and *Peace Is Inside You.*

I pointed to them. "Are you your best friend?"

"No," said Stuart.

"Have you found peace inside you?"

"No."

"Maybe your best friend found it?"

"No and stop and fuck you."

The basement had a high window from which we could watch for Megan Rose. The road ran sideways across the hill, and her house was on the uphill side, towering above us. It really was the exact shape of a brick. The architects of the seventies clearly had *Star Trek* in their eyes and cocaine in their noses.

It was the perfect setting for some solid staking out. All we lacked were binoculars, whiskey-spiked coffee in Styrofoam cups, bitter ex-wives, and a pinboard with pictures of our suspects. But Stuart's mind quickly drifted.

"I'm stuck," he said.

I looked over. He was sitting on the couch. "Hmm? You miss the tissue?"

"I'm trapped and forgettable."

"Yes, I remember. We went over this in the cafeteria. What losers we are." I gestured across the street. "Do we have to rehash that now? Don't you want to talk to Megan Rose and find out what's going on with Melvin?"

"That's exactly it."

"What is?"

"She's never wanted to talk to me."

"Did she say that?"

"It's implied."

"Okay." I took a good look at Megan Rose's house—all quiet—turned around, found a chair, pulled it over to where Stuart sat. "Are you all right?"

He wasn't. Stuart wasn't all right, and it was a subject he was quite up-front about, I was learning.

"I've read all these damn wisdom books"—he gestured toward the shelf above the couch—"and they're full of lies. They all say you only have to extinguish desire and you'll be happy. But how do you extinguish desire? You need desire to stay alive! If we didn't have a desire to eat, we'd starve. They lie, the books. They're a deliberate, intentional lie."

"By who?" I asked.

"By who what?"

"Who's lying?"

"Man, are you even listening? Society. Those who've rigged

52

it, in between flying private jets to Africa to shoot famous lions for fun. Megan Rose is joining them any day now. Brad Stone is in the club, too—that's why he can beat you up and no one cares. Meanwhile, because I've oh-so-conveniently given up desire, I get to work the fastener aisle at Lowe's until the day I die. And you'll be in the next aisle over explaining to moms what kind of Spackle they should use when little Austin kicks a hole in the drywall. Don't you get it? It's rigged!" He threw up his hands. "And now Melvin is MIA. This week has been the worst. I should just goddamn quit. You ever feel like quitting? Like, for good?"

"All the time."

"Yeah? Really?"

"Yeah. Really."

He cocked an eyebrow, gauging if I was serious. "So why haven't you?"

I stood up and looked out the window to give myself a minute. Again, no sign of Megan Rose out there. A minute stretched to two. I didn't want to answer Stuart's question, because I didn't like to think about the answer. I didn't like to think about that feeling, the quitting one. A couple of years after Ma died, when Dad and I were living in a cabin in Wisconsin with only fat mosquitoes and the hum of a nearby Jackduke power plant for company, darkness hit me like a black Humvee. Then it backed up and hit me again. And then again. And again. Under the wheels and everything. And it never really went away. Every few months, just when I was feeling halfway decent— *Bam!* Again!

Mega D, I'd started calling it, this SUV of relentless misery. Mega D, as opposed to what I'd been dealing with up to that point, Kinda D. Kinda D: the type of sadness I could manage by cleaning my room or doing a juice fast or jogging for an hour. Kinda D was weak sauce. Mega D was an ocean, with me dropped in the middle of it, like that jewel by the old lady in *Titanic.* (Side point: I'm still mad she did that. Donate it to a rain forest!) Was it depression, as defined by doctors and therapists and other such people who think the key to health is telling you exactly what's wrong with you? I don't know. I avoided them out of habit. All I knew was that a couple of times a year I felt broken and that everything in my life was proof that my life was not what it should be; that, to give an example, if I was having a conversation, it was nothing but a judgment on all the other times I could have been having real conversations but didn't. *I could've been a person who talks to people, but it's too late for that now.*

I understood from talking to Stuart that this Mega D demolition derby—he was in it, right this minute.

That didn't mean I knew what to say to him. Dad would've said something like, "In rural China, they leave deaf babies on the sidewalk" or "Here's a twenty, go to a movie," neither of which I ever found helpful.

Meanwhile, it was getting dark. I was no closer to talking to Megan Rose.

Then the curtain in the giant front window of her house snapped open.

I ducked down instinctively. After a minute, I raised my

head to look. A man in a black suit and tie stood in the window, backlit by a chandelier. Slicked-back hair, lined face, trim-fit build. He looked like a stock option brought to life. He was motionless, with a drink in one hand, face lifted to the sky.

Megan Rose's father.

Stuart came over and whisper-explained that Megan Rose's parents were lawyers, successful ones who had moved to North Homer from New York City ten years earlier, under murky circumstances. He often overheard Mr. Rose yelling things like "Buybacks!" and "Residuals!" at his hand-free phones.

Lawyering, my father had once told me, was the art of grabbing money when it passed through the air from one account to the next. "I thought it was about figuring out the truth," I'd said. ("Don't be an idiot," my father had responded.)

Mr. Rose lowered his head in our direction. Had he seen us? A door opened at the side of the house-brick, and two girls stepped out of it and headed toward a blue CRV parked in the driveway. The taller one had that straight posture and regal jaw. Megan Rose.

"There she is," I said. "I'm going to shoot my shot, Stuart. Thanks for having me over."

"You never answered my question," he said. "How do you keep going?"

"Yeah, next time, I really should—"

"Did you extinguish desire? Is there peace inside you? Are you happy?"

I turned to him. Goddamn but he had the expression of a three-legged mutt at the end of adoption day.

"Look, Stuart, my life is no great shakes," I said. "Fyodor. Giannis. Stevie Wonder. I've named the ants in my apartment— I've spent that much time with them. And look." I pointed to my eye, the one welcomed to town by Brad. "This happens quite a bit. And the world, on top of everything, the world is a shitshow. What keeps me going? Peace? Happiness? Hell, no. Honestly, at this point it's mostly pain and aggravation. Like life is an itch that I have to scratch."

"And then what?"

"And then? After I scratch it? I don't know. I wish to God I knew. Maybe life gets bright and shiny and shit-free."

Stuart stared at me in disbelief. I didn't think I was doing a good job of cheering him up. Bucking people up was really not one of my strong points. Swap in an *f* and I could help you.

"Bright and shiny and shit-free," he said.

"All right," I said. "No need to mock. We all got our stuff. I really got to—"

"Melvin was talking about that. Before he stopped answering my texts."

"Melvin said he wanted a bright and shiny life?"

"Not exactly." Stuart's face was white as a sheet. "He said he'd found it."

My hand on the doorknob, my fingers frozen, my heart pounding, a thousand seconds in one.

"You better text him again."

SEVEN

A FEW LAST shards of daylight punctured the sky as I shut the basement door and ran around the rhododendron bushes. And it was warm still, disturbingly warm. The seasons were playing rock-paper-scissors—and summer was cheating, throwing late. I reached the road in time to see the blue CRV pull up to the gate at the bottom of Megan Rose's driveway. The gate slid open, and the car turned to where I stood.

Megan Rose sat in the passenger seat. The driver was the compact cheerleader with the painfully tight blond ponytail, the one who'd pulled Megan Rose away in the cafeteria on my first day. Both of them wore red football jerseys and had eye black smeared on their cheekbones.

The homecoming football game—that was tonight. I'd forgotten about it.

Megan Rose's head was down. When the car drew close, about twenty feet away, the driver said something, and Megan Rose looked up. She saw me, and her face cycled rapidly through several expressions—surprise, then disbelief, then a moment of suspicion, then something truly unsettling.

The unsettling thing was that she looked terrified.

I raised my hand. At the same time, the cheerleader-driver took one hand off the wheel and, without slowing down, stretched her arm in my direction, over Megan Rose's lap, and extended a single long finger.

I reached the football field at the end of the first quarter. The parking lot was packed with pickups the size of tanks, the bleachers were packed with texting students, Snapchatting students, Instagramming students, and drunken parents in *Stand Your Ground* hoodies. The field was immaculately cut, chalked, and lit, and on the fifty-yard line beautiful blue letters spelled out *POET^C*, running out of chalk halfway through the *S*. Young children ran about behind the end zones, slamming each other to the ground in a lighthearted approximation of the game. The whole scene looked airlifted into place from a Hollywood movie about small-town folk going through hard times, but gosh darn it, how they cared for their town. It was almost poetic.

In the game itself, Brad Stone hit people so hard they forgot how to walk for a few minutes and even then could do it only with assistance. The wounded got polite applause, a water bottle, and encouraging calls to "shake it off." I didn't see the appeal, if we're being honest. Young men ruining themselves for our entertainment is a long-standing American tradition but not one of my favorites. And where was Megan Rose?

Gunshot signified the end of the first half, and she materialized next to Brad Stone at midfield. He was sweaty and massive; she was regal and remote. They received the crowns of homecoming king and queen. There was more polite applause.

What was important about the game was this: I watched Megan Rose all through the second half; she was standing at the edge of the bleachers, putting her foot up on the railing and stretching out her leg. Her leg was quite long and flexible. She'd taken off her crown. Around her, friends were talking excitedly. She was next to them but not a part of the conversation.

Behind one end zone was the parking lot and the school. Behind the other were a few acres of woods. All through the third and fourth quarters, Megan Rose kept worriedly glancing in the direction of the woods. I followed her gaze. The trees she was looking at, the ones right at the edge of the forest and the field, were aspens, and they were doing that thing aspens do, where every single leaf in the entire tree moves at once. Aspens are, I think, one of the more underrated trees. They take every breeze as an opportunity to express delirious excitement, as if the wind were delivering shade-grown espresso shots or crystal meth. And these aspens, the ones past the end of the field, had something extra in their excited shimmering, like they were actually glowing, like beneath each leaf was a pin-sized white glow stick.

A trick of light off the bleachers' floodlights, clearly.

I watched the aspens shimmer all through the second half, through the final gun, and through the postgame, the teams shaking hands, the field and bleachers clearing of people, the parking lot emptying of trucks, until at last there was no one left and the floodlights above the field were turned off.

Then the field was dark, and the bleachers were dark. But the trees stayed lit.

This deserves repeating: the trees stayed lit.

EIGHT

THEN MONDAY, MELVIN returned. Also Monday, he went full hysteria. Then I did.

On Monday, in other words, I started to get the hang of things.

All weekend I ate leftover pizza and conversed with the ceiling ants, too spooked by tree behavior to go outside. I did monitor the three oaks out front, and they seemed like perfectly normal, nonwaving, appropriately lighted trees, but how could I trust that? And then at lunch on Monday, after another morning of disappointing teachers and ducking Brad Stone, I grabbed chips and Twix and went to eat at my locker in the dusty hallway—and it was full of screams.

They bounced me two feet off the ground. They came from the direction of the cafeteria. I ran to it. And there, on top of a table, in a T-shirt honoring a band made entirely out of eyebrow rings and skull tattoos, Melvin screamed his head off.

His face was a blur. His voice was a sonic nuke. His inked forearms thrashed. His legs kicked trays of Superfund slop in high arcs, kicked milk cartons clear across the room, kicked air.

Students stared, some still holding their lunch trays. Stuart was up front. I made my way to him.

And it appeared, as I got closer, that Melvin wasn't screaming exactly but whooping, like he'd just scored the touchdown that won the homecoming game. I mean that there was joy in his cries.

He was gone, in other words. Gone-in-space gone, off-the-grid gone, so gone he had nowhere left to go, so it felt like we, the witnesses, were the ones actually in danger. Because we still had the possibility of staying or leaving. And I looked around at the other students, and they, too, were looking around, asking that question: Am I really here? How do I know? How does anyone?

Two panting overweight male teachers ran through the crowd and approached Melvin from each side. They *One-two-three*'d and grabbed him together. Melvin kicked them away. They grabbed him again.

"Biter!" yelled one, spinning to the ground like he'd been hit by a sniper.

The teachers backed off, yelling strategy and *You go!* at each other. More teachers ran in, and then the long-bearded janitor, followed by Principal Rathschild, and they finally pulled Melvin off the table and pinned his arms and carried him flailing out the door that went to the parking lot, and the janitor lay on him on the pavement, whispering into his ear until the ambulance came.

In the cafeteria, no one moved. No one spoke. The air was a sheet of glass that could shatter at any second. Rathschild came back inside, panting, the top of her blouse unbuttoned, her jacket sleeve torn.

"Go to class," she said.

We shuffled out of the cafeteria. Policemen flew past us, all blue uniforms and gun belts and righteous purpose. I backed away and hit the wall; it felt electrified. There was a humming in the air. Stuart was bug-eyed and breathless, like a cartoon character who's run off a cliff but has not yet begun to fall. In a daze, we walked past a bathroom, a water fountain, a collection of Mathlete trophies, and a photo display of marine animals that'd eaten too many yogurt containers.

"I'm next," Stuart said.

"You're not next," I said.

"I am. This thing is coming for us. Melvin was our type. The forgettable type."

"Not that again. You're not forgettable. You're not a loser."

"He was my friend."

"I'm sorry."

"I'm next."

"Stuart . . ."

"Don't," he said. "Just don't."

A clattering—the janitor turning a corner, pushing his cart. He wore a gray uniform, a black vest covering where his name would be. Only a few patches of skin were visible above his chest-length beard. His hair stuck up in places like he'd just wrestled a kid to the pavement.

He stopped his cart in front of us and stroked his beard.

"You're scared," he said to Stuart and me.

"Well, yeah," I said.

"Don't be scared," he said. "This is the best thing that ever happened to your friend."

"But he's gone," I said.

"Exactly."

Stuart's jaw hung open like a broken glove compartment. The janitor raised his eyebrows with great pity.

Then he left. Stuart moped off to class, after disparaging the janitor's intelligence, hygiene, and career. I had to jam my hands in my pockets to stop them from fluttering all over the hallway. The sun came through the windows and ignited a floating city of dust. I turned a corner, and there, leaning on my locker, was Megan Rose.

NINE

SHE LOOKED NOTHING like the student-body president I'd met in the cafeteria. Pale, weary-eyed, dressed in disheveled-poet black, she wobbled awkwardly on her long legs, like she'd just found them propped against a wall.

For a minute we looked at each other, too scared to speak. Or maybe I should speak for myself. I was scared.

"Wallace. I've been trying to find you all morning," she said.

I blushed, surprised, and hid it with a fake cough, which became a real cough, which went on for an uncomfortable amount of time.

"Did you hear what happened in the cafeteria?" I said when I could talk again. "Melvin caught it."

"I heard. It's upsetting."

"It was intense. What do you think that's like, catching it? Is it all at once, or slow? Do you not know until it's too late, or do you get like a check-engine light a little bit before? And then what?"

I thought these were good questions. Megan Rose didn't answer.

"I'm leaving, Wallace," she said.

"Oh." My heart dropped a sudden distance, like a broken elevator. "Leaving? Really? You sure?"

"I'm sure. Tonight."

"Where are you going?"

"Princeton."

"I've heard of it."

"Yes. It's crunch time for my college applications," she said. "And I'm falling apart. All these years of tennis camps and five a.m. study sessions . . . and I've lost my last four singles matches. The girl from Lansing who beat me yesterday is legally blind. My practice scores have nose-dived. And Princeton—it's my first choice and I'm a double legacy there, but my parents haven't donated nearly enough. My father says the faculty has become too politically correct for him to give in good faith. That's a quote. He also thinks he has an enemy in the provost's office."

Good-faith donations and a double legacy with a provost enemy—I'm not going to lie, I didn't understand half of that. Nor how they made someone fall apart. I mean, what just happened in the cafeteria, I could see how *that* did.

Megan Rose saw my confusion. "It's an SAT workshop," she said. "I've got a singles tournament at Princeton, and then an SAT workshop. And I'll be meeting with the admissions office."

"So you're not leaving town for good?" I asked with relief.

"For good? Who just up and leaves their home for good?"

"Right. Who does that?"

"I have to ace the SAT. With a poor score, my admission will be shot. I'll probably have to go to Tufts—and I really don't want to go to Tufts."

Wait a minute. Getting into Princeton? *That* was Megan Rose's concern? Now, of all times? When hysteria was vibrating through the school hallways? Had I completely misunderstood her?

"I'm surprised to hear this," I said.

"To hear what?"

"Tufts. You're worried about Tufts."

Megan Rose's eyes were suddenly evasive.

"Odd name for a school. Makes you think of old people's ears."

"It's near Boston."

I felt frustrated. Why was this so difficult? There had to be something she wasn't telling me. Or something that I was supposed to say.

"Are you okay?" I asked. "You look tired."

"I haven't slept in three days," she said.

"That's not good for you."

"I know."

Okay. Enough.

"The trees, Megan Rose. In the cafeteria on my first day, you told me to watch the trees. Then at homecoming, I saw you. You weren't watching Brad Stone and the game—you were watching the aspens behind the end zone. They were lit up. What was that?"

She looked up. "You saw that?"

"I stayed at the field until midnight. They didn't dim one bit."

"They're getting brighter," she said. "Have you noticed that? Brighter and bigger and louder."

"Why are they doing that? What do they want?"

Megan Rose didn't answer right away. She stared at the floor or at something miles under the floor. And when she spoke again, it was to say one of the strangest things I'd heard in my life.

She mumbled it first. I had to ask her to repeat herself.

"I hate tennis."

"You hate who?"

"Not who. What. Tennis. I hate it. I've never liked playing. My father's sport. Not mine."

"We're talking about tennis?"

"She doesn't leave me alone."

"Wait—not tennis?"

"I can't sleep. I can't think. I have to get away from her."

I was having trouble keeping up. "Someone's following you? Have you told the police?"

Megan Rose laughed at that last question, a bitter chuckle that seemed uncalled for.

"A tennis ball," she said. "You ask who's following me? A tennis ball is. A tennis ball. A big round yellow felt tennis ball, about four feet tall, with yellow felt hair and little arms and big clown shoes. She can barely walk. She keeps falling over. And she never stops talking. She never leaves me alone! That, Wallace, is who's following me. That's what keeps me up at night. Aren't you glad you asked?" She grabbed her hair with both hands and pulled. "I'm trying to study synonyms and modifiers, and this four-foot tennis ball runs after me, crying, 'Don't leave me!' and then falls down! She can't walk in a straight line. A drunk penguin has better balance! What do you think of that?"

In my mind, alarms went off. Lights started flashing. Phone calls were discreetly placed to the proper authorities. This was the hysterics. That's what I thought.

"Okay," I said. "Let's talk this through. A tennis ball is following you."

"Yes."

"One with T. rex arms."

"Don't mock me."

"Four feet tall." I held out a hand. "So, about this high? Or this?"

"Don't."

"With big feet or just big shoes?"

"Don't! Don't make fun of me!" Her lip curled. "You think I don't know this is crazy? You think I'm not scared . . . ?"

"Have you asked her to go play with a wall?"

"Of course I tried that! Many times! She cries if I do. So loud I can't even think. But I've got things to do, Wallace! I've got the SAT! I've got plans! I can't take care of a freaking tennis ball!"

Sometimes you hear something so strange that you question the very act of hearing things. Like, maybe words didn't mean what you thought they did. Their meanings changed overnight, and now the word *love* is actually another way of saying *egg salad*. Or maybe all this time you thought you were alive you were dreaming and the few moments you caught yourself dreaming were actually the only time you were alive.

This was one of those times.

Megan Rose watched me with frightened eyes. It felt imperative to choose my words with great care.

"Princeton sounds nice," I said. "I've heard good things. Getting out of town sounds like a good idea."

Her shoulders relaxed when she heard that. Then we didn't say anything for a while. I wasn't sure why she didn't walk away. What could I do for her? I wasn't going to help her ace the SAT, for sure. I sucked at tennis. And all I knew about plans is that they got ditched when Dad said, "Pack your stuff and get in the truck." I wondered sometimes what happened to them, my ditched plans. Did they wither away to dust? Did they roll on to the next occupant? Were they waiting for me to return, lonely dogs sitting by the door?

They weren't, to be fair, being battered by a four-foot tennis ball.

"You wanted this, right?" Megan Rose stepped closer.

"What? Wanted what?"

"To know what's going on. It's why you've been stalking me."

"I haven't been stalking you," I said.

"Okay, Wallace."

"Hey, you're at my locker."

"You were at my house."

"Okay!" I held up my hands. "I do want to know."

"Good." She leaned over and whispered like she had in the cafeteria, so close I felt her lips. "They're waiting for you."

And as my internal alarms blared again, louder than before, in an all-systems-overloaded kind of way, Megan Rose explained exactly who *they* were and where *they* were waiting. The *night people,* she called them. They were in the trees, as I had already seen. And the state forest behind her house—that was a sea of trees. A half mile into it there was a stream, and down the stream was a clearing, a glade. It was an odd place, with strong energies. Megan Rose had found it when she was a kid. That was the place.

The place where they were waiting for me.

The night people.

"Got it?" she asked.

My heart pounded so loudly I could barely hear her.

"Why there? I thought the tennis ball follows you everywhere?"

"She does. She's in here." Megan Rose pointed to her head. "But out there in the glade, the night people energy is strongest. To understand what's going on in here, you need to go out there."

"Makes sense," I said. It didn't really. "It is kind of scary, though."

"Yes," she said. "It is."

TEN

THERE WAS STILL the afternoon to get through. Art was next. It was held in a second-floor classroom with so much collage on the walls they appeared to breathe. A handful of shell-shocked students sat on high stools, blankly thumbing their phones while the teacher, wearing a dress that may or may not have been a gray blanket with a hole cut out in the middle, led a dialogue. I say *dialogue,* as that's the word she used, but no one else spoke. "It helps me to draw my feelings," she said several times.

What was there to dialogue? Hysteria was in the open now. Anyone could get it.

That feeling you have when presidents tweet about preemptive nuclear war as a bargaining strategy—that was the feeling of art class.

As soon as school let out, I ran up the hill to the apartment, dropped my bag, then ran through aching thighs and oppressive heat to Megan Rose's house-brick. There were no cars there, so

I hopped the fence. Rang the doorbell, but I could tell the house was empty. I peeked in the big square window, just in case.

A week. She would be in New Jersey for a week.

Because of a tennis ball.

I walked back to the road and looked up at the ridge behind her house. A mile straight back, she'd said. Over the top of the ridge and there it is. There *they* are. I could be there and back by dinner, all my questions answered. No biggie.

I crossed the street, went around the side of Stuart's house, and knocked on the door to the basement. Stuart opened it, holding a book titled *Living Fearlessly in Fearful Times,* his mouth full of potato chips.

"Have you heard from Melvin?" I asked.

"Not a word," he said. "It's like he went into witness protection."

"You doing anything right now?"

"Got a shift at Lowe's in fifteen minutes. Why?"

"I talked to Megan Rose. She said what happened to Melvin and the others starts in the woods back there." I pointed up the hill. "I'm going to see what it is. Come with me."

Stuart pulled back, spraying chips on the floor. "Are you insane?" he asked.

"No."

"Do you want to be?"

I nodded to the book in his hands. "Seems like you might be missing the gist of that."

He looked down at the cover, put it behind his back. "Shut up," he said.

Alone, I crossed the street back to Megan Rose's and jumped

over the fence again. I walked up the driveway and around the house-brick. At the back of the smoothly manicured yard, the forest came right up to the fence and violently pushed against it. It looked very easy to get lost in there.

It was hard going. Thick bushes. Vines. Thorns. Spiderwebs. Bugs. Tree branches clawing for my eyes. Stepped-on twigs snapping like they were calling for backup. I struggled uphill for an hour . . . and then fell out of the forest onto another paved road.

Shoot. I could have just walked up the road and been here in five minutes.

I crossed it and continued uphill.

The sun lowered and the shadows grew longer. Darkness began to gather in random places, one bush twice as dim as the next one, the trunk of one white birch a shadow of the one beside it. For no obvious reason, spots of forest floor glittered like Christmas lights. I crossed an overgrown wagon trail. I passed under giant groaning maples older than the country. A bear crept in the brush behind me, I was sure.

See, Stuart? Nothing to be afraid of.

I reached the top of the ridge at sunset. The ground sloped off in two directions, and it was hard, in the gloom, to tell which direction to go. I took a guess and descended. Shortly after, I hit a small stream a few inches deep. My heart quickened—Megan Rose had mentioned a stream. I walked right down the center of it, faster now, getting my feet soaked, tripping over unseen rocks covered in slickness, and then all at once the water sparkled in the starlight and the forest cleared and there it was.

The glade was the size of a tennis court and filled with tall grass and goldenrod. It sloped in on itself, like it had long ago been the crater of a volcano. Three sides were bordered by forest; the creek ran along the other side and then curved off down the hill. At the lowest point in the middle of the glade was a single tree, the only one in the entire clearing. This central tree was a weeping willow, a small one, no more than fifteen feet high, and old, with an elaborately mottled trunk and gnarled branches tapping the ground, like they were, well, weeping. The name fit.

Okay, Megan Rose. Made it. I'm here. At the glade.

Now what?

Fear.

Fear was what.

My mind hit overdrive. What would the night people look like? What would they sound like? Where would they be coming from? How would I know when they had arrived? How would I keep from catching the hysterics?

I wasn't going to. I was going to go full hysteria, wasn't I? Why exactly had I gotten myself into this?

I walked into the glade. The grass and goldenrod were knee-high. Past that, along the edges of the field, bare branches of dead trees waved frantically, like the rescue ship was leaving without them. Past that, a sky with no moon. Polaris shone directly above. I tried to remember where it was in relation to the Big Dipper—the handle, the lid, the stove? I thought of Megan Rose. Megan Rose: dressed like Sylvia Plath and standing against my locker. Stretching her leg up the railing at homecoming. Upset about a tennis ball. Her features changing with her moods. Megan Rose: I am here. Where you told me to go. You sure about this? Have you considered that the pressure you put on yourself is enough to make anyone start seeing things, Megan Rose? Those are some ambitious and specific plans you have. We could talk about this. A real talk. Picture it: I'd swing by your house when you return from Princeton, knock on the door, and you'd answer it, hair down, eyes soft, no bra, collarbones emerging from a loose sleep shirt like guidewires for my lips or handholds on a free climb and—

"Hey! Quiet!" A loud echoing voice.

I jumped, smacking into some willow branches. They smacked back.

"Who's there?" I yelled.

No answer.

I crouched low, scanned the field.

"I know Brazilian kung fu!" I yelled. "It's the deadliest kind!"

Nothing.

"Fine, the Russian kind is deadlier! But other than that!"

Calm down, Wallace. Nobody was out there. Was I even sure I heard anything? No, there was nothing.

That's what the hysterics are, hearing things that aren't said.

Don't think that, Wallace.

I just did think it. Want to watch me do it again? There.

Breathe.

Right. Breathe. Okay.

It was obvious now that the only things I'd find in this place were churning terrors, spooky-ass noises, and, undoubtedly, small latching insects that caused chronic diseases that didn't show up on standard blood tests. I'd have to go from doctor's office to doctor's office for years, my joints aching, strange rashes on my skin and ringing in my ears. "Why'd you go to the woods?" the doctors would ask. "To find the source of hysteria," I'd say. "And for love."

They'd call in their colleagues and ask me to repeat myself. Ridiculous.

I should leave.

A squirrel materialized ten feet away. Cheeks stuffed with acorns, it nervously rubbed its paws and assessed me. Was I planning on leaping the ten feet between us and tearing the acorns out of its mouth one by one? You got me, squirrel. How'd you know my intentions? *Intentions*—the word brought Brad Stone to mind. It wasn't intentional on my part, so why was I a magnet for guys like him? What did he get from keeping me out of the cafeteria? Is the part of the brain normally dedicated to kindness repurposed for petty hatred in alpha males? Do they not understand that they are walking, talking clichés, after-school-special villains? Have they not seen every single teen movie in the last thirty years? They didn't get the girl at the end. They got comeuppance. A great word, criminally underused. *Comeuppance.* A word of yore. *Yore.* Another fine word. Yore in a world of shit, Wallace—

"Hey!" Another shout.

"What?" I yelled.

No answer.

"What? Who's there?"

Nothing.

I backed my way through the willow branches until I was underneath them, touching the tree trunk.

"I've killed a man with my bare hands!" I yelled.

Okay, this was . . . okay.

Breathe. Nobody here. I took a few steps forward, emerging from the canopy of the old willow and into the field. All clear. I took a few more steps. And turned. Turned again. And like that, I was walking around the willow tree.

A walk. Might as well. Foot down, foot up. Step. Step.

Then I heard it.

A hum.

A hum? No. Yes. But not an audible hum. Not audible but prickling, in my skin more than my ears. A sensation that something had arrived and it was everywhere. Or no: I was the one arriving. I had transported into a living room, transported right onto the shag carpet as the TV played evening comedies with brittle laugh tracks. And the room was filled with this hum. It wasn't new. I was. And I knew the room. We had lived there in New Mexico, and Ma and I had watched sitcoms while she was on sick leave, Dad at work, the medicines tunneling through her, and her favorite sitcom was one called *Roseanne*— the original, not the botoxed racist reboot—in which, in the very last episode, it was revealed that the husband in the show, the best thing in it, a great, happy, hardworking, heart-the-size-of-Delaware fat guy, had actually died of a heart attack the year before and the whole last year of the show had been a dream. He was stone dead. And they had pretended he was still there, his family. For a whole year. It was a sucker punch of an ending, and it shocked Ma and me, and we sat on the sofa in that shock.

And I had heard humming. I remembered it now.

It's her sickness, I had decided.

"Please," I had said to it, the hum, as my mother and I sat stunned in front of the TV. "Don't take her."

It didn't answer.

"Is it something I did? Do I not love her enough?"

"No. You're fine," said the hum. "You eat your veggies when she asks?"

"Sure," I said. "Usually."

"You're fine. This isn't about that."

And then the hum said: "This is how you'll learn that death is not the end."

I was ten.

I had never told my mother or anyone else about this conversation. That it appeared to me in the glade, clear as the night it happened, made no sense. I had honestly not thought of that episode of *Roseanne* since we watched it. I had not thought of it now, actually. It had just appeared, fully formed.

I turned again, and the willow tree came back in view.

And now I saw how, when Ma put me in bed that night, the shock of the show we'd just watched (Life is a dream? Death is?) had made us open and raw, and so we were completely with each other and not in our worries or mental preparations for the next morning. We were with the moment. We were with her death. We were really with it. It was right there.

Death.

Mother.

Night.

Then I was lying in my bed under my Snoopy covers, Ma's hand on my hand. Her eyes, a shade of gray that looked blue if she had on a dark sweater, shone with wisdom and troubles. A look that made her seem to be in two worlds at once, the strain of giving attention to both beginning to show. She wore a white robe pulled tight up to her chin, hiding her wasting frame.

Her cool, thin fingers stroked my wrist. I asked her the obvious question:

"Is this real?"

She didn't answer.

"Are you dead?"

Her hand stopped. I sensed that for her to say yes would expose a sadness too large for words, but to say no meant going through the looking glass to a whole other kind of world.

She saw I wasn't ready for that. So she walked me right up to the mirror.

"Who really dies?" she asked me.

"Roseanne's husband?"

"He's alive in reruns."

"You?"

"I'm here with you, Wallace. Always."

"But he was made up. You're not."

"We all are made up," Ma said. "That's the secret."

I didn't understand the secret. It felt like there was a fragile bubble of water where my heart should be.

"He should've watched what he eats," I said. "He should've eaten more kale, less bacon."

"He should've," she agreed. "But you do see how their love kept him close? Everything we love we keep alive."

"That's beautiful, Ma," I said. "What a beautiful world that lets you do that."

"Yes," she said.

And I had a spine-chilling feeling, walking in the glade, looking at my ma sitting on my bed, that something was really off. And I realized it was because I would never have said anything like that—what ten-year-old lying beneath his Snoopy sheets in the glow of a SpongeBob night-light says it's a beautiful world? And further: I had never had any such conversation with my mother. We had watched *Roseanne* together, true, that last episode where the show tumbled in on itself, but we had not talked about dying. She never liked to talk much about feelings with me, really—talking in general wasn't her thing. She was married to my dad, after all. What had really happened that night was that she'd turned off the television and lain down on the couch while I put my cookie plate in the sink, and when I came back to the living room and tried to tell her how upset the show had made me, how it had hit too close to home—feelings I didn't have words for—she had asked if I'd finished my homework and was ready for bed. That was our *only* conversation that night. And then I'd gone to bed by myself. And lay awake for hours.

So this conversation had not happened. What I had just remembered in the glade had not happened.

It was as if the story of my life was being erased before my eyes and written all over again.

Who was writing it?

How did it end?

And here she was, my mother, sitting on the edge of my bed, holding my ten-year-old hand. Tears dripped off her eyelashes and floated over to my face.

"Who are you?" I asked her, suddenly terrified.

The door to my bedroom flew open, and by the light of SpongeBob, Roseanne's husband stepped in, nodded to my mother, pulled a chair right up to the edge of the bed, flipped it around so the back faced forward, and sat down in that dramatic, man-of-large-feelings-on-the-verge-of-sweating-through-his-shirt way he had.

He grinned a big grin. "Hey, kiddo," he said.

"Mr. Roseanne? Ma?"

"You liked the show, eh?" asked Roseanne's dead husband. He tilted the chair forward. "Bit of a mind-screw that ending was, though. You may have been a little young for it." He leaned forward even more. His giant frame blocked out the SpongeBob glow, and the room became darker and darker; and then, as he leaned right up to the bed, a thin white line split his chest down the middle. It spread open. White light poured forth from it. The light lit up my face, my bed, and then the whole room.

It began to lift the bed off the floor.

And someone said: Let go of the past, Wallace. Let go of the pain. I heard this, but nobody's lips were moving.

"You, Wallace," said Roseanne's husband, getting even brighter, "have never been hurt."

"I got beat up last week."

"Irrelevant. Never been hurt."

"My ma is dead."

"Never been hurt," he repeated. "Are you ready? Do you want to live without fear and loneliness? Do you want to know what really happened to your mother? Do you want to see the source of the light that holds up the world?"

"Ma!"

"Hey!"

"What?"

"Hey!"

ELEVEN

BREATHE.

Okay. Breathe.

Okay. I am hysterical. This is it. There is no other explanation.

I mean, what else did I expect to happen? This is exactly what was supposed to happen. You go to hysteria's nightclub, you join the party.

I trembled, waiting for the next thing.

Breathe.

It was pitch-black. A cloud covered the sky above the glade. The old willow tree rustled in the wind. The squirrel twitched darkly ten feet away.

"Hello?" I said, cautiously.

Not a sound.

"Hey, uh . . . Mr. Roseanne? You there? I'm ready now. You were going to tell me something about my mother?"

Nothing.

How did things get started last time? Walking. Walking in circles around the willow tree. Okay.

For the next hour, I walked around the old willow. I walked in a hurry, and then I walked medium-speed, and then slower and slower. And the slower I got, the faster my thoughts went. They spun. They bounced and hit walls. They bungee jumped, they mosh-pitted, they played hide-and-seek, duck-duck-goose, and truth-or-dare (truth: is this stupid or really, really stupid?); they ambushed each other, hurricane-nuked each other; and toward the end of the second hour of walking, they flat-out screamed.

And then, right when I was about to give up for good, they got quiet. Eerily so.

I tried again.

"Hello," I addressed the glade.

And the old willow tree said, "Good evening."

I—okay, so now the tree was talking. We were going to do this.

"So it was you," I said.

"It was me what?" said the tree.

"You were yelling at me before?"

"I was?"

I held up my hands. "I apologize, I didn't mean to scare you. I don't really know kung fu. . . . I—I'll get right to it. My name is Wallace. I have some questions. A lot of questions, actually. We could do simple yes-or-no questions, if that would be easier. Like, for example: Have I lost my mind? We could start with that."

The old willow said, "Wait."

"Sorry. Are you busy?"

It gestured toward the edge of the field. "They're coming."

This confused me. "Who? Coming from where?"

"Shh."

"Friends of yours?"

"Shh."

I'd never been shushed by a willow. It wasn't easy to be quiet. I bit my tongue.

Where the willow had gestured, the glade was empty. And past that were the trees, but they were empty, too. I mean, they had leaves and branches and stuff, but they weren't, as far as I could tell, having conversations.

And I don't know how to describe what happened next, other than to say that the emptiness opened up. And I . . . I disappeared.

The lonely boy called Wallace, with dirty jeans and no friends, with a lot of unanswered questions, with a dead mother and a father with the nurturing skills of those probes sent on one-way missions to deep space—he just disappeared. He was gone. All gone.

For a long minute, I forgot everything I had been looking for, forgot everything that hurt. It was beautiful. It was the most beautiful thing.

"Wow," I said to the willow. "This is . . . wow."

"Glad you see it," the willow said.

"It kind of makes my life seem pointless in comparison."

"Glad you see that," it said again.

"That my life is pointless?"

"That your life is so much more than you thought it was."

"Oh. It sounds nicer the way you say it."

"Truth is always nice to hear."

"You know, not a lot of trees talk like this," I pointed out to the willow.

"Actually," it replied, "we all do."

A bird sang a song too tender for a name. The willow chuckled as a squirrel ran up and down its trunk. Another squirrel joined the first one, and the willow's drooping leaves shook with laughter.

I did not know the meaning of this peaceful and contented vision. Or if I was worthy of it.

"Worthy? Why ask such a question?" said the willow. "This is just what is. You have forgotten that life is magic. We in the woods—we know it. We live in magic all day long. Wanting nothing, we can have everything. Like children. Like gods."

We live in magic. A magic world behind our own, more fluid, more colorful, less defined—trees could speak wisdom, tennis balls could talk, mothers died but returned to visit from time to time. It made sense. Maybe. Maybe. Just let go of trying to understand it—

But wait. Hold on. I had to understand.

"I have to get some answers," I said to the willow.

"I know."

"Well, what the hell is going on?"

The willow shook gently. "That's not the right question."

"What happened to Melvin?"

"Not the right question, either."

"Who are you?"

"Nope. Not it, either."

"What? How can it not be?"

It didn't say. Instead, what happened next was that the willow began to shimmer. It shimmered brighter and brighter, so that I had to shut my eyes; when I opened them, the willow was gone and I wasn't in the glade anymore, there was no grass or trees or sky anymore. A field of white light stretched to the horizon, which was made up of another field of light, that one a pinkish silver. It was like I was on a star.

And then the light parted like a curtain, and my mother appeared again, lying in a hospital bed under a thick quilt, heart monitor beeping by her side, as she had been in the last hours before she died. Then she sat up, swung her legs over the bed rail, and walked right out of the room.

That was impossible. She couldn't walk at the end. I'd had to drag her to the bathroom, her arm over my shoulders, the heaviest thing about her body the bathrobe that draped it. Placed her on the toilet, waited by the door until she was done. *Family time,* Dad had called it.

I followed her. She'd gone into the kitchen. She was looking out the small window above the sink at something a thousand miles away. Her hair blocked her face, and it was thick hair, far thicker than it had ever been when we lived in California. It had fallen out fast at the end.

"Ma?" I approached her. "You're feeling better?"

"Yes, Wallace," she said. She ran a hand through the brown curls, lifting them. "How are you?"

How was I? That felt like the hardest question I had ever heard.

"School okay?" she asked.

"Yeah. Sure."

"Your father okay?"

"Sure. Hard to say. You know. We moved again. We're in New York now." My tongue started to unstick. "I met a girl. Her name's Megan Rose. She's smart. You'd like her."

"I'm happy to hear that," Ma said.

"Yeah," I said.

"Yeah," I said again.

Ma's gray-blue eyes, normally strained and half-present, were shining in a full way I wasn't used to and found hard to look at. She seemed content to stand there in silence. But I was afraid if we didn't talk, she would leave again. I didn't want her to leave again.

I said, "Last year I wrote an essay about you for a contest. It was about the time we went swimming at Jennings Pond and tried to swim all the way across and six thousand geese attacked us when we were halfway."

Ma smiled. "I remember that day. The geese were so loud. Did I tell you how proud I was of you for trying?"

I looked down. "Actually, I never wrote the essay. Dad and I were driving across Nebraska, and I saw the contest in a magazine and I thought if I entered it, that's what I would write about."

Really? A chance to talk with my mother after seven years and all I can think of to say is a dumb, unnecessary lie? Stupid.

"Sorry, I shouldn't have said that," I said. "I don't know what I'm doing."

"Wallace."

"I've been talking to a tree."

"Wallace. Look at me."

I looked up. Her eyes, still with that full-on shine. And then I got what they were saying.

And I couldn't believe it. Wasn't I a weird malcontent doomed to a meaningless life on the margins of other, better lives? An annoyance? An oof? A loser?

It had to be a mistake. And yet.

And yet her eyes said: Wallace, you're everything I ever wished for.

And: I miss you.

And: Your sadness is my love keeping you from the cliff.

And: This is all you need to know.

Then I couldn't look at her eyes anymore and looked out toward the edge of the glade. And my mother wrapped me in her arms.

I don't know how long I spent like that. Minutes, years. At some point, I sat up and wiped my tears. I was again sitting in the glade underneath the willow tree and the starry sky.

Had it all been a dream? It had to have been. A fantasy born out of longing, hysteria finding the most vulnerable places in my heart and telling them exactly what they wanted to hear. A dream.

But then the willow gently reached down and brushed the dirt off my face.

TWELVE

QUESTIONS.

What was this town, this forest, that opened you up and filleted your soul? And then tenderly tended to the carcass?

And what did it want from me?

THIRTEEN

YOU KNOW THAT feeling after opening your eyes, when you're not sure if you are awake or still dreaming? And the feeling lasts for a second or two, until you blink a few times or hear a garbage truck outside? *Hypnopompia,* it's called. I looked it up. The next morning I had that feeling for thirty minutes. Eventually I got out of bed and went around the apartment picking up things—a plate, a cup, a sock—to make sure they were there. They were, it seemed, but what did that prove? I felt my face to make sure it was actually my face.

It appeared to be. *But how could I be sure?*

The part of my brain that ordinarily autopiloted past such questions was on the fritz. Like hot water and world leaders who don't stare at the sun, we don't properly appreciate this autopilot until it's fritzing. We don't normally stop and ponder: Why is this called a *shoe*? It took heroic concentration to shower, dress, eat the egg-and-sausage sandwich my father had left on the kitchen counter, lock the door, nod good morning in response to the greetings from the street's three oak trees—

—and do what?

I looked at them, the oaks. They stood there in the dim morning light. Their branches extended like the gnarled hands of arthritic giants. Dark shapes moved through their leaves.

And they said good morning.

"Good morning, Wallace!"

"Um, hi?" I said.

"Buenos días," said the smallest of the three. "Muy buenos días a todos! Did you have enough to eat?"

"Sure," I said.

"Breakfast is the most important meal of the day," it said.

"Actually, that's been discredited," said the first.

"It has?" said the third tree.

"You can't generalize like that. People have different metabolisms. Different internal clocks. Wouldn't you agree, Wallace?"

I didn't answer. Was I absolutely sure I was awake?

At the front entrance of the school, two enormous security guards stood with their arms crossed. They were Brad Stone–sized, among the largest human beings I'd ever seen in person: six and a half feet tall, ninety-five percent forearms and sunglasses. Five percent don't ask what the other five percent is, fuckface. I wasn't sure how I was supposed to get inside. Then Principal Rathschild stepped out from behind them.

The bags under her eyes were dark and round as bowling balls. She looked like an unethical experiment on sleep deprivation.

"Jesus," she said.

"Hi," I said.

"You're late, Wallace."

"Just five minutes."

She looked at her watch. "Seventeen."

She flipped through sheets on a clipboard until she got to the very last one, where I saw my name written by hand at the end of a long printed list. She put a check next to my name. The security guards behind her glowered.

"Can I go to class now?" I asked her.

"I don't know, can you?" she answered. Maybe you have a disease that prevents you." She rubbed her eyes with the back of a wrist. "I'm tired of this, Wallace."

"Sorry. I overslept."

"Come to my office immediately after school."

"Why? What'd I do?"

"Why? You've missed four classes in one week. Your father completely blew off his meeting with me last Thursday. I need a reason not to expel you. How's that?"

"Oh," I said. "Sounds reasonable."

"Go to class."

A straightforward order, but at my locker I got sidetracked again. The combination had completely slipped out of my mind. I stared at the lock for ten minutes, hoping that the combination would slip back in and I wouldn't have to beg the mean-eyed secretaries for it. But my brain was no help at all. It was back in the glade, talking to trees.

Hey, trees.

That's when Stuart showed up. Bent double, face pale, eyes glassy, his forehead covered with sweat—he looked like he'd just returned from one of those pointless wars they make poor people fight.

"Holy shit," I said.

"A simple 'Good morning' is more polite," he sniffed.

"Who did that to you?"

"Wait. I have a message."

He reached into a back pocket with a shaky hand, dug around in there, and produced his middle finger.

"This is from Brad Stone," he said. "He wants you to look at it carefully."

"Thank you."

He pushed his finger up close. "From all angles, like so."

"Got it," I said.

"You can sit on it, too. And spin in circles. I don't really understand the logistics of that. Seems like it would hurt unless he has a very strong finger. Make it dirty, at least."

"Stuart? Dude, you sound a little—"

With the same arm, Stuart pushed up the left sleeve of his T-shirt. "This message is also from Brad."

His upper arm, slack, scrawny, thin as a deer leg, was covered with an enormous black-and-green bruise. It pulsed to his heartbeat and grew a little with each pulse. It looked like it hurt like a mother—

"Fuck," I said.

"The message is," said Stuart, "and I quote, 'Tell newb: don't infect people or this is his face.'"

"Don't infect people?"

"Brad heard you were talking to Megan Rose in the hallway," Stuart said. "Ergo: infecting her with your foreign germs. 'Infections need to be excised quickly.' His words."

Goddamn it. Why now? Why the hell did Brad Stone hate me so much? What would get him to back off?

And how could he be so oblivious to what was happening? For God's sake, trees were talking about the meaning of life and breakfast grains.

"I'm not infecting anyone," I said. "He can go screw himself."

"You sure?" said Stuart. "You sure you want to take that tack? You should know that if I lift my arm above my shoulder it will land on the floor."

"Well, don't lift it."

"Okay, then. My job is done. I'm going to the nurse."

"I'll go with you. You going to tell her Brad did this? The principal will nail his ass." I snapped my fingers. "I'm meeting her later, actually. I could tell her."

Stuart grimaced. "Don't be stupid. I walked into a door."

The nurse's office was in the school basement. I hadn't been down there before. One hallway had a massive water stain on the ceiling the shape of Antarctica. In another, paint had dripped onto the floor in hard puddles the color of dried blood. The few classrooms down there had the feel of secret prisons.

It was an appropriate match for Stuart's mood. Brad had knocked Stuart a mile deeper into Mega D, and he'd already been cruise-ship-wreck deep. He bitterly recounted society's ingrained injustices as we walked down the hall.

I finally interrupted him. "I went to the woods last night."

Stuart shook his head. "You really did it? Damn."

"I'm not sure I can describe it. It was powerful."

"So, are you hysterical now?"

"No. I mean, I don't think so. Maybe. Maybe I need to go back. Will you come with me?"

"Dude." He gestured angrily, wincing at the pain it caused his shoulder. "No. Can't you just drop it? Is it worth risking everything for this—your body? Your face? My face? I like my face."

We'd reached the nurse's office: a heavy door, a frosted window reading URSE in big block letters.

"I don't think I can drop it," I said.

"Right. Of course," said Stuart. "No one ever listens to me. That should be on my tombstone."

He pushed the URSE door open. It thumped behind him, and I was standing alone in an empty hallway. A fluorescent tube flickered, and I had a flash of memory of a light splitting Mr. Roseanne in half.

What was that worth? What did it even mean?

The bell rang, and classroom doors swung open. Students filled the hallway. They avoided eye contact. They looked terrified, like farm animals that had just come to understand what would happen to them.

Two grim-faced football linemen walked quickly in my direction. I turned around and pretended to open a locker; they passed; a few seconds later the locker's owner, a gum-chomping girl in red sweats, elbowed me away with impressive force.

Another bell, the start of second period. The hallway thinned out. What did I have next? Math. My math class—where was that? I started walking in what I hoped was the right direction. But what was the way out of the basement? The other way. No, the *other* other way. My brain was still fritzed. I started to worry it might stay that way. Maybe that's what hysteria was: permanent brain fritz. And then, when the hallway cleared, leaning against the wall opposite, arms crossed, brow furrowed, in black pants and a brown jacket—Dr. Rathschild.

"Wallace Cole, in the hallways when he shouldn't be," she said. "What are the odds?"

"I was just on my way to calculus," I said.

"Why rush?" She straightened up, rolled her shoulders. "Why do anything?"

"Well, actually, that's something I—"

"Don't answer that."

FOURTEEN

THE WALLS OF the administrative offices were the color of a prison cell. Yes, a prison cell is mostly bars and the space between the bars, and that's not exactly a color, but that's what they were. The color of hopelessness. The color of broken-backed old men drinking booze made from urine and guards yelling, "Closing number four!" The color of pure and unexpected happiness smashed by merciless authority figures.

The secretary pointed me to a chair in the waiting area, and from there I listened while someone in Rathschild's office, a man, spoke to her with very loud and pointed opinions. As I listened from my seat, his voice stabbed her repeatedly. After ten minutes, the door flew open and the angry man emerged. He wore a three-piece suit, a hundred-dollar haircut, and an expression of pure fury. I realized with a start that it was the same man who had been standing at the square window of Megan Rose's house-brick. Her father. He charged through the waiting area, then stopped abruptly in front of me, studying my face.

I looked down, so he could see only the top of my head.

"I know you," he said, his voice a poison-tipped dart.

I didn't say anything.

"Who are you?"

Who am I? Well, I'm the guy walking through your yard yesterday. I'm the guy outside your house every afternoon before that. I'm the one your daughter trusts with her secrets.

Probably best not to mention all that.

"Nobody," I said to the floor.

"Look at me," he said.

I didn't move.

"Wallace Cole, get in here," called the principal.

"Wallace Cole," Megan Rose's father said, committing my name to memory or a hit list.

I ducked past him and went inside.

Rathschild's inner office: desk, chairs, file cabinets, bookcases, precariously stacked folders on each of those. On the wall behind her desk, a clock, crooked diplomas, and aerial pictures of the school. On one side of the room, a large fish tank, which appeared to hold no fish, just those vertical, spiky fish-tank plants that wave desperately, like they're trying not to drown. On the other side, a small closet held a few coats and a stack of books. The desk was made of battleship steel.

"Sit," said Dr. Rathschild. She picked up a coffee mug.

I sat.

"Not there." She pointed to another chair, which looked completely the same.

I switched.

I avoided her eyes. They had the stare of principals all across the country: the stare of the verge. Principals were always on the verge of having had enough. Or the verge had been crossed. They had crossed over to the other side of the verge.

"You know why I brought you here, Wallace?"

"Because I missed first period?"

"You did? Right after our conversation? Good Lord, do you really think the point of a high school education is to wander the hallways? This is not okay, Wallace. It is something we need to discuss. And we will. In detail. But later. I think you know why you're here."

She stared at me again. Harder.

"You're right, I didn't oversleep this morning," I admitted.

"I know you didn't," she said. "And I know your type. Authoritarial disrespect born from poor parental relationships, subversively anarchic literature, and blood-soaked video games—and a surprisingly above-average IQ."

"I don't play video games."

"You think life is a game."

"What? No. That's not what . . . Principal Rothschild, last night, I—" How would I even begin to explain the glade and how it had made me late for school? That a willow had brushed away my tears and I had walked on a star? "You're right. I'm sorry," I said. "I won't miss class again."

"Oh, you definitely won't."

"Right. Can I go?"

Rathschild slapped down the request. "Your father, Wallace,

agreed to meet me and then never showed. I spent an evening in the office by myself. He lied to me. That's not on you, but do you not think I had better things to do Thursday evening than eat a moldy tuna-fish sandwich at my desk? So tell me, did the apple fall far from the tree, or did it get wedged right in the branches?"

"I'm not sure I—"

She lifted a three-inch-thick folder from the top of a pile on her desk and cleared space with a violent forearm shove, decking a phone and a hole puncher. She dropped the folder there.

"Your records, Wallace," she said, "finally faxed to us yesterday from your high school in Kentucky. And earlier faxed there from"—she opened the folder and flipped a couple of pages—"Laramie, Wyoming. And some town in Washington State I've never heard of. Before that, Mississippi. Fourteen high schools in three years, to be exact. This is remarkable. I've never seen anyone move around like this. And then quite a truancy record when you *are* settled somewhere. Look at this!" She stabbed at the folder with her index finger. "Listen to these reasons you've given for missing class: a dental appointment to have a tracking device removed from a molar, fatigue from a long night following a rogue asteroid for NASA, you got trapped in a Costco after closing, mild malaria, an abnormal growth on your elbow that doctors wanted to research for sentience—"

"Psoriasis."

"What?"

"That was supposed to be psoriasis. I misspoke."

"Somehow I doubt that. And, my favorite: you missed a

field trip because you were busy with a detective investigation into the nature of existence. Come on. An existential detective?"

"Well, I've often wondered what the point of life is," I said.

"You don't say! Me too! Every day! Right this moment! But why wonder in the hallways? Why not in class?"

She rubbed her face with her large hands, hard, like she was trying to rub it off and put a mask on. Or rub a mask off and put on her face. Like the disguised aliens would.

"Wallace, look, I'm sorry for what you've been through. Truly. And it's understandable, with your loss—again, sorry—and your transient living situations, to want to believe you have big secrets and secret missions. But understand that the world doesn't run on people's pity. It runs on upholding responsibilities. Even for detectives! Why, Encyclopedia Brown went to all his classes. He got straight As, then went to college, got a law degree, earned a name partnership at a medium-sized Boston firm, did pro bono work for asylum seekers, and paid off his student loans in just sixteen years. Little-known facts."

"Who's Encyclopedia Brown?"

"Never mind. Point is: hobbies and schoolwork are not mutually exclusive. You can solve crime and go to math at the same time. Or better yet, you can just go to math and solve crime at home. You can stop getting in fights you can't win. You can start caring about yourself and your life in a way that has some practical value. Can you do that?"

"Absolutely."

"You sure?"

"Yes."

"You promise?"

"Yes, Dr. Rathschild."

"Great. So why are you lying to me?"

My breath caught. Rathschild leaned over the desk and knocked her knuckles on the folder between her elbows. My folder.

Her voice dropped but got harsher at the same time. "I have time to think things over when phone calls from parents and the blowhard chief of police keep me up the entire night. I got students filling the nurse's office, convinced they're seeing little green men. I got teachers saying they need leave for bite rabies and insisting that the school pay for therapy for their PTSD. I got the school board ready to nail me to the wall if this isn't settled by the PTA meeting next week. And yet, with all that, here's the thing that I keep coming back to." She hit the folder again. "Why would a kid move so much? So suddenly? Is he in the circus? Is he a spy?"

"I'm not a spy."

"I didn't think you were. But I did something called Google late last night. And found out that every one of the high schools you've attended was right next to a Jackduke power plant. And a lot of these plants have had strange 'incidents' "— she air-quoted—"right around when you and your father arrived in town."

A missile rocketed up my spine. It carried a North Korean payload. The payload detonated. My Seoul trembled.

"I'm right, aren't I?" she said.

"About what?"

"Your father. He's involved."

"Maybe it's a coincidence?"

"What does your father do for Jackduke?"

"I don't know. He won't tell me."

"Does he hurt you?"

"No."

"Is he part of a cult?"

"What? No."

"Like Heaven's Gate?"

"I don't know what that is."

"It's a cult. A death cult."

"Oh."

"They all died."

"Okay."

"Are you Russian?"

"What?"

"Does your father travel to Russia?"

"What? No. Dr. Rathschild, I don't know anything. Please!"

It was quiet for a minute. Rathschild blinked several times without moving a single other muscle, an expression conveying that she was uncertain if I was capable of intelligent thought and also that she had no choice but to hope I was.

She got up and locked the door.

Back in her chair, she lifted the coffee mug but put it down without a sip. She tapped the folder on the desk, pushed it away from her. When she spoke again, her voice was much less harsh than it had been.

"It's getting worse," she said. "Last night was by far the worst we've had. It was like someone was out there all night, pissing off whoever's behind this. Two students went to the

ER. One girl was medevaced by helicopter to Syracuse at first light. And that's on top of the breakdown in the cafeteria at lunch yesterday. You saw that." She rubbed her face. "I've been going through lockers for drugs. Been eating cafeteria food for three weeks to see if there's LSD lacing it. Nothing. My one job, keeping the students safe, and I'm failing. Starting tomorrow, there're going to be a lot of changes. It's going to be hell for all of you. I'm already sorry about it."

She rubbed her face again, harder.

"You kids . . . I get it, you know. I think I'd do the same. It's all breaking the hell down. It's already broken. Honestly, my generation, I don't think we can help you. The world has passed us by. We don't know what's going on anymore, but we don't know how to admit that. You're going to have to figure out new rules for the new world while we punish you for having the temerity to do so. You're totally screwed."

It was a sudden, despairing confession, and it surprised me and appeared to surprise her, too. For a minute neither of us said anything. I saw then that Dr. Rathschild wasn't my enemy, just a tired woman flailing against the pain machines, rubbing her face with disturbing intensity.

No one knew anything, it seemed, except maybe the trees.

"What can I do?" I asked.

"Nothing," she said. "There's nothing you can do. No, wait, there is one thing."

I drew in a ragged breath. "What?"

"Go to class."

FIFTEEN

THERE FOLLOWED A week of fear.

How can I describe what that felt like? Every morning landed in the North Homer High parking lot like a hijacked plane. The plane was wired with explosives. Terrorists in the cockpit made demands. The president was notified. But the president was clearing brush from his ranch. The president was golfing with sixteen internet billionaires. The president spelled *ransom* with a *u* and an *e*. We were on our own, in a world that had no leadership and made no sense. That's what it felt like.

Three more students disappeared.

In classes, kids discussed the missing in low voices and how they personally felt off. In the hallways between classes, there was a thrumming, aching nervousness—even Brad Stone felt it. When we passed each other outside the cafeteria on Tuesday, he didn't shove, insult, punch, or wind up and pretend to punch me. That had never happened before.

Ah, that's not true. He punched me in the arm so hard I felt it back in kindergarten.

"Leave, newb," he said.

That hadn't changed.

On Wednesday in social studies, Mrs. Durkins wrote a few lines about Franz Ferdinand on the blackboard, then stopped midsentence and said, "None of you are listening" and "I need a new car seat," and sat down and pulled out her iPad. At the end of the period, the PA ordered us to the gym. We filed onto the bleachers, all four grades, Dr. Rathschild eyeing us from the Fighting Poet painted at center court. She looked more haggard than ever, blouse untucked, short hair stringy with sweat. Behind her stood a half-dozen rumply dressed men and women who gave off the ragged vibe of stuffed animals at Goodwill.

After hushing us by glaring into our souls, Rathschild explained that we, the students, were going to get to try something different. Unusual. Starting immediately. *Being there,* she called it—we were going to *be there* for each other. If you see a friend spacing out, *be there* for her. Check in. Talk to her. Ask her what she's thinking. Ask her if she knows where she is. If what she tells you is disturbing, notify myself or one of—Rathschild gestured to the people behind her—our county's mental-health experts. They will be at North Homer High until we get to the bottom of this. Or until the crisis fund runs out, which is next Tuesday. But we can't get to the bottom of this if you don't talk to us.

"Stay with me on this, guys," Dr. Rathschild added, her voice straining. "If this doesn't work, things are going to get rough. But it's going to work, I know it. I know you. It's going to work."

She introduced an expert named Dr. Howard, who stepped to the microphone, smiling like he'd just found a puppy for his inner child. His suit coat had elbow patches; his bald head gleamed like a sick pearl.

He also spoke about being there for each other. We don't listen to each other anymore, he said. And while this problem starts with everyone tweeting instead of listening, and for sure some blame goes to a societal overemphasis on standardized testing and too early toilet training—he had a number of theories—he'd formed a listening group right here in North Homer and people picked it up quickly—listening, that is—and the group is for adults, but kids can come, too, and his daughter was in the auditorium, actually, right there in the third row, don't be shy, Melanie, and we could ask her about it, the listening group, because it meets in their living room and—

Dr. Rathschild leaned into the microphone.

"What Dr. Howard is saying is all of us must become each other's helpers," she said. "Each other's protectors."

"It's *Mr.* Howard, actually. I just have a certificate in family counseling. But you can talk to me about anything."

"Including demons?" a boy called out from the bleachers near the back.

"Say what now?" said Mr. Howard.

"Can we talk to you about demons?" yelled the boy.

"There are no demons," said Rathschild. "We're not talking about demons."

"How do you know there are no demons?"

"Demons aren't real."

"How do you know they're not real?"

Gasps swept through the gym, back and forth. Rathschild white-knuckled the edges of the podium, as if she were going to rip it off and chuck it, pro-wrestling-style, at her interlocutor. "Because they're not."

"But what if they're out there?" the boy cried. "What if they're coming for us, one by one? The demons! They'll break our heads open! They'll eat our minds! What if they've already started!"

Two of the men standing behind Dr. Rathschild stepped forward and ascended the bleachers toward the boy. Assembly ended shortly after that.

All week, I chewed over Dr. Rathschild's suspicion that my father was behind the outbreak of hysterics in teenagers. But how? By blowing cigarette smoke in their faces until they went hysterical? By ignoring them until they became emotionally stunted, overly imaginative loners? I mean, for sure he was as friendly as a heavily accented Terminator from the future, and no question his job was exposing him and me to chemicals that would lead to fierce cancers later in my life, but trucking around the country, directly hurting kids—wouldn't he have to take an interest in them before he could do that?

It couldn't be him.

So, what the hell was going on? What was hysteria?

And then on Friday, I was sitting with Stuart in the cafeteria, having taken advantage of the general mood of unrestrained terror to overlook Brad's threats and eat there. Nobody was laughing. Nobody was flirting. Nobody was jumping in anybody else's lap. In the aisles between the tables, Dr.—Mr.—Howard and a couple of other mental-health experts strolled about, kindly whispering, "You need someone to talk to?"

"They don't have a fucking clue," I said. "Not one."

"And you do?" responded Stuart.

"Tonight. Come with me. I'm going back to the woods."

"To talk to the trees?"

"Yes."

"Have you listened to yourself?"

"I know how it sounds. But the world doesn't just stop making sense."

"Wrong!" Stuart said. "Maybe that's exactly what it does!"

He was in as pleasant a mood as always. I was beginning to wonder if his Mega D was of the permanent kind. Might be time to check.

Though maybe it was warranted, considering.

Just then a compact girl with bulging deltoids rushed toward us like an attack helicopter. Students ducked out of her way or took an elbow to the back of the head. She skidded to a stop in front of our table. She had a facelift-tight, blindingly blond ponytail—she was the one driving the CRV outside Megan Rose's house-brick. The one who gave me the finger.

"Wallace," she said.

"Kelly, right?"

"Keely. I'm having some people over tonight."

She bounced on her heels.

It took me a minute.

"Wait, you're inviting me?"

"Whatever," she said.

She spoke as if she were being forced to by an evil government but was about to rebel against them. It wasn't a friendly
invitation.

"Not you, loser," she said to Stuart without looking at him.

"Aw, I'm crushed," he said.

I was surprised. "You're having a party? For real? With
Rathschild's new group-therapy state in effect?"

"It's not a party," Keely replied. "Well, it wasn't meant to
be. A few of us decided to get together. Other people heard and
wanted to join."

"Is Keely your first name or last name?" I asked.

"What kind of dumb question is that?"

"Just curious."

"Don't go, Wallace," Stuart said. "Brad Stone will be there.
Your ass will get kicked if you go. Then mine."

I glanced at the other side of the cafeteria, where, at a table
stuffed with football-uniform-wearing minions, Brad Stone
watched us intently. In his tight gray T-shirt, he looked like a
war-robot prototype.

Keely bounced impatiently.

"Why am I invited?" I asked her.

"You're a freak," she said. "You stare at us in the halls
like you're looking under our skin. You smell like a fasting
vampire—"

"Not sure that answers the—"

"Megan Rose wants to talk to you."

* * *

Okay. A party. Tonight. With Megan Rose. With other students, possibly including Brad Stone. Away from adult protection. With everyone tense and terrified, still without a clue as to what was going on.

Across the table, Stuart violently shook his head, mouthing the word *no* over and over.

"You're *so* gonna get your ass kicked," Stuart said after Keely choppered off. "I'm *so* gonna get my ass kicked again. And life already has my ass kicked. Look at this—" He rolled up his sleeve to show me the Brad Stone–inflicted bruise. It was now the shape and color of one of those Pacific Islander shoulder tattoos. Those tattoos usually had some muscle under them, though. Skin and bone ruined the look.

He touched the bruise and groaned. "Brad kicks my ass. Lowe's kicks my ass. Getting out of bed kicks my ass. I don't think all this ass kicking is healthy."

"Well, you heard Keely. Maybe I can get some answers."

"Dude. It's a keg party. There are no answers at keg parties. You think when Stephen Hawking was stuck on the nature of black holes he went to a keg party?"

"It's more of a Supreme Court thing."

"Ha, ha. I hope it's worth it when you're dead."

"I'm not dying."

"I'll say a few words over your grave. If only he'd listened to me, I'll say."

"Stuart! You're not helpful. It's either the party or you're coming with me to the woods."

"I know," Stuart said. "I'm just afraid. Everything's going to shit."

"Well, did you ever think that maybe out there is the thing that frees us from fear?"

Stuart's jaw dropped open; mine did, too, honestly. Sometimes you don't know what you're saying until it's been said.

Though once it's said, you realize you've known it all along.

"Hey, boys." We looked up. Mr. Howard waved. "You two got anything on your mind?"

SIXTEEN

AFTER THE LAST bell of the day sounded, and after the extra five minutes the bio teacher spent expounding upon how he would accept no late assignments, despite whatever odd things were happening, and that this was an important life lesson that would serve us well like when, oh, for example, our wife left us for the sideburned graphic designer who had put together her craft-jewelry website, I rushed to the apartment. I had just enough time to grab a change of clothes and get them washed at the Laundromat before Keely's party. I was going to look my best or at least not smell like the fasting undead.

At the apartment door, remembering my manners, I braked and greeted the three oak trees.

"Wallace, por favor, is it summer already?" the middle one asked. "Because it feels like summer."

"It's not summer."

"Fall lose a bet?"

"World might be busted."

"Oh," the tree said. "I was afraid of that."

The trees had not, all week, offered an explanation for why they were now speaking or how exactly they were doing it. But they were effusively polite. They thanked every breeze. Their branches extended toward each other and through each other but never once blocked each other's light. There was a lesson there.

Then I turned, vaulted up the stoop, opened the door . . . and ran into my father.

He was sitting at the kitchen table. It had been a few days since I'd seen him last. Longer than that, at least a week, since I'd seen him in daylight. He had on a wrinkled flannel shirt and worn jeans and a blank expression, but that goes without saying. He held a half-eaten sandwich in one hand and a cigarette and a glass in the other.

Did he look like he caused children across the country to get hysterical? Hard to say. Not really.

His ball cap was on the table, and next to it was a bottle of Wild Turkey, three-quarters empty.

Oh. Right. Once a year he drank.

Dad raised one eyebrow on seeing me, then the other, then lowered one, then the other, then took a drink from his glass, a deep drag from his cigarette, and a bite of his sandwich. I can't imagine how that made his sandwich taste. The act of chewing seemed to involve every functioning brain cell.

I didn't mind him like this. He wasn't an angry drunk or a

sad drunk or a sloppy one. He was stripped down, acoustic. He was chewing a sandwich.

"Your ma," he said.

"Yeah."

"Twenty-one years ago today. Vegas."

"Yeah, Dad. I know."

"Love of my life. Love of a hundred lifetimes. Like a flower. Like a sun."

"Dad—"

"In the sun. A flower-sun."

"Dad. Maybe some water?"

He drained his glass. "Special. Wallace. You're special. I wish I could explain. Here. It's like"—he beckoned—"like this. Come."

I walked over to him and bent down.

He slowly raised a hand, reached out, and pushed my face. And then slowly, hand still raised, his head fell forward until it rested on the table.

I put him to bed. I went to the laundromat. When I came back to the apartment to shower, he was gone.

"You see him leave?" I asked the oak trees.

"Yes," said the oak tree in the middle.

"He seem good to drive?"

It shrugged, a rustle like a small wave. "It will be okay," it said.

"Yeah? You sure?"

"Sure," it said. "But then again, I'm a tree."

SEVENTEEN

KEELY'S HOUSE WAS impossible to miss: a large white Mc-Mansion at the end of a dead-end road, a half-moon driveway circling an enormous maple tree, cars lining the street, lights and music thumping out of the windows, the whole house appearing, in that house-party way, to suck up all the energy in the neighborhood. I watched the front door from behind a garage two houses away. Students arrived in pairs and groups, on foot and piled in cars. They looked nervously around as they pounded on the door and waited to be let inside, and when the door opened their greetings were forced and rushed. A police car drove by every few minutes, flicking on its strobe light so everyone at the party knew they were being protected—or watched.

More likely watched. Or is that what protection is?

No sign of Megan Rose. I took a deep breath and cut into the woods behind the garage.

In the woods, invisible sticks snapped under my feet and

bugs dive-bombed my eyes. Spiderwebs reached for my mouth and ears and found their way down my freshly washed shirt. Late October and the leaves on the birches and black walnut trees were still green, the thornbushes were still lush and full, the insects still loud and aggressive. Perhaps there could be a new season called *still*. It would grow and grow until all was still.

I stopped at the edge of Keely's backyard.

A couple a dozen students milled about on the broad, floodlit back porch a hundred feet away. Most of them had the mopey body language of hoping that someone would tell them that everything was okay. That was a lot of pressure to put on other people, especially similarly insecure people, so everyone was avoiding each other. The only exception to this generalized anxiety was in the corner of the porch where the keg was. Football players had gathered there to oversee the keg's use and cheer each other in same. I've never understood how pouring liquid into your stomach is improved by chanting variations of "Hey, pour that liquid into your stomach!" or "Holy shit, did you see the liquid go into his stomach!" or the inevitable "Would you look at that liquid leave his stomach!" but it's something I've heard at every stop in the country, and North Homer was no different, save for the odd player raising a plastic cup of beer high and yelling, "Fuck you, demons!"

Then he'd chug, and everyone would cheer.

No sign of Megan Rose on the porch, either.

Two of the football players separated from the crowd and walked down the steps. They beelined straight across the yard to where I stood. I froze, easy to spot if anyone was paying attention. The football players came closer. One of them was none other than Brad Stone himself. He looked, as always, like a cement foundation had come to life and poured itself into a pair of jeans. Moving back into the woods was no longer an option. I stood as motionless as I could.

They stopped at the edge of the lawn, not five feet from me. This was it. I clenched my fists.

They unbuckled their pants and pissed.

Go home, Wallace. Stuart is right. Coming to this party was a dumb idea. You are outnumbered. You are not actually invisible. You are, right at this moment, talking to yourself—never a good development. You are five feet away from Brad Stone, and he doesn't see you. Take it as a sign of your good fortune and go.

This is called intuition. Intuition is very important.

I ignored it.

Brad Stone buckled up and headed back to the porch with the other player; the two of them were greeted with full-throated cheers and full cups of beer. The party found its rhythm, haltingly at first, as there was a lot of fear to work through, then steadily picking up, the alcohol pushing people out of their nerves and into their hormones.

It started to look almost like a normal party in a normal town. To look almost like fun.

And then Megan Rose glided out of the house.

Megan Rose—tall, thin, in jeans and a red tank top, hair wild, spine straight, cheekbones sharp, skin the glowing paleness that only deep-sea bioluminescent fish and moon people can achieve—she was magnetic. I stared. Everyone did. Even the music seemed to quiet down and stare. At the bottom of the porch steps, Keely, who had been chasing behind Megan Rose, caught up to her and took hold of her elbow. She tried to turn her, but Megan Rose refused. She shook herself loose and stepped out onto the lawn.

Everyone watched her go.

The party grew. Students spilled into the yard. Chuggers were cheered while face suckers got to work sucking face. They made it seem like a competitive sport.

I watched Megan Rose from behind the branches of a willow at the end of the yard. She greeted friends but said little. Mostly she looked over their heads at the growing crowd. I knew who she was looking for. It made my heart pound.

Patience. Too soon and I'd be seen. I counted to fifty in a British accent. Counted the number of bro-hugs in a five-minute span and computed the party's bro-hug-per-minute rate. Did a set of ten push-ups so my chest would have a little bit of pump. Did another. Finally, when the party had grown to the point where the lawn was packed past the reach of the porch lights, I stepped out of my hiding place.

Megan Rose was facing the other way, looking up at the house.

"Nocturnal beings," I said.

She started to turn.

"Don't turn," I said. "Wait five minutes and meet me under the willow."

This willow was enormous, the size and shape of a fairy-tale universe. Drooping branches covered the ground like a tent. Megan Rose arrived, four and a half minutes early. I checked to make sure that she hadn't been followed.

I was suddenly nervous. It's amazing—your long-gone mother appears, oak trees talk, a forest is full of visions, and it's the girl you like that scares you most.

"Megan Rose. It feels like you've been gone forever," I said.

"Four days," she said. "I left Princeton early."

"It felt longer. Are your SAT scores much improved?"

"They're probably worse."

"So why come back?"

"Because I missed her."

"Who, Keely?" It took me a minute. "Wait. The tennis ball? You missed the tennis ball?"

Megan Rose winced, apparently as surprised as I was.

"I spent weeks wishing she'd go away and leave me alone," she said. "And then when she actually did that, all this week down in Jersey I couldn't stop worrying about her. The whole time I was away I worried. Listening to the very guy who started the Princeton Review explain the seven secret keys to a perfect test score, keys that apply to admissions interviews and job interviews and numerous kinds of grown-up life situations, and all I could think about was a giant clumsy tennis ball. What if she fell down and couldn't get up? Rolled into a storm drain? Got lost at a dog park?"

"I understand," I said.

"You understand? Really? That doesn't sound nuts? I think it sounds nuts. I think I sound completely nuts."

"You don't. At all."

She looked at me, into my eyes. "So you did it. You went to the glade."

"I did."

"You saw them?"

"I did."

"What did you see?"

I'd been anticipating the question. Preparing for it. But all the answers I'd come up with seemed pathetically inadequate: I'd found my mother in the glade, a wise willow tree, a light growing inside a dead make-believe man—each of those descriptions accurate, sure, but all of them capturing just a sliver of the experience and not anything close to the most important sliver, that most important sliver being something I could not articulate, even to myself, but which, nevertheless, had nestled in a deep corner of my heart from which now and then it sent out little shocks of awe.

I tried my best to describe it anyway.

"But what are they?" Megan Rose responded. "The visions, the night people—what are they?"

I'd anticipated that question, too.

"They're our desires, I think. Our deepest, most aching desires, like thorns stuck in our souls, blown up a thousand times normal size."

Megan Rose considered this. "So you mean Susie is what I most desire?"

"Who's Susie?"

"The tennis ball."

"Her name is Susie?"

"Yes. That okay?"

"Yes. Sure. Susie is a nice name."

"Glad you approve," Megan Rose said. "So you're saying the ache inside me is that I don't want to play tennis, that I'm sick of approaching every task in my life as another match I have to win, and I'm sick of feeling that if I dare take it easy, I'll fall helplessly behind?" She frowned. "So you're saying what's inside me is that I hate my life?"

I knew better than to respond to that.

"Shit," she said.

A strand of light from the porch illuminated Megan Rose's features so she got that sharp, dangerous-ninja look when she turned a certain way, and she turned that way now. I held my breath.

"But what about the trees?" she asked.

"What about them?"

She explained. "If the night people come from inside us, why are the trees talking to us? I mean, I can understand having unresolved feelings about tennis—but about trees?"

"You're right," I said. "That doesn't fit the theory."

"And why is it only affecting people in high school?" she added. "I thought it might be some kind of poison or drugs in the water or air, but my parents seem completely the same. Teachers, too."

"Yeah. You're right."

"And what started all of it?" she asked, voice rising. "Forget what they are. Why? Why are they? Why the heck is this happening?"

"Also a good point," I admitted.

Now I felt useless, out of my depth. In trying to figure out what was going on, I hadn't thought to ask any of these questions. They'd called us hysterical, and I had just agreed with it.

"Megan Rose!" called a voice from the porch.

She turned toward the party, peering through a willow branch to see who had yelled. She turned back; I looked away at a fascinating branch.

"Here's the other thing I can't figure," she said. "Everyone expects me to be perfect, right? So I had this idea at Princeton that the problem was I cared too much about that. That I cared too much in general. So I decided to work on that, on not caring. Is my backhand in rhythm? Do my friends think I'm intelligent and fun? Am I on the right test-score trajectory? Probably not! But why should I care! And today, Susie's been the calmest she's ever been. She hasn't been talking in my ear nonstop. Simple, right? Just don't care. Just don't care about anything. Today was *nice*! But then, what *does* matter, Wallace? What the hell is the point of my life?"

Her hands moved to cover her face. Something in that movement pushed her against the willow branch behind her, and it caught her, kept her from falling over.

I wanted to catch her myself, to comfort her, but I didn't know what to say. While the night people had also led me to ask existential questions of my life, in important ways that didn't change much, I had nothing to lose—my plans for my life were still sitting in some broken-down apartment I had passed through. But Megan Rose—she had everything to lose.

"I'm glad you're getting along with Susie," I said.

She didn't say anything.

So, what then? But I already knew.

"We're doing this all wrong," I said. "We need help."

"What do you mean? Who can possibly help us?"

"My father."

"What about him?"

"He works for Jackduke."

"Half the town does."

"All over the country. They send him wherever there's trouble."

"This is trouble."

"Yes."

Megan Rose nodded, catching on. I nodded also, though I was the one who had to actually talk to the guy. And then, you know, get him to talk.

"You're right, we can't figure it out ourselves," she said. "It's time to bring this out into the open. Wide open. I'll talk to my father, too. He knows people—he's the lawyer for every divorce in town."

"Megan Rose! Megan Rose!"

Her name was shouted like she was a toddler who'd fallen in a well. It sounded like a search party was forming.

"I should get back," she said. "Thank you, Wallace."

"What for?"

"For listening. For believing me. I'm glad it's you."

And that should have been it. I should've gone. Slipped away into the woods and back to the apartment before anyone saw me, cherishing those words. Dad would open the door at some ungodly hour, flick on the light, and see me sitting at the kitchen table, arms crossed. The cigarette would fall out of his mouth in shock. "The beans," I'd say. "Spill them."

But I didn't go.

"I thought about you while you were gone," I said.

Megan Rose had turned but now stopped. The shoulders bare in her red tank top, shuddering with her breath. There should be a rule that when the world stops following rules, you get one thing you really want.

Just one. I wasn't going to be greedy.

I found her wrist first, a hair tie around it. Then I found her palm. I found her fingers and the space between her fingers. I found her thumb. I found the space between her thumb and fingers, the soft flesh part. She turned around, her eyes looking right at mine. I put pressure on her hand, and I found her hand putting pressure to meet my pressure, and the pressure between our hands was equal, which spoke to an undeniable connection, forged in a mysterious other world.

Or, at least to, you know, consent.

I leaned toward her lips.

A giant hand clamped down on my neck.

"What a nice surprise," said a voice I knew. "I've been looking everywhere for you, newb."

EIGHTEEN

BRAD STONE PULLED me out of the woods and up the lawn. It was like being dragged by a waterskiing rope—my body was just along for the ride. Megan Rose was right behind us, yelling the whole way.

He stopped when we reached the porch lights, dropped me to the ground.

"Here we go, newb," he said. "Now you can properly join the festivities."

My neck burned from his grip. "Thank you," I said. "I'd been hoping."

"Let him go," said Megan Rose.

"I did," said Brad. "See?"

He whacked a nearby kid to cue him in on the joke; the kid fell right over.

"I meant home, Brad. Let Wallace go home."

"Ah," said Brad. "I can't do that."

Partygoers looked over to see what was happening. They elbowed their friends. The elbowed friends turned, froze. A space instantly cleared out around Megan Rose, Brad Stone, and me, as though we were contagiously diseased or starting a dance-off. Same thing, maybe. The doors at the back of Keely's house slammed open, expelling jumpy cheerleaders and jacked-up football players, who buttoned their jeans and ran to where we stood.

A distant police siren said: Woo-hoo, not my problem.

"What are you talking about?" Megan Rose said. "Of course Wallace can go."

Brad shoved me. "I'm talking about he's behind this. This . . . crazy stuff. This infection. Everything got worse when he got here."

"You have no idea what it is!"

"Negatory. I know exactly what it is." Brad shoved me again. "*It is* . . . the breakdown of strength in society. What else do you think is sending our classmates to the emergency room but weakness, mental and otherwise? And we've got to take care of it ourselves! You think the wackjob therapists at school are going to save us? We've got to be strong!"

"Strength isn't the answer to everything," said Megan Rose.

"Welcome to America!" Brad raised his arms. "It most definitely is!"

There were cheers. I took a few steps toward the woods but hit a mass of football players.

"Stay awhile," said one.

Megan Rose looked back and forth from Brad to me. I didn't think she needed to do anything. I'd made my bed. I'd had my warnings. I should never have come to the party. And Brad was flat-out impossible, a city-sized ego mainlining steroids and deep web conspiracies.

And how could Megan Rose explain that what was really happening was a four-foot-tall tennis ball named Susie was laying waste to her life? How could she explain that it felt like the worst thing in the world together with the best thing in the world?

Which is to say that what Megan Rose did next surprised us all.

She pulled off her shirt and threw it as high and as far as she could.

The red tank top disappeared into the dark sky. All she had on were faded jeans and a plain white bra. Her skin glowed silver in the light from the porch.

I held my breath. A lot of people held their breath. When I did breathe again, it felt like different, thinner air.

Megan Rose extended her arms to Brad.

"Hey. Whoa," he said.

"You're the strongest," she said. "You're the champion. Okay, then." She unbuckled her belt, whipped it off her waist in one snapping motion. "Stupid male stupid shit. Get on with it."

"Stop!" yelled Brad, raising both hands up. "You see? Everyone seeing this? Newb got to you, too. The only question is when they're gonna take you to Syracuse. And who he's going to infect next."

The shovel-jawed king and the shirtless queen of North Homer High School stared at each other. A minute went by, during which everyone seemed to at once remember that they were not at a normal party in a normal town but that actually they were in a terrifying place where kids were disappearing. It had been an impressive act of self-denial, this party, maybe even a necessary one. But the jig was up. No, the jig was fucking blasted.

"It's beautiful," I said.

"What?" said Brad.

"Complicated. Mysterious."

"What is?"

"What's out there. I'd love to talk about it with you sometime."

"Newb, shut up."

Keely appeared at the front of the crowd. She was holding the red tank top. On her signal, she and a few friends took hold of Megan Rose by her arms and waist. Megan Rose stiffened against them.

Keely said, "We're going inside, Megan Rose. You need to sober up."

"I'm not drunk," said Megan Rose.

"Yes, you are," Keely said loudly. "Everyone got that? Too many Jägerbombs. I called your parents. Your father is on his way."

She started pulling Megan Rose toward the porch. Megan Rose resisted, but more friends surrounded her, more hands pushed her. One girl was pulling the red tank top over Megan Rose's head in the midst of it, and I saw that if Megan Rose fought them off, it would mean expending a lot of energy, a wild and fierce energy that would be misunderstood and would frighten people who were already frightened plenty. She saw that, too, and I caught her eye and gave her a nod, and she was like, *You sure?* and I nodded, *Sure, don't worry, we'll stick to the plan,* and she went limp and was dragged off, up to the porch and into the house.

Then, as before, as always, I was facing a wall.

The wall knew what it wanted. It knew exactly how to get what it wanted. It was a brute trauma-inflicting force that had spent its life receiving praise and awards for doing what it wanted.

"This is all your fault, newb," it said.

"Hey, Brad," I said. "You can call me Wallace."

"The hell I will."

Most of the other partygoers had followed Keely back to the porch, and those who remained were the most hostile. They had gelled hair, tight shirts, and pushed-up sleeves, like an Abercrombie & Fitch ad for mob justice.

Goddamn it. There was a world-shaking mystery out there in the woods, but it didn't matter. They just wanted a scapegoat to punch in the face.

"We're better when it's just us," said Brad.

"Just who?" I asked.

"It's always the unwanted newcomers breaking down society with their filth and disease."

"That's kind of racist."

"The truth often is."

I tried one last appeal to reason. "Brad, what's happening

in North Homer is huge. Bigger than us. I don't understand it. Megan Rose doesn't. I understand if you're scared."

"Fuck you, I'm scared. I'm not scared. You're scared."

"Okay. Right. But if we all look out for each other—"

"Nope."

Yeah, that was never going to work.

A squirrel ran past with a very concerned expression. A single cricket rubbed its knees together, tirelessly. A vein in Brad's temple throbbed like a countdown.

"Hey," I said. "How do you confuse a self-important idiot?"

"What are you talking about now, jackass?"

"Yeah," I said.

I got to see Brad's fist before it hit my jaw, got to watch it cut through the air like a missile, bearing, in its solidity and purpose, a certainty that was refreshing. No inexplicable visions. No dead mothers or clumsy, needy tennis balls. The next thing I felt was the cool grass beneath my cheek, faintly wet and sweet, a handful of it already in my mouth. And then there was a foot in my stomach, air leaving my lungs with surprise and regret, and I closed my eyes and flew over the moon to the trees.

NINETEEN

TWENTY

THE POLICE STROLLED leisurely into the backyard, nightsticks swinging. The panicked scattering of partygoers alerted me to their arrival. I waited facedown in the grass. The concerned squirrel watched me from behind a nearby branch.

A pair of black boots emerged next to my face. I smelled them before I saw them.

"What's with him?" asked the boots.

"He drank too much," answered someone—Keely.

"Who is he?"

"I've never seen him before."

"How do you know he drank too much if you ain't ever seen him?"

A fair question, I thought.

A boot jabbed between my shoulder blades. "Hey. Hey. Can't hold your booze?"

"Not exactly," I said.

"Well, then. Get the fuck off the lawn."

I got the fuck off the lawn. I somehow walked all the way back to the apartment—fell forward the whole way, really. I dreamed of journeys through space all night and woke up uncertain I was on the right planet. At dawn, I dragged myself out of bed and sat down at the kitchen table and commenced waiting for my father.

The pain didn't help. My eye, my mouth, my ribs, my soul—I knew the exact shape of my right orbital bone, could tell how it fit underneath the skin, could tell how it reached places I had not known it could. The back of my left eye. The underside of my tongue. The memory of the first kiss I ever got, at fourth-grade recess. My balls.

I waited at the kitchen table all day. I waited the day after that. I waited the nights, too, in the dark, listening for the front door, for the lighter's click. All that waiting began to feel not so much to see my father but to see what fate had been decided for me.

Monday, I blew off school to wait some more. Wasn't so keen on seeing Brad Stone and other glaring faces from the party. Wasn't keen on talking to the oak trees out front, either. It rained all day, a warm, slow, May kind of rain, like condensation dripping off a locker-room ceiling. It was late October. Why was there May rain in October?

And as I sat in the kitchen, waiting, Mega D, on top of everything, revved up the SUV.

Think, Wallace, think. What was going on? LSD in the town reservoir? But adults weren't getting it. Next-gen DMT in the school water fountains? But teachers weren't getting it. A bleed-through of aliens living in another dimension? A virus transmitted through social media? A reaction to insecticides? A reaction to atmospheric carbon levels? A reaction to reactions, to being a teenager in a world with so many things falling the hell apart?

And on that note, said Mega D, every land animal you learned to love as a child is going to die. Goodbye, rhino. Goodbye, red-faced spider monkey. Goodbye, koala—would have loved a hug.

At six, there was a knock on the door. Dad, at last?

No, it was Stuart, holding a bag of potato chips.

"Damn," he said, looking me over, "you get beat up a lot."

"I am aware," I said.

We went to my room. The chips had vinegar on them, and who does that to potato chips? They made the cuts in my mouth burn. I felt edgy, aggravated.

Stuart said, "I'm not going to say I told you so, but I do recall one of us predicting that going to Keely's party was a terrible idea."

"That's the exact same thing as 'I told you so,'" I pointed out.

"So, what answers did Megan Rose have?"

Nada, is what. No answers. More questions than answers. Her carefully planned-out life was being wrecked by a tennis ball.

"She really got naked?" Stuart asked. "Everyone at school is talking about it."

"She didn't get naked."

"So . . . almost naked?"

"Dude. She was making a point to Brad."

"What point was she making? Was it about being naked?"

"Stuart, you are seriously pissing me— Is there a reason you're here?"

"The PTA meeting's in an hour," he said. "We need to go."

I looked at him: cross-legged on the floor, his limbs like scattered chopsticks, grinning, his eyes glimmering—

"Wait a minute," I said. "You haven't bitched once since you got here. You're not moaning about being a loser or about the chosen ones who have it better. What's going on? What's got into you?"

Stuart stretched out his skinny frame, cracked his neck. Then his fingers. His wrists. His shoulders. His lower back. His neck again. More fingers.

I knew before he answered.

"I saw them," he said.

"I was home. Alone. You were at the party, getting your ass beat. I decided I had to give it a shot. Ghosts or trees or ghost trees or whatever. You told me they like to hang out in the state forest, but I wasn't going to walk in the woods in the middle of the night like some crazy person—"

"That's not—"

"—so I took a flashlight and went and sat with the birches in my backyard. And waited for hours. And nothing happened. Around midnight, I saw lights in the bushes. I thought: This is it! The ghosts at last! But they turned out to be fireflies. It's almost Halloween—we never get fireflies after August, so you

138

understand my confusion. At that point, I thought the night was a bust. I mean, I was hungry, I was sitting on an anthill, and black ants were crawling in my butt crack—"

"Good visual," I said.

"All the way up there. Licking the sweat."

"Thank you."

"It actually started with those ants. Their tiny, dedicated annoyingness reminded me of something—all the tiny screws and nails and nuts and washers in the fastener aisle at Lowe's. That's my home at Lowe's. I know that aisle better than any-one in the county. And there's this old woman who comes in every day at four o'clock to find a particular screw. She's bent and has crumbs in her mouth and never remembers to bring in the screw she's looking to match, so every day it's 'I need some-thing this big, not this, not that, not that, that's too long, that's too short.' Every damn day. It's the worst. If I'm still at school when she gets there, she waits for me. If I'm helping someone else, same deal. And while I was in the yard, remembering that woman—or *not* remembering, it felt more solid than remem-bering does, like I was right there with her, actually with her in aisle seven—a feeling took me by surprise.

"You know what the feeling was? You'll laugh. It was: This isn't so bad.

"That was it. *This isn't so bad.* The thing I hate most in the world, and it was fine, actually. A small feeling, maybe, but I swear it knocked me sideways. It seemed to shine from behind every single object in the aisle. I found the old lady the screw she wanted. She had trouble keeping her purse on her shoulder, so I helped her with the strap. Then she floated down the aisle.

"Floated," he repeated. "Then I stacked boxes of roofing nails. Swept the aisle with the big broom. Fixed up the shim display."

He smiled. I had never seen Stuart smile before. It was kind of cute, actually.

But it also made my brain hurt. Another life-changing vision that had fuck-all in common with the other ones? My mother . . . Susie the tennis ball . . . an old woman missing screws. Were they beautiful? Sure, they were. And the trees talking were beautiful. But put it all together and it didn't make a lick of sense.

"Who is she?" I asked Stuart. "The old woman?"

"She lives in the senior apartments near the mall. Widowed, I think. Has this kind of hunchback. Her name's Edith."

"Why her, you think?"

"I was hoping you might have some ideas."

"I got nothing."

"Yeah, I know. But the PTA meeting. It starts in ten minutes. They're going to talk about the hysteria."

I looked at him. For a second I felt hopeful. Mega D revved its engine again.

"Stuart, it's nice you got to talk to Edith," I said. "I'm happy for you, really. But I have to wait right here for my father. And everyone at that school hates me. They think I'm a border-crossing virus. I've got bruises in places I didn't know I've got places. And it's a goddamn PTA meeting. Nothing interesting has ever happened in all of history at a PTA meeting. So, no. I'm not going."

"Megan Rose sent me to come get you," said Stuart.

TWENTY-ONE

THE RAIN BEAT down, sticky and warm. The wind was a mouth breather with no concept of personal space. Stuart and I walked through North Homer's empty streets, the last people left in the world on the last day of the world . . . and arrived to nothing less than the entire county at the school. Men clumped in hunched huddles, smoking cigarettes, draining cups of coffee. Women held young children in their arms and tried to keep older ones in sight while saying things to each other like "Her grades are in the toilet," "He never leaves his room," and, if I heard correctly, "I found her curled up on the couch with mud painted on her face, holding a live chicken." Some kids were throwing a football, and some men were shouting, "Stop throwing the goddamn football!"

I knew these folks. I'd seen them in every town I'd lived in from Washington State to South Carolina to Kentucky. Solid, hardworking people limping along from paycheck to paycheck, who did not complain about their lot in life as a general rule. They sucked it up. They rubbed some dirt in it. They got by.

But this—freak-outs, disappearances, chicken-cuddling daughters—they couldn't make sense of this, they didn't know how to get by this.

The doors to the gym were closed, and standing in front of them was a tall bearded man wearing a long gray robe. His arms were outstretched like he was being crucified.

"Repent from the path of Satan!" he shouted.

No one responded.

"The devil is ascendant because you have turned away from God!"

It wasn't clear who he was addressing.

"That your father?" Stuart joked, his good mood continuing.

"You don't want to meet my father," I said.

The doors opened. Stuart and I were carried inside by the crowd. On one side of the gym, a couple dozen rows of bleachers looked down on the basketball court. They filled quickly, and we found a spot in the very last row. From there we watched the crowd swell to the point where the bleachers were packed and latecomers had to sit in the aisles and on the floor. Several hundred folks, at least. The gym was designed to amplify noise, and it succeeded in its design; the commotion was deafening. There was a pungent smell of tobacco and wet clothes. I saw plenty of students, faces I recognized from the hallways and the cafeteria and Keely's party, but no sign of Megan Rose.

In the center of the basketball court, over the stenciled logo of a poet in a toga ready for fisticuffs, a folding table had been set up. A podium was next to it. Principal Rathschild sat at the table with several other men and women I didn't recognize.

A man walked up to the podium. A gavel banged.

"Good evening, North Homer," he said.

The commotion continued. He raised an arm, and at this signal the doors to the parking lot were closed with a tremendous slam, startling the room into silence.

"Good evening," he said again.

He was an older guy, with a round, hard stomach, big shoulders, and long white hair that fell on those shoulders. He looked like a retired pro wrestler or George Washington. If he were a wrestler, his finishing move would for sure be called "The Constitution."

He said, "My name, if you don't know it, is James Govacoff. I am your county executive. Next to me is Victor Soares, the school-board president, and our principal, Dr. Eleanor Rathschild. And here"—he motioned to the end of the table—"is someone you may not recognize but will be, I think, as grateful as I am for her presence: Jackduke's executive vice president and national spokesperson, Ms. Marguerite Hoch."

There were loud murmurs at the last name.

"Arrest her!" yelled a man from the bleachers.

"What's she paying you?"

"Satan is in your heart!"

BAM! BAM! BAM! the gavel shouted at the interlopers.

"Citizens of North Homer," said the county executive, "this is a difficult time for all of us. Beware of flinging insults and unsubstantiated accusations. Marguerite Hoch is here completely voluntarily. Join me in giving her the courtesy of our attention and our decency."

Grumbles from the crowd but deflated ones. I'd never met Ms. Hoch, the CEO's daughter, but had heard my father mention her. *Jackduke's PR maestro,* he called her; she was often on the news, talking as quickly and precisely as a dental drill.

My father . . . Was he here?

Bracing myself against the wall, I stood up on my top-row seat and scanned the gym.

And there he was, at the very edge of the gym floor, standing against the wall padding, arms crossed, ball cap down low, working over a toothpick and scanning the crowd. Next to him stood a tall, thin man in a brown sports coat, shifting from foot to foot, wiping and rewiping his glasses. With his cap, his stubble, and his general vibe of having just returned from burying a body in the woods, my father looked like a man you don't mess with.

Was that where he had been all weekend?

At that exact moment, he caught sight of me. His eyes narrowed. I ducked down for a good minute. When I looked again, he was still staring.

"But first," the county executive was saying, "we have a statement from the North Homer chief of police, Martin Turnblad."

The county executive stepped to the table and took a seat. A wide man in a blue uniform wearing a wide belt and a wide flat-brimmed hat strode over to the podium from the side of the gym. Something about his width and how he swung his hips accentuated the fact that on each hip was a shiny steel gun. Everyone noticed. Does a roomful of throats tightening make a noise?

Chief Turnblad set his feet.

"I'll get right down to business," he said. "I am beyond disappointed with the students of this school. We trusted you. Per Dr. Rathschild's wishes—and against my instincts and experience—we introduced a program of passive surveillance, which depended on you looking after each other. You would have the responsibility of keeping each other out of trouble and danger. You would have mental-health professionals at your beck and call." He snorted at this mention of mental health. "Dr. Rathschild was sure you were mature enough for this approach. But what happened? Tarnation. A wild party, with criminal behavior, ending in a bloody fight, which my officers had to break up."

The audience murmured a "Darn—really?" murmur.

The chief continued. "How can I trust you? I can't. How can I be sure we are actually working together to destroy this ruthless enemy? Tarnation. I can't be. So, starting tomorrow at dusk, a hard curfew is in effect. When the sun goes down on Tuesday night, students or parents: be in your homes or you will be in my jail."

Wild party? Criminal behavior? There'd been no crime in Keely's backyard, save for tapping a keg and, I guess, bloodying Brad's fists with my face. But the police chief glared at us with such anger there was no question of our guilt. All that was left was to confess our crimes. He walked back to where a dozen police officers stood. They glared at us as well, a blue wall of disapproval.

"That's not what happened at Keely's," I whispered to Stuart.

"Who's going to believe you?" he whispered back.

I considered that. And had a realization.

"Shock doctrine."

"Huh? Shock what?"

"They want us to be afraid. When everyone's freaked, clamp down further. They're manufacturing a crisis to take further control."

"Who?"

"I don't know."

"Why?"

"I don't know! I'm trying to figure it out!"

"Shh!" Two women sitting in front of us turned around in unison.

The county executive returned to the microphone.

"At this time in our meeting," he said, "Principal Eleanor Rathschild is going to share a few thoughts about the situation at hand. Doctor?"

Rathschild walked to the podium. She reached down to adjust the microphone, as she was several inches taller than the men who had spoken. Hair stuck to her forehead. Her brown sports jacket rose up her neck. She looked like she had spent the weekend combing the woods with a torch and a club. She shook the jacket out, and something, a pen maybe, flew from a pocket. In a flat monotone, she spoke about the community working together and sharing burdens together and traveling in the same boat together. No one was listening, and she knew it. This was a formality. The chief had already cut out her legs from under her. And even if he hadn't, the facts had. There had been shrieking students on top of tables, medevacs by helicopter, a brawling party.

I kind of felt bad for her, to be honest.

The crowd, itching for real answers but scared of the chief of police, squirmed on the uncomfortable bleachers.

"Please remember," Rathschild said, trying a personal tack, "myself, the members of the board—we have children in the school system, too. We worry about what will happen next, too. What's imperative to remember is that in times of fear, the most important thing is to stay in control of ourselves, and to help others stay in control."

A shout from the bleachers: "Satan! Is in control!"

"Let Jackduke's liar speak!"

"I don't want you on my boat, Eleanor!"

BAM! BAM! BAM!

The county executive grabbed the microphone. "Order!"

As the gaveling echoed, the chief of police stepped forward into the thirty feet of open space between the podium and the bleachers. The empty space spotlit him in our collective gaze. He put his hands on his belt in a way that said: Look. Look how relaxed I am, all casual-like. And also: Look at my guns. They are shiny, yes? They make holes. The holes bleed. The EMTs are late. The grand jury says it's justified.

"I will call this meeting off," said the chief, no need for a microphone. "And start curfew immediately."

The audience wrestled into a tense quiet.

"They're going to kill people," Stuart whispered to me.

"They want us scared," I whispered back. "That's their plan. Don't buy into it."

"I kind of want to buy into it."

"Go ahead," the chief growled over his shoulder to Rathschild.

"Right. Um. In conclusion," she said, "to echo what a man named Franklin Delano Roosevelt once said long ago, we must remain calm and help each other to be calm."

But calm had left the gym. Calm had left the county. Calm had walked in on her husband and the babysitter in the laundry room. Calm had boarded a rocket with a frozen O-ring.

"This is bad," said Stuart.

My father had moved off the wall and now stood only a few feet from the bleachers. The chief turned from his spot in the center of the gym and looked at him. My father nodded. The county executive also looked at my father, as did the Jackduke spokesperson. My father nodded to each.

Wait a minute, was Dad in charge of this whole thing?

The daughter of Jackduke's CEO stood up at the table and nodded to all of us.

Ms. Marguerite Hoch, a tiny, concentrated woman in a purple skirt and jacket and four-inch heels, makeup sharp as a razor, a bun of hair on top of her head pulled tight as a stone, walked to the podium. Then she smiled. The smile was breathtaking in its size and commitment. The smile ate her face.

"Hello! Good evening! Hello! It's so wonderful to see so many of you here!" she trilled. "What a loving community, what a special town! Since Jackduke first came to North Homer, all the way back in 1983, we have been excited and honored to support the community in whatever ways we can. From Little League to bowling leagues to fun runs, Jackduke is there. When the ambulance broke down, who bought a new one? When the town hall desperately needed its stairs fixed, who paid for their repair? We did! We love the town of North Homer. We live here, too! Our kids live here! Our kids go to this very school! We are you!"

She pumped her head vigorously.

"When something hurts our community, we're as hurt as you are. Imagine, then, how we feel when we hear accusations that we are at fault for what's happening to our children!" She paused to imagine it, her hand on her chest. The audience seemed disarmed by the aggressiveness of her politeness, if that makes sense. "Oh, it breaks my heart. So you'll be happy to know, in the past few weeks we have tested everything at our plant, backwards and forwards. Which is something we do as standard business practice, but we went and did it even more, far beyond EPA regulations. We flew in top experts on plant safety, ethnobiology, energy physics, nuclear physics, and gave them free rein at the facility. And you know what they found?"

She nodded excitedly at us, from one side of the room to the other.

"Every single test in normal range. The North Homer power plant is clean and safe."

She continued her head-pumping. Did we, the audience, not

understand? How could we not understand? The corporation wouldn't hurt them. The corporation loved them. The experts had found nothing. The shareholders were covered. These colors don't run.

I glanced around—no one was buying it.

Ms. Hoch wasn't done. "Let me repeat: there is absolutely no connection between the Jackduke plant and the unfortunate situation here at the school. But we still want to help! Jackduke cares about this community. I personally update my father about the situation here, and he is very concerned! 'You are us,' he said. 'We are you.' So tonight we are very happy to announce that Jackduke has found a solution!"

She paused again, nodding vigorously again. Possibly she was waiting for applause, which was not coming.

"Yes. Please join me in welcoming Dr. Milos Lehmann, of the world-renowned Stanford-Harvard Institute on Transitory Sociology, to speak about a very auspicious discovery. . . . Dr. Lehmann."

Clapping—the only one in the gym doing so—Ms. Hoch looked to the side of the room. The nervous, eyeglass-wiping man standing next to my father picked up a briefcase and made his way toward the microphone.

"It's the shits," I whispered to Stuart.

"Huh?" he said.

"Stanford-Harvard Institute on Transitory Sociology? They're scamming us. I knew this meeting wasn't on the level. Let's get out of here."

But we couldn't leave, of course.

Dr. Lehmann arrived at the podium. With the fluidity of a drunken tin man in a hot tub, he opened his briefcase, pulled out a folder, and placed it on the podium. He rewiped his glasses.

"Greeting. As Ms. Hoch stated, Stanford-Harvard . . . um . . . Institute has analyzed the situation here." His accent was Eastern European and thick. "Nine separate episodes of transitory psychosis. Seven female. A clear age bias: four were sixteen years of age. Two were seventeen; two, fifteen. Three cases successfully treated with antipsychotics. Four cases moved out of the county; we assume full recovery after moving, as there have been no further complaint from that population." He closed the folder and bent down to the microphone. "No one wants to hear that there isn't a clear explanation. But there isn't one. That doesn't mean we can't focus on what we do know. And what we know is that while this outbreak doesn't have a clear cause, it has a clear diagnosis. These are cases of hysterics. Textbooks, you say? Textbooks cases. Recognize, please, that hysterics is a real disease. It was Sigmund Freud's very first identified illness. Method of transmission remains unknown, but one must assume psychological weakness in the patient. Which is why we are pleased to announce a new medication protocol combining two antidepressants with a new antiseizure drug made in Austria that has shown to be eighty-five percent effective in controlling stress-induced hysterics in canine trials. These medicines will be provided to the school nurse and North Homer family physicians, to give free of charge to all who need them."

Dr. Milos Lehmann put the folder back in his briefcase. He bowed awkwardly and went back to his spot by the wall. Ms. Hoch beamed her horrific smile.

Three separate drugs. My God, students would be catatonic.

But why? What was Jackduke's motivation? How could the power company be behind this? I mean, my mother watching *Roseanne,* Susie the walking tennis ball, old Edith in the fastener aisle at Lowe's—weren't the night people an expression of something inside of us? It didn't make sense.

And where was Megan Rose? She'd wanted me here. Had something happened to her?

Mind churning, I looked at my father. He was again staring at me. I ducked down.

Stuart: "Who's the scary serial-killer guy who keeps looking over here?"

Me: "That's my dad."

Stuart:

Me: "Yeah. Told you."

The county executive returned to the microphone, his expression saying, See? I told you we're the good guys.

"There you have it," he said. "Courtesy of Jackduke, purely out of altruistic concern, a way to help our children that is eighty-five percent effective. Now, we know this is all very sudden, so at this point Ms. Hoch has graciously agreed to take a limited number of questions. We're going to ask you to line up at the microphones set up in the aisles"—he pointed at two microphones standing on the steps of the bleachers—"in an orderly fashion."

Immediately, the gym exploded with noise. Pent-up emotion burst into a rush toward the microphones. Within seconds, a line of parents stretched up each aisle all the way to the top of the bleachers and back down again. Seated parents who'd been boxed in and missed their chance loudly voiced the injustice.

"Quiet!" shouted the chief of police.

I sneaked another peek at my father. He looked like the guy in the movie who walks away from the explosion without turning back. Though he didn't move, save for the toothpick doing circuits around his mouth, and though he hadn't said a word throughout the entire assembly, it was now clear beyond a doubt that he was running the show. Again and again, Ms. Hoch, the county executive, and the chief of police all glanced over at him.

In a way, it was heartening to see that other people were terrified of him. Welcome to my world!

In another way, it was just terrifying.

The first question for Ms. Hoch, from a short lady with short gray hair who took short breaths yet spoke in long pauses, wasn't really a question so much as a lament: she was afraid, her insurance didn't have mental-health benefits, and her daughter was refusing to shower and was weaving live herbs into her hair, and was anyone listening to her?

"I am listening," said Ms. Hoch. "I feel your pain.

"If she truly is unwell, we will give her the new medicines, free of charge," Ms. Hoch added. "Then she will be well."

"Really?" said the small woman. "My daughter has named the chipmunks in our yard after the saints. She speaks for hours to her grandfather, my father, dead twelve years. She climbs the apple tree and crouches and talks to him from there. She also—"

The chief of police: Next question.

The next question was from a mother in a gray sweat suit whose daughter had missed the past week of school. She, the daughter, had been having a recurring dream of being stuck in a carnival full of excruciatingly slow rides through cubicled office spaces. She had been put on a regimen of antipsychotics. But the drugs made her lethargic, spacey. She had been on the cross-country team, but when she ran now it was as if she were under the surface of the lake. Would the new drug regimen have the same effect? When would she be normal again? When would she, the mother, get back the child she had raised? Soon?

"Soon," said Ms. Hoch. "The new medicine protocol has minimal side effects. I believe, in fact, that the main side effect is duodenal ulceration—easily manageable—and not lethargy. Correct, Dr. Lehmann? So let's get her switched over and see what happens."

"Next question," said the chief of police.

It went on like this—I'm sorry, I understand, I feel for you, medicate, be patient, trust me, next—for half an hour.

How damaged the town was! I had no idea. No one did, I think. The outbreak was much more widespread than anyone knew. Or maybe everyone knew but me? I could tell people were asking themselves that exact question. They looked around the gym warily.

None of the questioners appeared convinced by Ms. Hoch. But the overall effect of her measured, soothing answers was that the crowd was being lulled to sleep. After a while, it was like they were discussing crop cycles, not their children.

And may I mention here that as the question-and-answer time continued, the ceiling of the gym dissolved into a shimmering silver cloud, and out of the cloud a samurai appeared, stroking his beard? He wore a robe of scarlet and gold. His sword was sheathed in a scabbard studded with purple jewels. The cloud behind him slowly faded, revealing a battalion of soldiers. Some wore scarlet and gold and had shields and helmets, and some were naked, save for loincloths, curved scimitars, and elaborate facial tattoos. Others wore hoods and carried bows and arrows, glinting knives. They stood in bedraggled lines in the clearing mist, drinking from their canteens, rubbing sore muscles and sweaty faces, ready for war.

"Stuart," I whispered, not taking my eyes off the floating army. "Don't be afraid."

"What? What is it?" A pause. "Oh."

The next questioner to the microphone was a man in a black suit that fit him like it had been licked on. It looked breathtakingly expensive. It looked like it went to secret meetings for shadow banks. There was nothing like it in the gym.

"Chief Turnbald, thank you for your hard work," he said. "Mr. Govacoff, Dr. Rathschild. And Ms. Hoch, a pleasure to make your acquaintance." His voice was as expensive as his suit. "But let us not insult each other."

"Oh, I don't want that," said Ms. Hoch.

"My name is Archibald Rose," said the man—Megan Rose's father. "I have worked in the law for two decades at some of the biggest firms in the country. I have had among my clients Firestone Tire and Rubber, Trump International Hotels, Coca-Cola, New Balance, former Speaker of the House Newt Gingrich, and an actor named William Smith. You may be asking what I'm doing here in North Homer—"

"I am not," said Ms. Hoch.

"I love it here," said Mr. Rose.

"Of course, of course," said Ms. Hoch, smiling. "How could you not?"

"I'll get to the point. In my twenty-six years of practicing the law, I have never witnessed a bigger steaming pile of bullshit than the one you've been shoveling here this evening."

A gasp rippled through the gym, jolting the sedated crowd upright.

"To begin with: the obvious fraudulence in the fact that you say these are hysterics, and hysterics are nothing but 'textbooks,' and then you offer medication for them? If they were nothing, how would medicine help? Steaming bullshit."

"Watch it!" barked the police chief, hands near his guns.

The county executive raised his gavel. "Archie, you of all people should know such language is not productive."

"Got it, got it." Mr. Rose tapped his forehead. "Me 'of all people.' Interesting phrase, Jack. What does it mean? Am I different from all of these people? Do you know me better than all of these people? Do you know what goes through my mind?

156

Or are you just assuming you do, as Ms. Hoch is doing with my daughter and *her* mind?"

His daughter. Megan Rose. She was here?

I stood up and scanned the crowd.

"The way you must feel," said Ms. Hoch. "You're right. I can only imagine—"

"Don't imagine!" Mr. Rose's voice seethed across the air. "Enough with imagination in this town! Enough with fraudulent answers to things you do not understand. I am tired of the imagining and excuses and panaceas you offer us. Henceforth, let us be clear and not incantatory. I will tell you exactly what goes through my daughter's mind. I will describe it for you. Not 'I will imagine it.' Do me the favor of listening. And then you can explain to me again why I should swallow the bullshit you're shoveling." He held up his hand to the county executive. "Withdrawn, Jack. My apologies."

Quiet. Deathly quiet. You could hear atoms in the gym knocking against each other. My father stared at Mr. Rose with eyes as fixed as laser sights. Next to me, Stuart's jaw hung almost to his waist, and he didn't know whether to look up or down. I glanced up; the lead samurai was testing the sharpness of his sword blade with his thumb. He found it satisfactory.

Mr. Rose tightened his grip on the mike. "My daughter," he continued, his voice low, "is not well. Megan Rose was, up until just a few weeks ago, enjoying the kind of high school career you dream of for your children. President of the student body. Captain of the tennis team. Straight As—though she likes to hide that side of herself from her friends, as so many of our children do. Still: ninety-seventh percentile on her boards, outstanding collegiate options. She is a legacy at Princeton, and I do believe she would fit in well there, despite its recent socialist turn. Volunteer work at the veterinarian's office two afternoons a week, wearing scrubs and everything. She loves animals—clichéd as that may sound. I'm proud of her, Ms. Hoch. I think she's special, as we are all wont to think our children are special. But know also that people have come to me—people now sitting at that table with you—and said, 'Mr. Rose, your daughter is special.'

"And when all this started a few weeks ago, she was fine. She kept her distance from the sick girls—I am sorry, I do not mean to offend anyone, but you all know what I mean. She kept on going to tennis practice and games, kept on going to her standardized-test study sessions, kept on traveling toward the wonderful, rewarding, and rewarded life that you imagine for your children. Yes, I imagined! And now? Now? First, her tennis game has fallen apart. Second, her grades have cratered. And the final straw—after nearly a week with the finest standardized-testing tutors in the Ivy League, tutors I paid top dollar for, this past weekend, for the weekend's entirety, instead of reading comprehension or essay techniques, she talked of nothing but whether trees have souls and what it means to die for our sins. Specifically: If a tree dies because you betrayed it—what price do you pay? It happened fast, Ms. Hoch. What am I supposed to do with this question? Where does it come from? And what about her college interviews? Yale is next week. Why isn't she prepping for her Yale interview?

"Other parents have confided to me that they are having the

same experience. We want to talk to our children about algebra and biology and college essays, and they want to talk about the qualities of light in a dark room and the soul's journey at death. How are we supposed to bridge this distance, Ms. Hoch? With your pills? Really? Does medication get you early admission to a big-three college? Does it lock down an internship in the Financial District? Am I really supposed to believe that a dozen healthy, self-assured young women and men are all of a sudden seeing flying turtles and that it's no big deal and has nothing to do with the biggest power plant in central New York State?"

He paused. With his eloquence, his style, his suit, the slight quaver in his voice as it got louder, his confidence tinged with sorrow, Mr. Archibald Rose had drawn us all in so skillfully that by the time he arrived at this pause, we trusted him completely and also felt like we had come to this trust by ourselves, of our own free will.

Clearly, the guy won a lot of cases.

Everyone waited breathlessly to see what he would say next.

Ms. Hoch shot a quick glance at my father before speaking. "Mr. Rose, my heart goes out to you," she said. "Hysteria has been extensively researched and documented. It is especially prevalent among teenage females put under severe academic stress from overly involved parental figures. Top psychiatrists—"

"Of course you have to say that. I'm a lawyer. I know the liability issues you are facing."

"Trust me, liability is not the issue. We at Jackduke care about this community—"

"I'm sure it's not an issue," said Mr. Rose. "But if it's not, can you tell us what exactly is going on out there at your plant?"

"It's a power plant, Mr. Hoch. Coal- and natural-gas-fired. We supply electricity to four counties in whole or in part, and we adhere to all the EPA regulations."

Mr. Rose's voice grew sharper. "I don't understand why you persist in this game, Ms. Hoch. It's our community that works at the plant, and I know you have ironclad nondisclosure agreements and state-of-the-art security systems and work very hard to ensure there are no information leaks. But I got a tip on Friday night and spent the weekend investigating, while my daughter contemplated the atomic weight of a tree soul."

"A tip?"

"From someone personally involved."

"Who?"

"Not your business, Ms. Hoch. But my sources tell me that things are being tested at that plant that the world has never seen."

Ms. Hoch gasped at this. All of us did.

"I don't know what you're talking about, Mr. Rose," she said.

"I will tell you. You're pursuing a new energy source."

"This is all getting a little outlandish."

"Is it?"

"Frankly, you're on the edge of defamation, which, you know—"

"Cold fusion. The holy grail of the industry. *Creatio ex nihilo.* Energy out of thin air."

The gasps of the audience rose in volume. My own breathing choked off. Here at last was an explanation. Or was it? What did cold fusion have to do with a samurai army—or my mother? I looked up: the lead samurai scratched an arm, considerably less impressed than the rest of us.

The county executive rose to his feet. "That's enough, Archie!"

"Mr. Rose, as an attorney, you should know it is dangerous to hurl accusations without any shred of—"

Mr. Rose held up his hand, stopping Ms. Hoch. She looked to my father, who was again bomb-sighting Mr. Rose, the muscles in his jaw now furiously fighting. Megan Rose's father took the microphone out of the stand and walked down three steps to the bottom of the bleachers and hopped from there to the ground. It was a dramatic move that heightened the tension even more. He walked toward the table in the center of the basketball court and the people seated there. Halfway, where the chief of police had stood earlier and threatened to arrest us all, he abruptly stopped and turned around.

When he spoke next, it was to us, the town.

"Friends, they want us to believe that it's all a passing cloud. That our babies are just having bad dreams. That it's in their heads—when it's clearly not—and that little pills will make it go away. That we imagined it. They want us to deny what our own eyes and ears tell us. Meanwhile, my friends and neighbors, our children slip further and further away. Is this not the case?"

Shouts of assent.

Mr. Rose held up his hand. Immediate silence.

"Proof, they say. Where is your proof that Jackduke is

involved? You have no proof, and we have research. World-renowned research with Stanford and Harvard. Well, okay. Don't take it from me. I'm just a parent. Take it from one of the affected. Take it from my daughter."

He raised his arm to the crowd.

And there she was at last, Megan Rose. She was sitting about halfway up the bleachers, a hooded sweatshirt hiding her face. A woman, her mother, I guessed, tastefully dressed as a retirement-fund commercial, slid Megan Rose's hood off and pushed her to her feet.

Megan Rose stood. Everyone looked at her. Light shone upon her like the light on paintings hanging in art galleries behind bulletproof glass, focusing our attention, emphasizing her features, but also, like those museum lights, pointing out how fragile and alone she was. How fragile and alone we all were. Her mother pushed again, and Megan Rose shyly made her way down the bleachers to where her father stood.

I believe that this was when I realized I would do anything for her.

"Megan," said Mr. Rose, motioning toward Ms. Hoch, "tell this nice woman what you just told me as we listened to her speak."

"I don't want to."

"Please, Megan."

Mr. Rose moved closer to his daughter, right by her side. He put the microphone under her mouth like a television interviewer.

Anything could happen.

"Really, I don't want to."

"It's okay, Megan."

"Please, Dad."

"Megan. You said you wanted to tell people what was happening. You said you wanted to help."

Megan Rose sighed and looked out at the crowd and then up at the ceiling and then back at the ground. The crowd followed her eyes.

"There is an army above us," she said. "Dressed in scarlet and gold. Holding swords. Ancient. Timeless. Ready to slice us all open so that the love can come out."

Many things happened at once, and these are what stood out:

A blast of screams. Hundreds of people jumping to their feet. The spokesperson of Jackduke disappearing. The county executive pounding his gavel. The samurai in the ceiling belly-laughing at the chaos. The cells in my nerves inhaling pure Ritalin. The chief of police pulling out a billy club the size of a baseball bat. Other policemen following his lead and rushing to the center of the gym and setting up a defensive circle around the VIPs. And my father spitting out his toothpick, pulling his cap low, and walking determinedly to where Megan Rose stood.

Of everything, this scared me most of all.

I could not take my eyes off Megan Rose. She stood right in the middle of the gym, the center of the tumult, the eye of the storm. But she was also somewhere else. I'd seen it before: in the cafeteria on my first day, that deep mental free dive. Before, I had seen that as a disappearing, as an escape, but I understood now that that was wrong. It was a finding. The finding of a strength deeper than what was out here in the shattering world. As the crowd surged off the bleachers, past her and toward the table where the school board sat, its rage rising and rising, the police tensing and tensing, Megan Rose did not move.

And this: she glowed. Like the moon on a clear night. Like the cabin in the valley in the mountains in the storm. Megan Rose held the microphone, watching the audience howling, watching her father thrust angry fingers at all the guilty parties, and she glowed. If only everyone could see it! The president of the student body, the queen of homecoming, the tennis star, the animal healer, the Princeton hopeful with a life of accomplishment awaiting, had become so much more.

I stared in awe.

The shouting grew louder, a hurricane of noise. The crowd surged forward. The bleachers thundered. Chairs rocketed across the floor, tumbling onto their sides. The police began kicking people's legs out from under them and zip-tying their hands together, working up the bleachers to where Stuart and I stood. I looked to Megan Rose again for guidance; she still stared inside herself. I looked up at the ceiling; the army watched the chaos beneath them, our human chaos, with less and less amusement, more and more rue. They sheathed their swords, hoisted them over their shoulders, turned back to the mist.

"Wait!" I called to them.

One by one they disappeared.

"Wallace!"

"Don't go!"

"Wallace!"

It was Stuart, holding my shirt in his fists, his face inches from mine.

"We've got to get out of here!" he yelled.

"Poets. Poets," said Megan Rose.

"The army's leaving!" I said. "What does that mean?"

"They're arresting people!" shouted Stuart. "Come on!"

"Poets. Truth always hurts when we first open our eyes. I know it. I know it. Listen to me."

Megan Rose's voice was kind. Mouths open, fists cocked, people froze in the middle of their movements, like they'd gotten stuck in time. Stuart dropped his hands from my shirt.

"I was afraid of it, too," she said. "Afraid of what was happening to me. Afraid of what would happen to my life and my plans and all that I had put into them. I was afraid I would be lost forever if I let go of what I planned to be."

Somewhere in the crowd, a woman started sobbing.

Above us, all the soldiers were gone except for the Fu Manchued leader. He turned back, cocked an ear.

"I misunderstood," said Megan Rose. "They're not hysteria. They're not here to break us. They're here to help us. To find a better way to be. We just have to be open to them. We just need to—"

Someone knocked the microphone from her hand. It squealed cruelly when it hit the floor. At that instant, Megan Rose's father bellowed and ran as fast as he could in his beautiful suit and launched his body at the policemen protecting the VIP panel. He assaulted them with such speed and force that he burst right through their defensive line; arriving at the table across from the principal and the county executive, he seemed unsure about what to do, and pounded the table with his fists as hard as he could before policemen gang-tackled him to the floor and zip-tied his hands behind his back.

The crowd surged wildly. The melee picked up where it had left off. And Megan Rose—she fainted.

It was, I saw, my father who caught her as she fell. He caught her cleanly, like a bride. Whispering into her ear—a disturbing level of intimacy, to be honest—he carried her to a far corner, and then Megan Rose was resting against a wall, and my father was walking out of the gym.

Above Stuart and me, our spot in the bleachers, the last samurai was gone. The ceiling was empty except for glaring, chicken-wire-wrapped lights. Below us: the frenzied crowd. We carefully picked our way down the bleachers. When we reached the bottom, powerful hands grabbed me from behind. They jerked me into a stranglehold, up under my arms and behind my head, nearly tearing my arms out of their sockets.

"This is the guy!" yelled my assaulter, breath reeking of Skoal. "This is the guy you're looking for!"

Not again. "It's not me, Brad," I gasped.

"This is the one who started all this!"

"Did you hear anything Megan Rose said? What her father said?"

"I heard. They've gone full psycho."

"She's telling the truth!"

"Feel that?" Brad tightened his grip. I felt tendons shearing off my shoulders. "That's truth. Not your fairy tales."

The doors to the parking lot burst open, sirens blaring,

flashing cruiser lights stabbing through the chaos. Ten more policemen ran into the room. They plunged into the crowd, clubs above their heads.

"Motherfuck!" Brad shouted, releasing me.

I turned, cradling my arms. Brad was bent over, holding the back of his head with both hands. A chair had hit him there. A few steps away, hidden in the crowd, Stuart whistled and looked at the ceiling.

He pointed to the door that led out to the parking lot.

We made for it.

"You two—stop!" a policeman yelled. It was Chief Turnblad himself. He moved between us and the exit, his billy club raised overhead.

I took another few steps, diagonally around him, pretending like I didn't hear him. He took a step to cut me off, raised his club higher.

I stopped. It was over. There was no way out. But then I caught sight of someone motioning at the far end of the gym— the janitor, standing next to a door, one that didn't lead to the parking lot but into the school itself, and without a second thought, I turned and ran for it, Stuart right behind me, the chief's angry shouts chasing us as we cut across the basketball court and past the janitor, slammed through the door and into a dark school hallway lit only by exit lights, and ran through the school, alarms blaring, past the library, past the science wing, down the stairs, out a fire exit, across a parking lot, and into the woods.

TWENTY-TWO

PAST THE FAR end of the football field was a grove of aspen trees, the one that had lit up during the homecoming game; somewhere past that, Stuart and I stopped running. We bent over, dropped to our knees. The ground was littered with crushed beer cans, cigarette butts, and candy wrappers. There was a faint smell of pot. It was a place for high school students to escape—but not the kind of escape that would help us right now.

Parents attacking the school board, policemen attacking parents, Jackduke coming for the student body with pills and lies—the school was pure, terrified chaos. The whole town was. A samurai army had wanted to slice us open.

And that had seemed like one of the better options!

Stuart gasped, his whole body shaking. "Holy shit! Did we just fuck-you the chief of police?"

"Did you just throw a chair at Brad Stone?"

"Hell, yeah. Right at his fat head."

"Nice shot."

The consequences hit him. "Shit. He's going to find out who did it. He's going to punch me so hard I'm going to forget my name."

Sirens burst through the air. I stood up, checked the aspen grove to see if we'd been followed—and where we could go. Where next? What next? What do you do after watching violence take hold of everyone you know? What do you call the last sane man in the asylum: the jailer or the prophet?

Bright lights sliced through the branches above our heads. The police—they were after us. Stuart and I took off running again, deeper into the woods. Arms up to keep from getting slashed or bonked, we crashed through dark, unfamiliar terrain. We fell out of the woods into the back of an empty parking lot—the town library—ran along the edge of the lot until we hit a road, crossed the road, cut through backyards, over another road, into a tract of marshy, undeveloped land.

The lights and sirens dropped away. We stopped, panting hard.

"It doesn't make sense," Stuart said. "It's not hysteria? How does a power plant do this? How does it make a sky army? An old woman in Lowe's?" He violently shook his head. "Honestly, until a couple of days ago, I thought you were full of it. Or, you know, did too many drugs in middle school."

"I kind of gathered that."

"You did, didn't you?"

"What do you think now?"

"I think if Jackduke is behind this, this is big. This is next-level Chernobyl. Fukushima on 'roids."

We stood there, staggered by that immensity. Then sirens

exploded on the nearest road. A fleet of cruisers stopped at the edge of the woods fifty feet away, setting fire to the trees with their strobes. Car doors opened and slammed, commands were issued in voices that sounded like MMA finishing moves, and a dog whinnied desperately that it knew everything.

"A dog!" Stuart hissed. "They'll find us. They know we know. They'll kill us!"

"Water."

"You're thirsty? Seriously?"

"No. We can lose them in water, right?"

Stuart pointed. "There's a creek this way."

We took off again, stumbling through the woods to a backyard, running along that yard and others until we reached a lawn that fell off suddenly. The creek below it was ten feet wide and rocky. It looked fast and cold. The shouts behind us were gaining.

I grabbed Stuart's arm before he could jump in.

"Change of plans," I said. "I'm going to wait here. You go."

"What? What the hell? They'll kill you."

"Go! Stay off the roads. Get home, talk to the old lady in the aisle, find out all you can from her. I need to do this."

I knew what I had to do. My father's secrecy, his evasions and denials—I was done. Enough. All the lies—he had been playing chess and letting me think it was checkers; he was a dark-side Jedi and I was a sap in white Lego armor, sweeping the floor while he charged up the planet-destroying ray. Screw that. Screw not telling me the truth. The chief of police had followed his directions at the PTA meeting. The county executive and spokesperson had, too. And Megan Rose had fainted in his arms.

Principal Rathschild was right. My father was behind this.

The realization calmed me even as the lights and sirens and dogs closed in.

"Question," said Stuart.

"Dude. Quick. What?"

"Who the hell are you?"

"That's what I aim to find out," I said.

Stuart took a deep breath, jumped down into the creek and started upstream, fell once, twice, and then, bent low, the water at his knees, one hand down to brace himself, he disappeared past a cluster of blackcap bushes.

A split second later a flashlight blinded me where I stood.

"You! Next to the water! Get over here! With your hands up!"

I raised my arms over my head and took a few steps up the lawn.

"On your knees!"

I dropped to the ground. One, two, three police officers materialized out of the darkness behind the flashlights. One of them held a toothy and passionate German shepherd by the collar. The chief of police came last.

He walked slowly, slower than everyone else, the slow walk of the boss, but his chest heaved. He'd been running hard. His face was shiny with sweat. One of his pistols was not in his belt but in his hand, where it gleamed like a star.

He walked up to me, walked slowly around me. "Disobey my. Direct order? Make me. Run across. The whole damn school?" He breathed like an asthmatic bull. "Tarnation. Do you understand. How stupid you are? What's this?" He stopped in front of me. "Are you now reaching for my weapon, son? Are you putting my life at risk?"

"No, sir."

"Deputy Sloane, do you see this criminal aggression?"

"Yes, Chief," said one of the deputies.

"Dangerous. So dangerous."

"Yes, Chief."

"I want to see my father," I said.

The officers chortled at that.

"Daddy can't save you, son," said the chief. "We're long past that."

"I'd like to see him right now, actually. You can give me a ride."

The gun handle felt hard as stone where it hit my skull. Then I was lying on the grass, my brain playing wind chimes, smelling gun oil and the creek.

Two of the cops stepped forward, holding more justice in their hands. The chief glared down at me, his expression conveying that he would be one hundred percent okay filling me with holes if only there wasn't that pesky thing called the law. And the law went missing sometimes.

Excessive police force, malfunctioning body cameras—was this how it ended?

"Deputy Sloane?" The chief motioned to a nearby officer.

"Yes, Chief."

"Arrest is being resisted."

"Yes, Chief."

Deputy Sloane was short but enormously wide, with those gym muscles that are allergic to clothes that fit. He reached down and took hold of my head in one hand and lifted it and the body attached. I was floating, weightless, and then there was an arm around my throat, cutting off the flow of air. I looked up and saw that I was under an oak tree and it had a great sideways branch and on that branch sat a white owl, seven gray doves, and a small blue angel nervously clutching a wing.

Mysterious. And as the deputy tightened his grip, I knew that I did not have to fear these visitors, that the night people—my mother and the trees and the rest—wanted the best for me, that my sanity was not what they were after but something deeper that I still didn't understand, and that the real danger had always been in the world right in front of me. The real danger was in those who said, Trust us. Who said, You're hysterical. Who said, Be afraid.

The edges of my sight became dark, then the middle and the inside of it. Just before blacking out completely, I managed to croak out one last thing.

"His name is Ronald Cole."

PART II

TWENTY-THREE

BACK WHEN WE lived in New Mexico, before Ma got sick, before we started moving every couple of months, my father got on a healthy-living, doomsday-prep kick. An odd mix, I agree—if the world is going to end, what's the point of outliving it? Regardless, he flushed his cigarettes down the toilet with ceremony, did fifty push-ups every morning, and started a seed bank in the garage. Every meal, he lectured me on melting permafrost and low-carb diets. Saturdays at dawn, he face-pushed me awake and chucked me a grain-free granola bar, and we climbed into the truck, drove, disembarked at a trailhead, and hiked at a fast-timed pace until the sun went down. Every break from hiking, we practiced wasteland survival techniques—starting a fire without matches, identifying edible weeds, that kind of thing.

Control of nature, Dad called it. Ma called it *abusive.*

One of those Saturdays, the whole Cole family went for a hike in a sky oasis. A sky oasis is a high-altitude rain forest with its own ecosystem, separate and distinct from the desert below it. (Side note: they're all being annihilated by climate change.) Around noon, we came upon an open field, and in the middle of this field was a small tree, its branches heavy with giant fruit. It was a pomegranate tree. The reddish-orange fruit was as bright and round as Christmas tree ornaments. The fruit distinctly called my name, which I pointed out to my parents, who exchanged a concerned glance.

The only thing: the whole field between us and the pomegranate tree was covered in poison oak. Even at eight I could recognize it—it's a distinctly pissed-off-looking plant.

My father looked at me. I looked at him. He looked at Ma. Ma looked at him. He was wearing shorts.

"Fortune favors the bold," he said.

"No," Ma said. She had peanuts and raisins in separate ziplock bags in her backpack. She reached for them.

Dad stepped forward.

The pomegranates were terrible. Like eating chalk. The worst fruit I've ever eaten. I suppose they had put so much energy into their beauty that they had nothing left for taste. There's a lesson there, perhaps. But here's the main thing: when the rash covered ninety percent of his body and cracked and bled, and my father spent every spare moment lying in an ice bath, I asked him if it was worth it, and he shrugged and said: "Wallace, it doesn't matter."

It doesn't matter.

I don't know if he remembered telling me that, but I did. I thought about it every time we threw our garbage bags in the bed of the pickup and drove off to another town. I thought about it when I arrived at a new school and was greeted by oversized bullies, over-the-verge principals, and further empirical evidence of the accelerating collapse of everything. I thought about it when girls I liked disappeared from my life, blips in the rearview, my plans for happiness puddled on the ground next to them. I thought about it night after night, when Ma was dying.

What matters?

Nothing, son. Nothing does.

I was eight when my father said this. Is it any wonder I was wandering the woods at night looking for something that did? That I had a counseling folder as thick as a Bible? That I had no idea what was real?

And that I was tired—really, really tired—of not knowing?

Police Chief Turnblad drove straight to the duplex from the creek, siren blasting the whole way. We sat in front of the apartment until my father pulled up a few minutes after we did. He lit a cigarette as he climbed out of his truck. The chief got out of his car and met my father under the porch light, and the two of them spoke very close together, like old soldiers. Then the chief yanked me from the backseat and uncuffed my wrists.

At the kitchen table, Dad lit another cigarette as he looked me over. I had scratches on my face from branches swiping it, to go along with the assorted bruises I'd picked up previously at friendly neighborhood keg parties and such. My clothes were a collage of sticks and mud.

"You look like you fought a swamp creature." He pointed. "Who gave you that bump on your forehead?"

"Your buddy outside," I said.

"He said you resisted arrest."

"And you believe him?"

"He said you mouthed off. I can believe that."

I rubbed my sore arms and shoulders. "You two seemed awfully friendly."

Dad carefully measured his words. "Chief Turnblad and I have an understanding."

"What's an understanding?"

"It's classified."

"Meaning you're not going to tell me."

He took a deep drag and tapped his cigarette on the ashtray. "Sorry, Wallace."

And just like that, our conversation was in the familiar territory of denials and vagueness and not-your-business. Next, I would snark, he would patronize, I would point out his dismissive behavior, he would say he had to go to work, and nothing would have changed.

No. Not today.

"You called the shots back there," I said.

"What? What shots?" said Dad.

"You ran the meeting."

"Uh, no. That was the guy with the Deadhead hair. The county executive."

"I saw the way he looked at you. The chief and the spokeswoman, too. They wouldn't do anything without your approval."

Dad shifted in his seat. His blank eyes blinked quickly.

"And I'm curious about what that Megan Rose girl was saying. An army in the sky? Everyone going to get sliced open by swords? What was that about?"

"Don't change the subject," I said.

"She's the one you fell for on your first day, right? Good choice."

"Thank you. She's special."

"That was sarcasm."

"Wow, I totally missed that."

Dad put his hands on the edge of the table to push himself up. "Okay, I'm going to go. Get some rest, Wallace. You need it."

"Why did you hurt her?"

His voice rose a couple of notches. "Hurt her? Come on. Do we really have to do this? The girl expressed agitation. Agitation that was not conducive to the general community discussion. It was dangerous, point of fact. I took the opportunity to help her release it."

"Agitation? She seemed pretty calm to me."

My father cocked an eyebrow.

"When she spoke," I explained. "She wasn't ranting like everyone else in the gym."

"Wallace, she got hundreds of people to riot. A calm person wouldn't do that. A calm person makes a tense situation calmer. She doesn't turn it into a cluster-event. Look, she's a striking girl. You have a tendency to fall for them. Runs in the family. Runs in the gender. But you got to put that aside and look at the facts. A golden army in the sky? Ready to cut us open? She's hysterical—that's a fact."

"So you *did* hurt her?"

"Knock it off. She's fine. She's home resting." His jaw muscles started that wrestling thing. "You know what? Fine. I *was* actually in charge of that meeting. And when I get back to the plant tonight, I *do* have to answer for everything that happened there. Do you know how much I have at stake? How much pressure is on *me*?"

Bingo. The opening I'd been waiting for.

"That's exactly it!" I yelled. "I *don't* know what's at stake. Because you don't tell me! You never tell me. You never tell me anything. You just disappear and leave me with this big hole in the middle of my life. Enough! No more hiding! I want to know the truth!"

My voice came out fast and high. My hands shook. My arms did, too. I wasn't used to speaking so bluntly, to him or anyone. And though the words had the pitch of a chipmunk squeak, it felt damn righteous to say them. I'd been waiting for years to say them.

And they worked.

"Okay," Dad said.

"Okay?"

"Okay!" He said that loud. "The truth. Let's do this. Just don't get upset when you wish you had never asked."

Dad stood up, walked to the window, looked out, walked back, opened the ancient fridge. It had that old-fridge, bad-tooth yellow going inside and out. He pulled a bottle of Yuengling off the top shelf. After a moment's thought, he grabbed another.

Fished his opener off the counter, popped them both, and placed one in front of me.

"Beer," he said, like I didn't know the name for it.

Our first together, actually. But it wasn't like the commercials. In the commercials celebrating such alcohol milestones, fathers and sons rested their elbows on wood fences, sweat rolled down their arms, pride welled, manhood was earned, and wild horses ran on beaches in slow motion.

This was not like that.

"I wish you weren't like me," Dad said.

"Well, then," I said. "We agree on something."

"The abilities I have, you have to be born with them. And you were."

"Being an asshole is genetic?"

He ignored that. "I know the suffering this life has in store for you. And I'll admit—I don't know what to do about it. I'd hoped that if I kept my distance, you wouldn't go through what I went through. That your life would be different from mine. Easier. But that's not working."

"Maybe you should stay farther away."

"Will you relax? You're missing the point."

"No, I get it. You think I'm screwed up."

"Screwed up? God, no. The opposite. You feel too deeply and you see too much. Way too much."

It was hard to hear that. Concern? Respect? Praise? *From my father?* My defenses glitched as something shifted from ice to water inside my chest. I quickly put up a new wall against it. Dad, look at my life: town to town to town, a skipping stone, a blur. And you know what a blur feels like? Nothing. So my life is nothing. Every potential friendship ends in departure. Every girl I like disappears before I can explore my feelings for her. Or maybe—plot twist—she gets knocked out by my father in an assembly.

"I don't need your pity or whatever this is," I said.

"It's not pity."

"You still haven't told me a thing. Like always."

He looked down at the table. He took a long sip from his beer. When he looked up, it was clear he'd made a decision.

"It's actually obvious," he said.

"What is?"

"Energy."

"What's obvious about that?"

"Energy is the truth. Truth is energy."

I still didn't get it. "What?"

"Human society has an insatiable need for energy," Dad said. "Now, Jackduke is an energy company. Meaning, we find energy sources around the world and refine and distribute them. And then people can run their hair dryers and laptops and Rokus and George Foreman Grills and so forth. The survival of society depends on our scientists and engineers and miners and oil workers doing their tasks successfully. That's not an exaggeration. We are essential to human survival. We, Jackduke, are as true as this world gets." He took a pull on the Yuengling. "However, there are two serious problems with conventional energy sources, as I am sure you know: first, they're going to boil us alive. I'm not one of those industry idiots who argues that we're in a climate pause or that atmospheric carbon-dioxide concentrations are determined by Jesus farts. Global warming is real. And second, they're running out. Easy sources of energy, that is. Which is funny, because the world is full of energy. The world *is* energy. Form"—he ran his arm around the kitchen, taking in the table, the walls, the fridge, the beers—"isn't actually solid. It isn't actually real. It is energy trapped in stasis, and that energy will be released when the form decays. And every form decays eventually. Bodies. Buildings. Even stars. If you paid attention in physics class, you would know this. This is basic stuff. Our bodies, our cars, our shoes—all of them: trapped energy. In some forms, like decayed and compressed primordial organic matter, that energy is readily available. In most, it is not. You follow, Wallace?"

"Sure. I don't see what this has to do with—"

"I'm getting to it. Patience."

Dad sat back, sipped his beer, lit a cigarette. He stretched out the pause, edging on my discomfort. I bit my tongue hard.

"Two serious problems." He counted them off. "Energy runs out, and energy sets the world on fire. Everyone's looking for sources that don't have these two problems. Renewables are one way, but they're not enough. Solar, wind—they're great on paper but always a dozen years away: inconsistent and hard to store, hard to ramp up and distribute, and impossible to make a profit from."

"I thought they were getting better."

Dad raised his eyebrows and shook his head: no, not even close.

"Here's the thing that we've figured out at Jackduke," he said. "There's another kind of energy."

"You mean cold fusion, like that lawyer guy said in the gym?"

"No."

"Nuclear?"

"No."

"Bacteria pools?"

"No."

"Algae? Undersea waves? Cow shit?"

"No, Wallace. Nobody has ever used this. And yet it's right in front of us."

I looked around the kitchen. Fridge, counter, window, table. Two bottles of beer. Cigarette smoke piling around the single ceiling lightbulb. Energy everywhere, right in front of us? I didn't see any energy. Dad held up his hands like a magician showing his sleeves. Was this another one of his verbal deflections, another stall?

"You're looking too hard," my father said. "As you always do. It's not German philosophy. It's not computer code."

"I don't always look too hard."

"Energy has energy, to put it crudely. It shakes. It floats. It moves around houses and lawns and trees. It's in rooms, in hallways, in corners—energy tends to cluster in corners. Go figure. You can really feel these energies when you're in an old house or an overpacked gym full of panicked parents. Did you notice that tonight? The intensity of that gym? Ask yourself: Why does an empty playground feel full in a way an empty parking lot never does? Why do you feel more alive on a trail in the woods than at the airport baggage claim? Energy is why. Subatomic elevated neutrino energy. Sen energy for short."

Disbelief joined the hostility I already felt. They gave me a bitter taste in the back of my mouth.

"Send energy?"

"Not Send. SEN. S.E.N. Sen energy. Neutrinos. All three kinds. Quarks, leptons, bosons. All that."

"In the corners of rooms?"

"In the corners." He pointed to the ones in the kitchen. "We gather up these ignored and aimless particles, excite them with an ultrasonic quantum bombardment process—I could explain how it works, but I don't have time and the gist is it really isn't that difficult: all energy wants is to move, so we help it do so, we help it move—and in this activated Sen form, we put it to use. And then we use it. And so."

He pointed up. Beneath the cobwebbed ceiling fan the single bare bulb gleamed dully.

"A lightbulb?" I said.

"Powered by Sen energy. The North Homer plant has been running on it and nothing else for"—he looked at his watch—"eighteen days, seven hours, and thirty-nine minutes."

It took me a minute, but then I grasped what Dad was saying, the audacity and magnitude of it.

A new energy source.

One that was everywhere.

Easily available.

World-saving.

Powering lightbulbs as we spoke.

In the corners of kitchens. In the gymnasiums. In the trees—

Dad sipped his beer. He didn't seem excited by what he just told me. He seemed subdued. And then it clicked.

"The visions," I said.

"Yes."

"It *is* you."

"We're still working out the technology," Dad said. "It's got some bugs."

"Bugs? Holy shit, there are bugs."

"We've pushed things a little fast. I admit that. We couldn't be completely honest at the meeting tonight. You have to understand . . ." Suddenly he thumped his fist on the table. "Look out there! I grew up near Albany, a couple hours east on 88. I can tell you it's supposed to be cold around Halloween! The leaves are supposed to be on the ground, Jack Frost nipping at your toes—hell, chewing them off. And instead, the window's open, and we're wearing T-shirts. Someone had to do something! You were waiting for Congress to do it? Facebook? Independent Vermont senators? Permaculture hippies in yurts? The Supreme Court? That's all a bunch of chimpanzees flinging shit at each other. We had to act!"

"And too bad for any kids who can't handle it."

"Yes. Well. High school kids . . . their energies are so volatile, their emotions so over the top, their boundaries so undefined. . . . You know this, you spend all day with them. Teenagers are a danger to themselves and others, to begin with.

Of course, some of them are extra-sensitive. One or two get a little freaked out by minute energetic charges. But most people aren't affected at all."

"Dad, I saw a kid lose his mind in the cafeteria."

"That's overstating it."

"He bit a chunk out of the gym teacher's forearm."

"If it makes you feel any better, that's where I come in."

"You—what?"

"Hallucinations are a side effect of Sen particle overflow. It's my job to collect the overly stimulated particles, to collect the spilled energies. My job." He smiled wanly. "I know you've always wondered. Now you know. Happy?"

Happy? Like a blind man living in a haunted house, waking up one morning and suddenly being able to see—that's what I felt like, listening to this. A veil was being pulled off my eyes, and the world I was seeing was impossible. Terrifying. And also absurd.

I said, "Your job is collecting broken souls?"

"I don't like using that word."

"*Broken*?"

"The other word."

"*Souls.*"

"That one."

"You collect them."

"Again, I collect energies from systems that have overflowed. And we're working to prevent this overflow from even happening. We're getting there. And when we get there . . ."

He may have said more. Or perhaps he tailed off. I wasn't sure. I couldn't listen anymore just then. It was a lot to process.

He and Jackduke were saving the world from boiling oceans and bleached coral and dying bumblebees. With a new energy source. One that had no greenhouse gas, no toxic smog, no radioactive cooling ponds, no broken well in the bottom of the Gulf giving dolphins blowhole cancer. But that did have a wee technical issue that caused minor bugs like, oh, cafeteria freak-outs, samurai armies, talking trees, clumsy tennis balls, Ma appearing with love in her eyes—

Wait a second.

"What about the good ones?" I asked.

"The good what?" Dad said.

"Bugs. Visions. The *good* visions. They're not all bad hallucinations. They're not hysteria. Some of them, they're trying to help."

"Wallace, they're side effects of overstimulated—"

"What about the trees?"

"What? What about trees?"

"Do they also overflow when you hit them with your whack technology? And, like, start talking like people?"

"No. It's—" He shook his head, twisted the neck of his beer bottle. "You worry me when you talk like this, Wallace. It's overstimulated energy. That's all. It's not *Toy Story*. It's not magic. It's not inanimate objects becoming animate. There's physics behind it. We've got teams of scientists that figured this out. Activate, then collect. Activate, then collect. That's all."

"That's all?"

"Yes, that's all."

"I saw Ma."

Dad jerked. Or no, he was still, still as always, but his blank, thousand-mile eyes twitched as if something had slashed across them. And in that split second I saw he wasn't being straight. He was bluffing. He was low-cards, off-suit.

He had to be.

"I did. A couple times," I said.

"Wallace, charging subatomic particles has side effects—"

"She knew my life. Everything that had happened since she died and—"

"Let me guess. She visited you in a ball of light. She told you that the world was larger and gentler than you knew. How good the creek smelled then! How sweet the birdsong!"

"Yes, exactly!"

"Yes. That's a hallucination, Wallace."

"She held me."

"That's not your mother."

"She forgave me."

"It's an ability. You have an ability—"

"Stop it, Dad."

"Bugs, Wallace."

"No! Fuck you!"

He didn't say anything. Then he said softly, "I'm sorry."

Dad held up his hands, motioned for a time-out. Went down the hall. The bathroom door was thin, and I heard him draining his beer down there.

I sat in the kitchen, shaking.

It had rained all day, tapering off during the PTA meeting, and the breeze that now came in the open window was like steam off soup. A couple of mosquitoes hummed against the screen, swearing they'd just forgotten their keys and would be right on their way.

I had wanted to know what was causing the visions, and now I knew. It was fuel. I had wanted to know what the hell my dad did, why we moved from town to town, power plant to power plant, why he spent every waking minute at the plants, and now I knew. He collected fuel. He collected fuel that could save the world.

And if souls got broken along the way, he came along with his broom and dustbin and swept them up.

So, yay? All good?

No. Not all good. Things were happening that he didn't fully understand. He didn't know how far the technology went. Or he was denying it.

And what I kept coming back to was this: if what he said was true, it meant the night people, and all their grace and wisdom, were false. That they were an industrial malfunction. Spilled coffee on the control-room panel. Screwed-up test pages of a new printer, fever dreams of monkeys testing breathing apparatus on one-way rides to space.

A mistake.

What kind of world was that? Did I want to live in a world like that? Did I have a choice?

Dad came back into the kitchen, buckling his belt. He took off his ball cap, palmed his hair, put the cap back on. Still standing, he reached down for his beer—empty—reached for mine, and took a long swallow.

"I've got to go to work," he said. "I'm glad we talked."

"One more question," I said.

"I've told you the truth."

"Just one."

He grabbed his cigarettes and keys off the table and sighed.

"What's the point?" I asked.

"The point of what?"

"Life."

A needle ground into the skin between his eyes. "I'm not following, Wallace."

"If all the visions—Ma and the other ones, good and bad—are just side effects of your technology, what matters? If deeply personal, life-affirming energies aren't important, then what is?"

Dad muttered something under his breath, looked at his watch. He sat down again. For a minute he violently rubbed the scruff on his jaw.

Finally, he said, "It's been a long-ass day, Wallace. I prefer to avoid theological discussions after midnight. Or anytime, as a general rule. But ask yourself this: Who ever said life has to have a point beyond what's in front of us? How many centuries of societal harmony have been squandered because of the idea that life has to mean something more than it does? Why not let that kind of mental torture die? Enjoy a football game. Take a trip to the beach. Go see a good movie, like that Tom Cruise alien one we saw last summer. Have a pizza and some soft-serve. Take a drive in the country. That may not seem like much to you, but for most people, that's plenty, that's more than enough. To most people, that right there is the American dream." He stood up. "At the end of the day, you've just got to make it to the end of the day."

"So nothing matters?"

"Hey, you wanted the truth."

"How are you so sure that's the truth?"

"Because they're hallucinations, Wallace."

"They're more than that. They told me."

"Stop listening to dreams!"

"Maybe you should start!"

"No." Dad shook his head at everything, up to and including shaking his head. "No. You don't know what I've put on the line. The sacrifices I've made. I've had enough of this. Hoch has had enough of this. Chief Turnblad has had enough, and he is now authorized to use whatever force he deems appropriate. You understand what that means? You understand the danger?"

"I can guess."

"Good. We leave Sunday."

"What? That's six days from now!"

"Yes."

"We just got here. I'm making friends."

"Then you might want to start saying goodbye," Dad said. "I'm going to work."

TWENTY-FOUR

(QUESTION AT FOUR a.m., after three sleepless hours)

If I wanted answers and if I finally got answers,

and if I had been waiting for an honest conversation with my father for my entire life,

and if I finally got that,

and if the night people are, in fact, side effects of a new technology, side effects that screw up teenagers, who, in fairness, are ripe for it,

and if the most convincing arguments for the night people were presented by a tennis ball, an old willow tree, and my mother in visions not entirely in sync with how she was in life,

and if the world is indeed on fire and getting more crispy by the day and could really use some Hail Mary, Tony Stark–level technology, and here's a solution,

and if Tom Cruise does from time to time make surprisingly

good movies, to the point where they honestly can't be said to be surprises anymore,

and if it already has been long established that my life is a skipping stone, a blur, a nothing . . .

. . . then why does it feel like my heart is breaking?

TWENTY-FIVE

THE NEXT MORNING, the police were everywhere.

I opened the front door, and North Homer was crawling with them. They drove past. They walked past. They flew overhead. They stood under awnings, like shadows of themselves. They ate breakfast in the Dunkin' Donuts parking lot, like parodies of themselves. They got out of their cruisers, weaponed to the teeth, like comic-book fantasies of themselves. They had body armor and handheld shields in addition to the body armor and guns with high-powered scopes. For sure, when aliens arrived from Orion to invade upstate New York, the police would be ready to kill them all.

And I saw that, to them, the aliens had already come. We, the North Homer High School students, were the aliens, the strangers who had to be dealt without mercy.

They swarmed the hallways inside the school. Deputy Sloane, who had choked me out in the woods, was easy to spot, as his uniform was several sizes too tight for his swollen frame. He spotted me as well and made sure that his path down the hallway went right into mine.

"Watch it," he said, stepping over my legs.

It wasn't the only time I hit the floor. A lot of the police lost their sense of direction around me.

"It appears that being a teenager is now a crime," I said to Stuart at lunch.

"Life sentence," he said.

A felony, class A. A disease. An epidemic. It did feel like that, like that's what they thought we were. And that we had always been seen that way and were just finding out.

In the basement hallway, a line of students stretched from outside the heavy wooden URSE door all the way to the stairs. Having learned their diagnosis at the PTA meeting, these students now waited for their cure, the radical, eighty-five-percent-effective three-drug regimen developed by the SHITS. They chewed their nails, barely spoke, didn't look each other in the eye.

Another development: Megan Rose was gone from school again. She didn't swing by her locker the one period I staked it out. None of her friends had seen her. None of them wanted to discuss where she might be, either, and some of them had again developed profound hearing loss around me.

At lunch, Stuart shared the rumors he'd overheard about Megan Rose. That she had been whisked away in the middle of the night to a discreet facility in the Adirondacks where Wall Street millionaires went to cut down on their abuse of prescription drugs. That she had undergone a "procedure," which was a "qualified success," and was now "resting comfortably in a quiet location" ("no other details at this time"). And finally that she'd gone full, one-hundred-percent-plus hysterical, past the reach of Jackduke's drug cocktail, and had been moved to a locked ward in Syracuse, where she was getting pumped full of the psych meds that leave you asleep sitting up.

"And drooling," Stuart added.

"I don't believe it," I said. "That's not what they're doing. You really think the night people want us cracked up and drooling?"

"No. Not at all. Quite the opposite." Stuart nodded across the room. "But *they* might."

In a corner of the cafeteria, two policemen stared at us, their expressions conveying that our very existence made their faces itch but they couldn't scratch their faces and that was agony—agony that was our fault.

Stuart wanted to talk more, so we agreed to meet in his basement after school. I hoped to stop by Megan Rose's house-brick on the way, but three police cruisers were parked out in front of her fence when I arrived. Two policemen were at the door conversing with her father; two others stood in the road, sipping coffee and doing that *Rain Man* talking-to-the-radio-on-their-shoulder thing.

They glared at me like I voted for an opposing party. I did an awkward cross-the-street-and-mind-my-own-business. What had happened to Megan Rose now?

When I knocked on the basement door, Stuart handed me a mug that smelled like rotten apples and pine needles.

"Tea," he said.

"What for?"

"Drinking, genius. With that hole in your face. And for freeing your mind from anxious states."

"There's a tea for that?"

He held up a book with the title *Tea for Freeing Your Mind from Anxious States.* "I followed the directions in this."

The mug smelled awful. "I had a girlfriend once who made her own teas," I said.

"What happened to her?"

"I moved. Never saw her again. That reminds me, Stuart. In a couple days—"

"Well, I'm glad," he said. "I'm glad you moved. You ended up here, didn't you? And I'm glad you're not dead or in jail. Both seemed very possible last night after I left you by the creek. I felt bad about that. We are friends, yes? I am glad we are friends. Friends having tea."

His voice was low and slow. I had never heard it like this. It had a quality that took a minute to place. *Kind.* That was it. It made my ears twinge.

"That's nice . . . of you," I said.

Stuart lit something with a match—incense. A stick of incense. He placed it standing up in a little bowl filled with dirt.

The tea was atrocious. Even Stuart gagged, though he tried to hide it. Between sips he explained how last night, after escaping along the creek, he had, as I had suggested, gone to the birches in his backyard and asked for help. The lady of the fastener aisle had met him there.

"And? Did she help you?"

"Edith gave me the greatest help of my life."

"Wow. That's great. What was it?"

"She taught me to meditate."

"Oh." That wasn't what I had expected. "You meditated?"

"We meditated." Stuart put down his tea. He had moved and now sat cross-legged on a cushion on the floor. From there he pointed up at the shelves. "I read all these books for years, and they never made sense to me. Calming the mind . . . how do you calm a mind? A mind, by definition, is a ruthlessly evolved freak-out machine. Humans only stayed alive because their minds panicked furiously when lions came around. But after talking with Edith last night, I understand mind-calming a little bit. You sit still. You breathe. You wait. And then it calms. It just does. I even found my *hara*." He pointed. "It's here."

He nodded that way spiritual types do, like he was in a vat of syrup.

"That's your penis," I said.

"Above that. Here."

"What's a *hara* do?"

"It calms you."

This logic seemed more circular than persuasive.

"You've no idea how long I've been looking for it," Stuart added. "You know what Rathschild always tells me when she sees me? That no one remembers high school. Basically, her one constant piece of advice to me is that someday I'll forget how awful my life is. But in here"—he pointed at his *hara* again—"it doesn't matter one bit."

He really did look peaceful in the candlelight. He wasn't even slouching.

"That's nice," I said.

So it appeared that right in the middle of a town-wide fubar, Edith, the old lady in the fastener aisle, had, in just a few hours, led Stuart to a new perspective on life, one that wasn't berating him about what a loser he was.

What a precious thing to not be oppressed by your own thoughts! What precious, strange friends the night people were.

I didn't have the heart to tell Stuart what my father had told me. That it was all a side effect. I would try to keep that to myself.

Stuart rang a bell and closed his eyes . . . and meditated, I guess. I watched the road, hoping the police up there would clear out before curfew so I could talk to Megan Rose. I also tried to find a way to reconcile my father's world, where no deeper experiences mattered, with the night people's, where all of them did. It got harder the more I tried.

After an hour, one cruiser started up and drove away. Then another did. Just one remained. There were about twenty minutes of daylight left. I would have to leave soon to beat curfew. A bird started singing from right outside the door. It sounded like the song of a person who'd lost his dog. "Aw, girl, aw, girl," the song went, "I miss you, I miss you, I miss you, I miss you."

"That's lovely," said Stuart, and I could hear it in his voice.

"Are you crying?" I asked.

"The bird, man. The bird."

We listened to the bird.

And then I told him.

TWENTY-SIX

OUTSIDE, THE RAYS of the setting sun Cheeto-dusted the trees. The last of the police cruisers had finally left. But it had been replaced. A gleaming black Mercedes with black windows was parked next to Megan Rose's fence, as threatening and out of place on that street as a spaceship.

The light was on in the giant square window of the Rose family house-brick. Here goes nothing. I passed the Mercedes, hopped the fence, walked up the driveway. Just before I knocked on the door, it opened. Megan Rose slipped out onto the porch.

Even though I'd been looking for her all day, it took me a minute to get over my surprise.

"You're here?" I said.

"Yes, Wallace," she said. "I live here."

Her hair was pulled back in a ponytail, and she was wearing yoga pants and a large formless sweatshirt. Her eyes sparkled warmly. Somewhere in the house behind her, animated voices talked with astonishing speed.

"I'm so glad you're here," I said. "I'm glad you're okay. I was worried. You were incredible at the PTA meeting, and then no one knew what happened to you. There were rumors about you in school." That sounded accusatory. "I didn't believe them, of course."

"What rumors?"

After some prodding, I told her what Stuart had told me at lunch, about procedures and drugs.

Megan Rose took it well. "They're not that far off, honestly," she said. "My father is sparing no expense in saving his precious, Ivy League–destined, tennis-champion child from the horror of having thoughts about life and death. Just this afternoon I met with a famous psychiatrist he flew in from Boston. She wrote a bestselling book about relational disorders in teenage girls called *It's Not Me, It's Uterus*. Have you heard of it?"

"I missed that one. Did she help?"

"Oh, I'm all cured," said Megan Rose.

We shared a quick smile. I motioned to the Mercedes. "That her car?"

"That, actually, is Ms. Marguerite Hoch from Jackduke Energy. You okay?"

The air had gone out of me.

"Next time," I said, "you can lead with that."

I listened more closely to the voices deeper in the house. They were behind a door, muffled. I couldn't make out any words, but it was obvious now that one speaker was indeed Ms. Hoch. She spoke with the roughshod determination of an anti-immigrant talk-show host to a liberal guest. Megan Rose's father was in there, too, his voice not quite as relentless but still plenty adamant.

The oddest thing was that they seemed to be getting along. Strident as their conversation was, they weren't fighting but agreeing. Why were they getting along?

I raised a questioning eyebrow to Megan Rose. She shook her head.

"When they're deciding your life," she said, "they make you leave the room."

"Or she's going to pay him off, I bet."

"So let her. Let him."

I took a step back. "Really? You're okay with that?"

Megan Rose raised her arms to the sky. "Susie is happy. The oak branches are full of blue angels. Love spreads like pollen, and we're all a giant sinus infection. Let them think their decisions matter. It's sound and fury signifying nothing."

"Nice. That Kanye?"

"Shakespeare, Wallace."

I took a deep breath; I was going to have to do it again.

"I finally talked to my father," I said. "And I know where the night people come from."

"Where?" She dropped her arms. "Tell me."

It was harsh music, and I tried to deliver it gently. After I'd laid it on Stuart—that the old woman who was teaching him meditation and self-love was an unwanted side effect of

Jackduke's Sen energy technology—he hadn't moved for five minutes. Hell, after my father had told me, I hadn't moved from the kitchen table for an hour.

Love, that pollenlike love? An accident. A hallucination. A bug.

"No." Megan Rose went pale.

There was no gentle way to deliver this information, I was finding.

"I'm sorry," I said. "I wish it wasn't true."

She stepped past me onto the edge of the stoop. She looked at the trees in the yard.

"A side effect?" she said. "Of what? Quarks? What even are those?"

"It's Hail Mary technology pushed too far. They're still figuring it out while they go along. And we're the guinea pigs. And my father, he's the guinea-pig wrangler."

"It can't be."

"I'm sorry. I don't want it to be true, either. But nothing else explains the night people."

Megan Rose's head dropped down and down, quickly approaching that isolating free-dive-level deepness. I felt impelled to find the words to bring her back.

"There is one thing I don't get," I said. "One thing. I've been turning it over and over in my mind all afternoon. My father says they're hallucinations, right? Like when you drop acid?"

"I wouldn't know," said Megan Rose.

"Okay. When you trip, everyone gets their own visions. Like Susie, for you."

"So?"

"The PTA meeting. *I* saw the samurai army. Scarlet and gold. Stuart, too. How could we see what you did?"

A minute passed in silence. Then Megan Rose looked at me.

"They don't actually know what the hell is going on," she said.

"That has crossed my mind."

"They're lying. Lying and covering their tracks."

There was a bolt of laughter in the room down the hall where the adults were planning Megan Rose's life.

"That's why she's here," Megan Rose said. "Has to be. . . . Okay. This could be okay." She nodded, convincing herself a little more with each nod. "Okay. Let's play it cool. Wait a few days. A week, even. Let Jackduke and the police feel like they have things cleaned up with their curfew and drugs. Then we'll go to the glade and ask the night people themselves who they are and where they come from and how we can protect them. We'll find it out for ourselves."

"That won't work."

She reached out and grabbed my hand, activating all the nerves in my arm. "It *will* work, Wallace. We'll go together."

"I leave town Sunday."

"What? For how long?"

"For good."

Megan Rose let go of my hand. The activated arm nerves missed her immediately. She dropped her head, falling back into herself.

"For good. Really?"

"Yes."

At a house across the street, a porch light went on. Night had completed its descent while we were talking. Curfew. Damn. No way I would beat curfew, and the police were out for blood.

"What do we do?" Megan Rose asked.

"Well, when I left other towns, I just slipped away," I said. "Didn't say anything to anybody. Didn't stay in touch with anyone. But maybe we could?"

"Oh, no." Megan Rose covered her mouth with her hand.

"Oh," I said. "Right." When you tell people you're leaving them forever, they tend to take it personally. "Okay. I understand."

"No, I meant— Wait. Wait a minute—I just realized something. Your father is the fix-it guy for Jackduke? Why would he leave town in the middle of this?"

"He wouldn't."

"Exactly."

"So? I don't get it."

"So, if you're leaving Sunday, that means they'll be done. By Sunday they'll have all the energy gathered up, Wallace."

"That would mean—"

"Yes." She waved at the yard. "All of them. Gone."

"But—" The ground rushed at me, and I grabbed a railing. "But they can't. They can't gather them all. How can they just gather them all? They're ours."

Megan Rose shook her head. In the house behind her, high heels impatiently hit a wood floor in a rising beat. The voices got louder and closer.

"Run!" she urged.

Too late. Abruptly, they were upon us. Ms. Hoch first, in a gray pantsuit and enormous robotic smile; followed quickly by Mr. Rose, immaculately dressed, also grinning.

Their smiles disappeared the instant they saw me.

"Wallace Cole," said Ms. Hoch.

"Yes," I said. "Have we met?"

"We have not," she said. "But I know who you are."

"Who is he?" asked Mr. Rose, trying to place me. "I've seen him before."

"Wallace and I were discussing our social studies homework," said Megan Rose.

"Yes. Right," I said. "Don't forget to read chapter six, Megan Rose. The French Indian War."

"French and Indian."

"That's what I said. I'll get going."

"Wait." Ms. Hoch stepped forward, uncomfortably close. "You missed curfew, Wallace. Why don't I give you a ride?"

"That's okay, I—"

"Ride with me."

TWENTY-SEVEN

WE SAT IN the back of the Mercedes on black leather seats while the driver sat up front. I hadn't known there was a driver. He drove slowly, and the houses of North Homer fell slowly through the windows, like playing cards falling into the void. Ms. Hoch sat perfectly straight, legs crossed, suit and blouse without a wrinkle. Her dark hair was glazed in iron. She opened a purse, removed a small object, and applied some dark red lipstick.

When you're next to someone very well put together, you become aware of all the ways in which you are not. I tensed.

The car slowed for a turn. It turned. The driver wore sunglasses, even though it was night. His head and shoulders never moved. I could feel my heart beating.

Ms. Hoch did not say a word. She appeared to savor my rising anxiety. We stopped outside the apartment, under the oak trees. One of them brushed the hood of the Mercedes with a branch and then recoiled. My father's truck was nowhere in sight.

I put my hand on the door.

Ms. Hoch put her hand on my knee, with just enough pressure to keep me in place.

"Wallace Cole," she said. "We've been watching you. I think you are a very, very lucky young man."

Her voice was a bear claw in a bee's nest, dripping honey and blood.

"Now, you're almost an adult. You're going to have to make a choice. Your parents, your remarkable parents . . . do you want to honor them? Or do you want to waste your gifts? What do you want to be? Everyone must decide at some point, though many choose by not choosing, until their lives drift away. Pitiful, actually. Avoiding fate, they determine theirs. Is that what you want, Wallace Cole? To be lost online, defaulting on student loans, making crescent moons in dairy-free lattes, dreaming of mystical Scandinavian paradises with twenty-hour workweeks and blaming your sad life on those who actually have the courage to get out and make their own? Do you want that?" She lowered to a whisper. "Or do you want everything?"

The car door swung open automatically, without my touching it. She let go of my knee. Air crashed out of my lungs.

"When you want to change the world," said Ms. Hoch, "you have to be where the world is changing. My father will be here soon. He will have an offer for you. I advise you to take it."

TWENTY-EIGHT

NOT FIFTEEN SECONDS after Ms. Hoch was driven off in her Mercedes, a police cruiser pulled up under the oak trees. Deputy Sloane stepped out, cricked his neck to each side, and leaned against the hood. He watched me unlock the apartment door. It took me a while, as I had trouble getting the key in the door with him there, with Ms. Hoch's words in my head, with the bottom dropping out of my world.

An offer? A choice? What did Ms. Hoch mean? What choice could I possibly have in any of this? I had four days left. The night people had four days left!

I'd been chasing after the truth since I got to North Homer, and damn if it didn't look worse the closer it got.

My life: don't get close.

The next day, Wednesday, the police were again at the school. And Megan Rose again was not. There was one new development: the media. Well, one—one media. A beat-up white van idled in the school driveway, its side painted with a radio station's AM number and its slogan, a cheerful (or maybe disbelieving) "You trust us." Next to the van, a blond reporter was interviewing no other than Brad Stone. I discreetly circled behind them. Despite wearing what looked to be four-inch heels, the reporter had to fully extend her arm to get the microphone close to Brad's face—he towered over her that much.

I couldn't hear what Brad was saying to her, but whatever it was had him very animated. As he spoke, the reporter turned around to look at her cameraman with an expression of incomprehension and panic. I knew that feeling.

Brad cornered me at lunch. I was distracted—the police in the cafeteria seemed to be part of a prison movie, all threatening eye contact and give-me-a-reason and failure-to-communicate. But then the students were in a movie that could not be more different: an art-house epic featuring a single black ant crawling along a white wall. The new drugs were strong.

If it was, in fact, the drugs that had them dazed. Maybe it was what Megan Rose had figured out, that the night people would be gone by Sunday. And they were already going.

It's not the most fun thing, honestly, contemplating why your world is imploding.

Brad smashed down into the seat next to mine, breathing hard. He wore a T-shirt tight enough to show the muscle striations under his skin. His shoulder was a theater-sized bag of Twizzlers.

"Been looking everywhere for you, newb," he said. "I was really hoping we wouldn't have to do this here."

That didn't sound promising. "Do what?"

He brought his right hand up, stretched out his fingers, spiraled them into a fist.

"Seriously?"

"Only for appearances," he said. "Don't want people thinking we're friends and shit."

"Why would they ever think that?"

His fist landed on my arm. Tiny nerves threw up into my eyes. When I blinked back into consciousness, Brad was pointing to a cork-sized knot on the back of his head. It looked to be the exact spot Stuart had beaned him with a chair at the PTA meeting.

That's what this was about? Really? We were out of time for this.

"You had me in a headlock when that happened," I said. "I didn't get a good look."

"I don't believe you, newb. And I need the truth. What are you infecting people with?"

"What?"

"You heard me. What is it?"

It took me a minute to gather exactly what he was asking. Far as I could tell, Brad Stone lived his life as if it were a reality show called *Yeah, I Kicked Your Ass*. The premise of the show was he kicked your ass. The *Yeah* came before or after. This was very different. His dip-swollen lip shook. His eyes looked hollow and chased.

Then I knew.

"Congratulations," I said. "I know you thought you were

immune. But they're not an infection. They're not our enemies. They even want to help us."

He snorted. "Say a word to anyone about this and your arms will hurt too much to jerk off for a year."

"I'm sure your mom will help. Congrats again. I got to go."

Brad grabbed my wrist, then picked up the milk carton from my tray and spit into it.

"I wasn't finished with that," I said.

"Listen," he said.

It involved football, his visit with the night people, a dream of a game. Maybe *dream* was not the right word, because he'd never dreamed so clearly. Also, oddly enough, he wasn't asleep during it. Regardless, in the pseudo-dream Brad Stone is the best player on the field, easily. He's middle linebacker, which, just so you know, is the most important defensive position. First down, he does a swim move, shoots past the offensive guard, and the quarterback is right there for a de-cleater—and the quarterback is a little kid! No pads, nothing.

Brad stops short and gets pancaked from behind.

Whistle blows, he shakes it off, goes back to the huddle, calls out the defensive alignment, and, two beats after the next snap, does a delayed blitz where he—get this—literally hurdles the center's cheap-shit chop block, flies over him . . . and there's the same little kid!

It happens a few more times. The most beautiful pass-rushing moves: rip, swim, stunt, and spin—and every time the quarterback is gone and the kid's there, right in the middle of the pocket. About eight, chubby, with freckles and a flattop, ears that stick out, droopy socks.

No one else sees him. Coaches and teammates look at Brad like: What's wrong with you, you're losing us the game!

Brad takes himself out. He grabs a water bottle and goes to the sideline—and there on the bench is the kid!

Fuck this!

He leaves the field—the kid's in the locker room!

Doesn't even bother changing out of his pads, drives his truck home in his cleats—the kid's in the fucking kitchen!

"Explain that, newb," said Brad.

"Did you talk to him?" I asked.

"The kid? I told him to leave me the fuck alone."

"That's not really talking."

"You mean, I should tell him nicely to leave me alone?"

I lifted my tray and eased, as inoffensively as possible, to a standing position. "I mean, listen to him. Get to know him. Find out what he wants."

"I don't care what he wants!" Brad punched me on the arm—hard, in the same place he had earlier.

The tray fell back to the table. A couple of policemen stepped toward us.

"Appearances?" I gasped.

"No," Brad said.

Look how beautiful they were, the night people! They had gotten their hooks into the Bully King of North Homer, their sworn enemy, and now they were slyly ripping his swollen ego into little pieces.

But they were going. Four more days. They had four more days and they would be gone.

Okay, where? Where were they going?

Fuel. They were becoming fuel.

Well, where would fuel go? What happened to fuel?

It burned.

The power plant . . . It hit me—they were going to the plant, the night people, and being set aflame.

All through my afternoon classes, I stared at the light fixtures, wondering what dreams they burned on.

After school, I dropped my bag at home, grabbed a sweatshirt and a slice of cold pizza, and prepared to walk the two miles out to the plant. I had to see it for myself.

But a cruiser was in the road. Two cops climbed out. Deputy Sloane himself emerged from the driver's side and strolled over.

"There's curfew, Wallace," he said.

"Not yet," I pointed out. "It's not dark for a few more hours."

"Looks pretty dark to me. What are you doing?"

"I'm looking for my mother."

"I'll keep an eye out for her."

"Please," I said. "You don't understand how important this is."

"Aw, rats," he said. "Back inside."

Deputy Sloane's partner silently illustrated how, if his hand were a gun, his thumb would be the safety and the safety would be switched off and his finger would fire bullets at my head, which would explode—*poof*—into a slow-motion mushroom cloud.

The original Stuart waited at my locker the next morning. By *original*, I mean that he was as deep in Mega D depression as when we first met. His lady-of-the-fastener-aisle-induced meditative serenity was no more. The glass wasn't so much half-empty for him as it was half-filled with colorless poison.

"You're cruel," he said.

"I'm sorry. It's really not my fault, you know."

"Cruel."

"I just passed along what I learned."

"Cruel."

"I'm trying to figure out what to do. We're running out of time. Help me?"

He considered that. "Cruel."

That day, Thursday, the school became its shadow. All the color fled from it, leaving vague flat shapes on the floor and walls. The students were there, of course—standing outside the nurse's office, sitting in the cafeteria, walking hallways and filling classrooms and writing down assignments—but they also weren't there. They were gone. Behind everyone's eyes was an empty field.

Wake up! I wanted to scream. But who would I scream at? The students? The police? The field?

I turned off the lights wherever I could.

Again, after school Deputy Sloane tailed me home. He parked under the oak trees, nodded a greeting, pulled out his phone.

Trapped. Forget the plant—if they kept me locked down, would I even see Megan Rose before I left town?

The apartment had a small back porch with just enough space for a grill and a chair, and at dusk, with my protector and server still out front, I went and sat out there. Ten feet from the bottom step was a wood fence higher than my hand could reach. The space between the fence and the building held trash cans, recycling bins, and a narrow strip of grass for curing dog poop.

It wasn't a glade in the forest, for sure. But look up and red maples leaned tenderly over the top of the fence, rocking their branches as if they were children being put to sleep. It would do. It would have to.

I closed my eyes. I waited.

Ma, where are you? What do I do?

Are you really leaving again? How could you come back just to leave?

Ten. I was ten when she died. She left her job at Jackduke and coughed and phewed and exhaled like an old man falling into a chair, and Can you play outside and Not so loud,

219

Wallace, and Don't bang your spoon when you eat your cereal, Wallace, and then . . . well, Ma and Dad said she was sick, but they didn't explain *exactly* what was happening—that, for example, there would be medicines that would take her hair, her muscles, her gums (Seriously, medicine, why do you need gums? It's kind of gross), plus her ability to smile, and that they—the medicines—also would give her body a burned-tire smell when she asked for a hug, which was less and less, as contact was nauseating.

And they didn't explain how a key part of her sickness was the disease taking the will to live.

And that sitting by the side of her bed, I would get to watch it go.

And that when it went—the will to live—what was left was a space.

And that this space actually isn't good or bad. It's just there.

And that there we all are, all of us people still alive, inside the space, blundering into each other.

They didn't explain this, nobody did; I figured it out on my own.

In a hospital bed in a spare bedroom in California, Ma died and became space.

And there on the back porch of the apartment, she came back. Not vibrant and awake, like she'd appeared in the glade, but the way she had been in those very last days: motionless, translucent, the will for life draining out of her. And it was all dissolving again and I was an abandoned ten-year-old boy again.

But I wasn't.

And so I thought: I'll do it. Of course I'll do it. I'll save you. What else was I going to do? What else mattered?

Some hours later, when I came inside for the night, the light was on in the kitchen. Dad sat underneath it, smoking a cigarette. He watched me but didn't say anything.

The next morning, Friday, my last day of school, two days before I left town, I saw Ms. Hoch.

I was on my way to social studies. She was at the far end of a hallway, facing the other way, but I could tell immediately it was her from the expensive sheen of her immaculate clothes. She was deep in conversation with Principal Rathschild. They went inside the administrative offices and stood talking in there. I listened from outside the door, as close as I dared.

"Jackduke's NDA terms are extremely fair," Ms. Hoch was saying. "Understand, it's a necessity in the business and not an admission of guilt. And you are aware that we have a generous college scholarship program for the families of underpaid and underappreciated educators? I'd like to make you an offer."

Her voice got muffled; I couldn't hear. I inched closer to the door.

"It's not about me," said Rathschild. "The students—"

"Eleanor, please. A few weeks of selfies and memes, and this will be a distant memory for them."

"My students aren't like that."

"They are!" Ms. Hoch declared, loud again. "Everyone in the world is like that! Forget and move on—it's the guiding principle of our nation. It's an evolutionary necessity. Entertainment is stronger than history! And the offer is final."

Suddenly Ms. Hoch was zooming out of the office, a missile in clicking heels. I spun around and fiddled with a locker. She grabbed my arm with uncomfortable tightness.

But no—it wasn't her. Principal Rathschild.

"Why aren't you in class, Wallace?" she asked.

It was my last day. Why play games? "I was listening to your conversation with the spokeswoman."

"That's not polite." She let go of my arm. "I heard it's you who's going around shutting off the lights. Is that true?"

"Yes."

"Can you not do that?"

"I'm protecting the night people."

"You're what the what?"

"The spirit energies. The lights are killing them."

Rathschild sighed. "Are you taking drugs?"

"You mean Jackduke's shit sandwich? Hell, no."

"Other people's?"

"No."

"Good. You'll be leaving us soon, won't you? Another company town?"

I nodded.

She gazed off down the hall. "Why are they doing this, do you think? Quarterly profit? An upcoming stock split? To win a bet?"

"To save the world."

Rathschild looked back at me. Her shoulders slumped. Behind her eyes, something large had imploded in a cloud of glass and dust, stranding her. "I'm sorry," she said.

"What for?"

"We failed. We failed you. You deserve a better world than this."

"Any ideas?" asked Stuart at lunch.

"One." I told him what it was.

"That's insane," he said.

"You got better?"

"Ritual suicide?" said Stuart. "Just plain suicide?"

"The plant is behind all this."

"They'll arrest you. Or worse. A lot worse."

To be fair, my plan did have many issues. To begin with: How the hell would I even get out of the apartment with Deputy Sloane keeping watch? But I had to do it.

"I'm not helping you," Stuart said.

"That's fine. What are you up to tomorrow night?" I asked.

"Sitting in the basement and weeping because you murdered my heart. With breaks to masturbate."

"Perfect. I'll stop by on my way. Can you get a message to Megan Rose?"

Arms crossed, a head taller and a foot wider than everyone else, Brad Stone paced in front of my locker after the last bell.

The last bell of the day. Of the week. The last one I'd ever hear in North Homer.

"Don't you have practice?" I asked him.

"I spoke to that stupid kid," he said. "Like you told me to."

"I don't think I *told* you to do anything. It was more of a suggestion."

"He says I should listen to you. And help you, even. Fuck that! I got all this fear now, newb. He's making me afraid. Says things are going to get worse."

"Cool, Brad."

"What?"

"That's deep."

Brad gave me a shove, slamming me into the lockers. "That's *deep*? That's it?"

I shoved him back; he didn't move an inch. "What do you want me to say? Forget him! Forget all of it. You don't have to worry about what he says! Ignore him! A few more days and he's gone. All of them are gone!"

"Don't you get it? He's me. I can't ignore him."

"Yeah," I said. "I get it. That's what happens."

"So, what do I do?"

A police officer appeared at the end of the hall, alerted by the bang I had made hitting the locker. He motioned us to get a move on. Everyone else had left for the week, drifting out of the school and into the numb and medicated rest of their lives.

And then, in my mind, it came together.

"You want to help, Brad?" I said. "Can you do something for me tomorrow?"

"What?"

224

I explained the thing.

"Unreal," he said.

"That a yes?"

"That's a your-mom-raised-you-wrong."

"Ah, you know, I really think she tried her best."

He took something off the next punch, at least.

TWENTY-NINE

THE POLICE WERE out in front of the apartment all night, a new pair swapping in every four hours. Saturday dawned hot and humid, and they were still out there, quickly extinguishing the small hope I had that they might take the weekend off. I didn't leave the apartment all day. I didn't even try. By noon I had stopped checking out the window. Let them think I had better things to do than be bothered by them.

Which unfortunately left me a long-assed day to worry over a half-assed idea. There were many ways my plan could go wrong. For it to go right would require broken laws and minor miracles and a faith that the arc of the universe really did bend toward justice and not toward, say, an offshore account in the Cayman Islands. I can't say I had that faith.

Also, if all went according to plan, I wouldn't be seeing North Homer's student-body president ever again.

But I had to do it.

Around six, the sun finally went down and curfew started.

Porch lights flicked on. The sparse traffic of rusty pickups and beaten-down Camrys eased. Sad mosquitoes asked, Hey, where'd everybody go?

At eight, I turned off the lights in the apartment so that it might appear to my watchers that I was asleep.

At ten, the agreed-upon time, I kneeled by the door, eyeing the road through the mail slot. Sneakers laced, hoodie pulled tight, I wedged a wooden spoon from the kitchen in the slot so my watching would be discreet.

But twenty minutes passed with no sign of Brad Stone. He'd bailed. Why was I surprised? Seriously, what had I been thinking? I had several body parts aching right at that moment from his fists, plus he had a football scholarship to protect, not to mention he had a worldview based on sociological theories that fall apart if you actually try and help other people, so you can't actually help other people, but you can make them think you will, so you get the drop on them.

But then, in the distance, a faint streak of paleness emerged. It grew larger. It looked like a sprinting flame.

It was indeed Brad Stone, running hard, yelling, waving his arms—completely naked, save for a pair of running shoes.

Well, now. That was unexpected. Points for creativity.

Ass and everything hanging out, Brad ran up to the police car from behind, pounded a drum riff on its trunk, roof, and hood, and then ran on, hollering. The driver turned on the lights and the siren, waited a beat—Go, go, go already!—and then Deputy Sloane got out on the passenger side while the driver peeled off after Brad.

Shit. So close. For a second there . . .

But I had to make my play. I took a deep breath and opened the front door.

"Get your ass back inside, Wallace!" Deputy Sloane yelled, starting toward me, one hand jabbing where he wanted me to go, the other on his holster. "This doesn't concern you!"

"Sorry! My mistake!" I turned back to the door.

And then took off.

Down the steps. To the corner. Around the corner.

Behind me, angry shouts. Ahead of me, an all-state linebacker, naked, pursued by a police car. I darted up a driveway, around a garage, over a fence, down another driveway onto the next street over, and then back in the direction of the apartment, doubling back to confuse the deputy chasing after me.

Bent low, darting from bush to bush, scanning every shadow, I was sweating furiously. Late October, ten p.m., and it was over seventy degrees. Where did it end? They were racing to put up oil platforms in the Arctic. They'd just finished a new pipeline delivering Canadian crude.

Focus, Wallace. Focus. They'll get the dogs soon.

Sirens ripped through town in a growing roar. I sprinted from yard to yard, staying clear of the roads except when I had to cross one. And as I was about to dash through a four-way intersection, a patrol car rolled up, with Brad Stone cuffed in back. I dove behind a tree. He was ranting loudly about his mother, Miranda rights, and the seat fabric scratching his ball sack. I couldn't tell if it was a performance or not—if it was, it was stellar. The officer driving had a spotlight clipped to his door, which he shined on the houses and trees at the intersection, including the one I had dived behind. The spotlight sniffed the air like a bloodhound on a scent. For sure, I was caught.

But the car continued onward to the end of the block.

Breathe, Wallace. Breathe.

Change of plans—I cut behind a house and started making my way through the backyards. I was certain traveling through backyards would startle many aggressive dogs and homeowners with hair-trigger shotguns and a cultivated terror of Central American street gangs, but I had no choice.

And it was a terrifying journey—but not because of that.

I saw a man in a bathrobe, thumbing a remote over and over, the channels full of riots, his eyes dead as stones. I saw a woman at an open refrigerator, staring at a music video on the fridge door. I saw a golden retriever whimpering unnoticed as his owner played a virtual-reality game. I saw a family of five in the glow of their personal screens, together but apart, the air around them as dead and distant as space. . . .

I crashed through swing sets and vegetable gardens, knocked over fences, triggered motion-detector lights, tied-up dogs, and the alarm system of a red Audi that screamed like it was on fire. Sirens roared near and far. But no one looked up. No one. Not one single person in the entire town.

That was terrifying.

Three police cruisers were parked out in front of the Rose family house-brick. Two officers spoke with Megan Rose's father at the front door, two others walked along the road, scanning the bushes with powerful flashlights.

Which meant Megan Rose had gotten away. Great.

Or they knew I was coming. Not great.

I reversed course to the road below and then cut up the driveway of the house directly behind Stuart's. Climbed the fence to his backyard, stealth-walked up the lawn, carefully tried the basement door—unlocked—opened it, closed it behind me.

And collapsed.

Stuart was there, folded like a paper clip into the deep couch, watching depressed cartoon animals.

"You made it!" He turned on a lamp.

I scrambled over and turned it off. "They're outside!"

"Right. Right." He fumbled for the remote and shut off the TV. Faint light from porch lights and police cruisers illuminated the room, enough to see each other. No one appeared to have spotted us.

"The house arrest?" whispered Stuart. "How'd you get out?"

"We might have underestimated Brad Stone," I admitted.

"That's not possible. He's perfectly estimated."

Before I could explain, the door jerked open and shut. Megan Rose fell into the room. She had on black sweats and a black bandanna, and her face was streaked with dirt. She looked like an assassin leaving on a mission. One of those people who whisper, "I was never here."

A finger pressed to her lips, she crouched, listening to the police on their radios, studying the basement.

"Been a while since we hung out down here," she said to Stuart. "Eighth grade?"

"Fifth," he said. "Everyone stopped coming in fifth."

"Really? That long?"

"Yeah, really."

"I'm so sorry," Megan Rose said. Stuart blushed intensely. She turned to me. "So, we ready to go?"

"We?" I did a double take. "This is where I say goodbye."

"The hell you're saying goodbye."

Ah, that was it. Always was.

"I know farewells are hard," I said. "Like I said, I hate them. I've learned it's best to leave a town without saying anything to anybody. Less hurt that way. But I'm glad you came. Thank you for risking it. It's good to see you one last time."

"I'm going with you," said Megan Rose. "To the power plant."

"What? No. You can't do that."

"That's not your choice to make."

"Yeah, it is," I said. "It *is* my choice. And my shitty life to risk. Yours is worth something!"

A police cruiser whipped up the road, braked harshly out front. Red, white, and blue strobes knifed into the basement window. We ducked, slid over to the wall. Tense voices shared information and expletives—it sounded like every officer in the county had been roused to look for us, and they weren't thrilled about it.

I tilted my head in their direction, as if to say, You really want to mess with that, Megan Rose? You could get a lot more accomplished inside the halls of power than down here, in the basement of the powerless, getting a criminal record.

I felt very strongly about this. I would kiss her if that would help to make my point.

But Megan Rose felt just as strongly.

"Wallace, they feed me pills three times a day," she said. "I spit them out whenever I can but not often enough. I feel like a graph-paper cloud. Then SAT study every morning. Drugs and tests, drugs and tests—I'm done with that! Done with a life focused on the perfect college and income bracket and medication regimen. I snuck out of my house hours ago—before curfew—because I realized I would rather sit in a bush in the dark than in my house in my life for another minute. Do you understand? So you don't get to decide what a good life is or a shit one! You don't get to decide what I'm going to do!"

I bowed my head, chastened, holding my heart tightly so it wouldn't fall at her feet. Stuart stared, bug-eyed, at her, recalibrating a lot of long-held theories.

"Good," she said. "So, what are we going to do at the plant? Blow it up?"

I'd thought of that. But having grown up around real power plants and not Russian-made or CGI ones, I knew that they didn't blow up. They didn't have self-destruct switches with countdown timers. There were no trapdoors for force-guided photon torpedoes. They had fail-safes on top of fail-safes, and the paid-for support of every congressman and congresswoman in a two-state radius.

"I'm not sure. My plan is a bit underdeveloped. Basically, I'm gonna go to the place where they're killing the night peo-

ple. And when I get there, I'm going to figure out how to stop them. And then I'll stop them."

Their silence said everything.

"I know. It's a lousy plan," I said. "Trust me, I know. But there's no more time. And one way or another, I'm gone tomorrow."

"No, it's good," said Megan Rose. "I like it. Let's go."

"You're serious? How can it be good?"

"We're all going," said Stuart.

"Not you, too," I said.

"Yeah, me, too."

"What about getting arrested? Or worse?"

"*This* is worse," he said.

Megan Rose pried open the basement door. Carefully, she stuck her head out, checked if the coast was clear, then slipped through. I inched out behind her, Stuart behind me. We crawled under the rhododendron bushes hugging the side of the house, stopping at the edge of the lawn. It was fifty feet to the fence at the back of the yard. Police chatter filled the air.

Slowly, slowly, we began to tiptoe down the hill. I still wasn't keen on the risk they were taking, but maybe, if we did this with care and discretion, we'd be back before dawn, with no one the wiser.

"Visual! There! There!"

Blinding light hit the bush behind us, then a bush in front, then slammed square on our backs.

"Stop! Right there!"

"Tarnation!"

"Go!" yelled Megan Rose.

She burst into a sprint, straight downhill, legs spinning in the flashlight beams, and vaulted the shoulder-high wooden fence at the bottom of the yard like an Olympic gymnast. I slammed into the fence, flopped over it, tripped on a hedge on the other side, tumbling hard to the ground, driving a triangle-shaped rock directly into my ass cheek but making a soft landing pad for Stuart—who pulled me up, and we ran, ran through yards and driveways, ran across streets, ran between cars, ran as fast as I ever have and then faster. Up a fence, down, across a squelching lawn, another driveway, across a street, another fence, lawn, lawn, grove of trees, backyard stream, splashing down that, lawn, driveway, gutter, street, driveway, stone patio, clothesline at neck height, jeez, run, run, run like hell.

You barely knew me, North Homer, but I knew your back-yards! The gopher holes, the hidden roots, the sagging garden fences, the black-mirrored lives . . .

The power plant was two miles north, a fast and straight-forward jog, provided we lost our pursuers. But then, exiting a driveway at the bottom of the hill, we nearly collided with a cruiser driven by none other than the chief of police. Shit. He blasted his siren. Megan Rose led Stuart and me across the street, and we jumped another fence into the marshy undeveloped backlots of North Homer's chain stores—Walmart, Kohl's, Dunkin' Donuts, ShopRite, Lowe's, Bed Bath & Beyond—as well as gas stations offering specials on malt liquor, fountain sodas, and foot-long Slim Jims.

We ducked through culverts, drainage ditches, and waist-

high grass as police cars zipped back and forth on the avenue. The commercial strip rounded a bend and abruptly ended in a neighborhood of sagging old houses and sidewalk-busting maple trees. The houses gave way to a park of swing sets, arc lights, and picnic tables. We sprinted across the park, avoiding the lights, sliding at last into a grove of black walnuts next to the lakeshore.

Then we started getting ready. We didn't have to discuss it.

The lake was a mile wide and stretched north for forty miles. Small waves hit the shore with impatience, as if the park were struggling to get under a blanket or kick it off. One side of the lake, the western one, was extensively developed, immaculate solar-roofed houses poking out of hillside trees, dozens of sailboats docked and bobbing. The other side was swamp.

That's where we were headed.

"You guys go," said Stuart. "I'll stay. Keep them occupied."

"Stuart. That's dangerous."

"Wallace. No shit. Look—" He gritted his teeth. "I can't swim. But it's all right. I'm amazed I got this far. The old me would have never left the couch. Just do what you promised."

"I never promised."

"Do it."

When the first cruiser turned into the park, Stuart ran toward it. The headlights picked him up, and he cut hard to the right, leading the car toward the playground. I had my sneakers off and jammed them into my shirt, tucked that into my jeans. Megan Rose and I waded into the water. The muck suctioned our bare feet. When the water reached my thighs, I felt in my back pocket. My phone. Forgot I had it. Well, too late for a power cord now.

Then I threw the phone as far into the lake as I could.

The water was cold, and my clothes were deadweight. But I could swim decently: on his doomsday-prep kicks, my father had made sure I had the technique for every stroke and that I had experience swimming past when it felt like my arms would fall off. And Megan Rose . . . well, I was no longer surprised. She moved through the water as if she'd been born in a giant clamshell to a race with gills.

We stopped to rest a couple of hundred yards out. Back on shore, cruisers and flashlights combed the park.

"Tarnation!" I called over the waves, adrenaline coursing through my veins.

A flashlight flicked in our direction.

"Careful," said Megan Rose, who wasn't even breathing hard.

"They'll never swim out here," I said.

"They have boats."

"Oh. Right. Good point."

We turned, continued north.

And then we stopped.

This is why we stopped: the surface of the lake was bubbling, boiling. And as we watched the disturbed water, a woman emerged. She was green. She had green hair. On her forehead lay a garland of white foam. On her body, nothing, she was naked. Droplets sparkled in the air around her. The stars shone through her face. She rose up and up, first her head, then her body, then her legs, then her feet, until all of her was hovering above the lake. She was a hundred feet tall.

My legs gave, and I nearly dropped like a stone. The spirit of the lake started drifting north and east, toward the plant. Slowly, she reached the shore, flew over that, up a hill and down behind it. Then she was gone.

A half hour later, Megan Rose and I dragged ourselves onto a rocky beach. We curled up, panting. In the sky above: pine branches casting spells, a nearly full moon, a plane blinking its way to Canada. After a few minutes, Megan Rose sat up and took off her clothes to wring them out. I followed suit. For a minute, I pretended not to notice the curve of her breasts and certain patches of darkness. But then I gave up on that. I looked at her body; she looked at mine.

"Just so you know," I said. "The water was really cold."

"What?"

"I'm not a virgin."

"What? Wallace, what are you talking about?"

Brilliantly smooth, as usual. Why was it that, of everything, not sounding like a loser when talking to Megan Rose was the hardest part of our escape? I loudly cursed myself inside my head.

"Nothing," I said. "We should get moving."

A half mile to the south, a single cruiser remained at

the park, strobes swirling. The rest had gone. Poor Stuart. I imagined the police shoving him into a dusty room with peeling gray paint, a bare table, a swaying lightbulb. A good cop and a bad cop—no, a bad cop and a worse cop—entered, rolling up their sleeves. From behind a two-way mirror, Chief Turnblad tells them the camera's broken.

We didn't have long.

Megan Rose and I headed north, following the shore. After half an hour, we angled up a steep rise that turned out to be made of thornbushes, no-see-ums, and invisible trip wire. We were tired and stumbling, eating cobwebs, snapping branches into private places. We reached level ground at last, falling onto a narrow trail. It was cleaved in half by a giant chain-link fence, fifteen feet high, topped with barbed wire and NO TRESPASSING signs. A siren hissed, and somewhere behind that was a distant thumping—a helicopter.

Megan Rose leaned back against the fence and slid right to the ground.

"Come on," I said, after a minute.

The air was heavy. "There's something very wrong here," she said.

"I know. And we have to find a way in."

The fence drilled a tube through the forest. We crept along it. Past a tall spruce, the trees and brush on the other side of the fence gave way to an enormous flat field. In the middle of this field, fifty yards distant, stood a single massive building. Gray with no windows, it was a concrete mountain. At its center was a tower two hundred feet tall, from which a plume of white smoke curled to the skies.

Dead quiet. Not a single person in sight. Four searchlights moved over the field.

I'd seen other power plants before, of course, plenty of them. Now and again, my father would take me to his workplace, usually because of some inconvenient federal holiday, a few times because I had nowhere else to sleep off a fever. Inside, all of them smelled like leaky engines, coffee strained through old tires, recycled air. Outside, all of them were massive; all of them were frightening.

But this plant was the most frightening.

And what could we do? How could we stop it?

Were the last night people already gone?

Then we saw them.

Winged and hooved, flippered and laced. In dresses and tails, ties and fins. In flowers, torn sheets, and spacecraft. Riding cars with eyes. Unicorns with saddles. Carriages with no horses.

A big red dog. A green ogre. Eight reindeer with round noses. A blue ox.

A little mermaid. A brave astronaut. An old lion. An oak tree, exactly like the one outside my apartment, holding donuts in each branch.

They crowded in the sky around a cavernous opening at the base of the tower. So many of them, beautiful as the stars . . .

They organized into a ragged line. And one by one they stepped forward into the tower opening. And were gone.

Gone. They didn't fight or scream. Wait—

I looked frantically all over, dread growing. But she wasn't there. She couldn't be. She wasn't like the rest of them. She was different. She was real. Whatever "real" was.

And then—brown hair, jeans, a white blouse—there she was.

My mother had found a spot in line behind a small old woman in a housedress. Welcoming her, the old woman offered my mother something from her hand, something small and shiny that I couldn't make out at this distance but appeared to be a screw. I watched Ma carefully, and as I did, I felt something else, something worse. My father—his energy—he was here. For a minute, I denied it—it couldn't be him, it wasn't possible—but then it was clear that the night people felt him, too. They moved away from his presence, which herded them closer to the tower.

And suddenly, I understood. A whole lot of my life made a lot more sense.

"No!" I yelled. "Dad! You can't! You can't do that! Stop!"

Two cars rounded the edge of the power plant, sirens and strobes on full blast.

I grabbed Megan Rose. "You need to get out of here."

She turned to me, horrified. Susie was up there, too.

"How can they do this?" she said.

"Go home," I begged her. "I was wrong. It was a mistake to come here."

"No. I don't care," she said. "I'm staying. I don't care what they do to me."

"Don't say that. It's me they want."

"What? Why do they want you?"

"They want to give me a job."

I let go of her. She took an uncertain step back, then another, staring at me. The two cars in the field sped toward us.

"I'm so sorry," I said. "I screwed this all up."

Megan Rose looked into my eyes one last time, for an answer I couldn't give. Then she turned and ran.

Three more security vehicles blasted around the corner of the plant. I reached my fingers into the chain-link fence and violently shook it and yelled, drawing their undivided attention, so Megan Rose could get away. I looked up again; the line moved forward, and more night people disappeared into the dark tower opening. Above them, the moon split in two, and a weeping peach-colored moon-diamond stepped out from inside.

The security forces drove right up to the chain-link fence across from me and slammed to a stop. Their high beams were dialed up to weapons-grade level. Furious voices shouted accelerating orders.

"Hands in the air!"

"Hands in the air now!"

"Hands in the air now, asshole!"

I gathered they wanted me to put my hands in the air. I put my hands in the air.

"I'm on this side of the fence," I said to the lights. "I never went onto your property."

"This is *all* private property," said a man behind me, ripping my wrists down into handcuffs. How did he get here? Was Megan Rose safe? He roughly turned me away from the fence and shoved me down the path that ran alongside it.

Out of range of the blinding high beams, I could again see

the plant. My mother was now one place from the front of the line. Then she was at the front. Then she went forward.

At the base of the tower, she dissolved into darkness; at that very same instant, outside the fence a shock went through my heart and knocked me out.

THIRTY

MY FATHER WAS driving carelessly, and the truck was jostling. Bouncing, bouncing—sometimes he was so up in his head that he drove with all the skill of a blind man. My own head was broken glass and black oil, like it had just been hit by an SUV. Something that I needed to find was in the strewn wreckage. It would change everything if I could find it. But I couldn't.

Broken glass and black oil, black oil and broken glass. That's it, that's all.

"Wallace," Dad said.

We kept jostling. I didn't want to wake up. I was tired. So tired.

"Wallace."

A real bump—

—and I was sitting in a chair.

Dad was crouched in front of me, his hands on my shoulders, shaking them. His eyes, direct and blank both, looked deep into mine. I rubbed my own eyes. That meant my wrists were uncuffed. I looked at them to check—they were.

"What? What's going on?" I said. "Where's the fence?"

"Take it easy," Dad said. "You were out for a while."

We were indoors, in a dark room. The shape of an airplane cabin—long and narrow, recessed lights in a curved ceiling, a dark gray carpet, floor-to-ceiling windows, dark curtains over them. Dad straightened up and stepped to the side, and directly in front of me, a few feet away, was an enormous desk of polished wood. Behind the desk, a man with iron posture, a deep country-club tan, and the lush white hair you can get only with money. He wore a black suit, a white shirt, a red tie, cufflinks that gleamed. Everything about him looked expensive, even his attention looked expensive, closing-a-private-arms-deal-with-a-Saudi-prince expensive—and his attention was squarely on me.

Dad sat down in a chair next to mine.

"You know who I am?" asked the man behind the desk.

"I do," I said.

"Do you know where you are?"

"I think so."

"Do you know why you're here?"

"You're offering me a job."

"Good," said the man behind the desk. "Very good, Wallace Cole. But you do know you could have just knocked?"

The CEO of Jackduke had a commanding voice. Not loud but resonant and without any hesitancy. A voice you'd broadcast in dystopian shantytowns, telling residents to get in line and accept their fates. I suppose this is what they teach in CEO class—how to speak like whatever you say is the right and perfect truth, even if other people must die for it—though perhaps that's more a skill you're born with.

I straightened in my chair, wiped my hands on my jeans. I was acutely aware that my clothes had been dragged through a lake, a forest, and half the backyards of North Homer. Not exactly how I'd pictured showing up to my first job interview.

My father had his cap off and was rubbing his head. The only other person in the room sat in a chair next to the CEO's desk, a woman in a gray suit: Ms. Hoch, his daughter, smiling like she'd planned this all along.

And my mother, where was she? A quick check. My mother was gone. Was she in my heart? No. In my heart she was gone. Maybe next to my heart, a little off to the side? No, off to the side she was gone.

Dad spoke. "I don't think tasing him was necessary, Lawrence."

"Nobody tased anybody, Ron," said the CEO. "Your boy fainted on his own. But so what if they did? He's a trespasser and a lawbreaker. He's on video trying to break through my fence. This is what we call a *confirmed threat*. Being that this is a power plant, it's a matter of national security. Being that this is a matter of national security, whatever response I deem appropriate is protected by the law."

"You can't be serious," said my father.

"Ronald. These are the times."

My father raised a hand toward the desk and opened and closed it a few times, as if pull-starting his vocal cords. It took a few tries. "I'm tired," he finally said. "We're all tired. We just finished an hour ago. The machines are powering down. The particle data is being analyzed and encrypted. It's been a hard push. The hardest one yet."

"Because of your screwups," said the CEO.

"We're figuring this out as we go along."

"That was the most poorly run community meeting I've ever heard of."

"Yes. Well. Our own workers' kids were getting violently ill," Dad said. "Classified proprietary information was being leaked to local attorneys. We were on the verge of a massive media firestorm. And all because someone launched a full-strength test, even though I told him we weren't ready."

The CEO waved my father's comments away. "You're boring me, Ronald. It was time. We couldn't wait any longer. The world couldn't! And the run is powering down, as you said. So it's all bygones." He nodded to me. "What's important right now is him."

"He's not going to be a part of it."

"Ronald," said the CEO, again with that total certainty, his face now growing red under the tan, the air around him growing red. "Whatever made you think that was your decision?"

Lawrence Hoch, CEO of Jackduke, the second-largest energy company in the country, one of the top five in the world, was worth billions. He owned sports teams and private islands and high-rises and yachts big enough to land planes on. He had senators in his pocket, representatives in his file cabinet, crusty cabinet members stuffed in his nose. State legislatures held emergency sessions to discuss how to best implement his cryptic tweets. The president of the United States of America called him for advice on energy policy. Jihadis chanted his name before detonating explosive vests in distant desert oil fields.

Even though we'd met a few times, I can't say that he ever seemed entirely real. The man was the living distillate of power.

"Wallace Cole," he said.

"Sir."

"I've been watching you for a long time."

"Sir?"

"You were at the PTA meeting, I take it. And before that, you had a front-row seat to the shenanigans at the local high school." He shook his head angrily. "What a farce this test run has been. I'll be handing every household in this township a nice sum to forget it ever happened. Marguerite has pulled every favor we're owed to get the networks to look the other way. And the Senate majority leader's re-election campaign is going to get another cool million, even though that turtle-faced fucker couldn't deliver a vote if it was jammed up his ass for nine months."

He paused, sipped a drink. I shifted nervously. Dad ran his hand through his hair again and again. The CEO's daughter sat as if moving were a crime.

"And yet, so what?" continued the CEO. "I'll pay the money. Marguerite will spin the spin. Because, Wallace, today we enter the final stage of the Sen energy project. We need you for this stage. And on this very day, here you are, banging on my fence, asking to be let in. After all the times that I've asked your father to bring you here! This is not a coincidence. This is a sign. Here it is, Wallace. Here you are."

"Lawrence." My father's fingers opened and closed. "We agreed when Claire died that he wouldn't be involved."

"I am aware," said the CEO. "And I respected your wishes . . . up until he showed up at my fence."

I turned to Dad. "Wait. Ma was involved in this?"

"Not now, Wallace," Dad said.

"Jesus. He doesn't know?" The CEO snorted. "Son, your mother ran the team that developed the retrieval technology."

"That's not what—I thought she—"

That couldn't be. My mother, she did . . . What was her job? Phone calls? She made phone calls. She watched old sitcoms. She washed dishes. She read me to sleep. She lay in the living room. She died.

"You promised her," my father said. "On her deathbed."

The CEO slammed the desk with his fist. It made a deep thump that the carpet swallowed. "Cole! Shut up! Don't bring that up! Enough! I gave you everything you wanted, and you repaid me by making a mess!" He searched the desk for something. An iPad? An iPad. He threw it over our heads. "This is the moment! And if it's good enough for you, it's good enough for him! Get out! Get the fuck out!"

He searched his desk again—found a glass of amber liquid; picked it up, drank it, and threw it, too. It landed somewhere behind us.

He pulled a handkerchief out and wiped his face. Composure returned as quickly as it had left, save for a throbbing tremor under his right eye.

"You can go, too, Marguerite," he said. "Make sure the plane is prepped for one extra and tell that fat police chief to lift the curfew tonight. . . . Or not. Let him have fun for a few days. And find this kid some clean clothes, for God's sake."

"Yes, Daddy," Ms. Hoch said. She gathered her stuff and stood, straightening out her pantsuit and bracelets. For a spokeswoman—by title and definition, a woman who spoke—she had been awfully quiet. She took a few steps toward the door, then stopped by my father's chair.

And Dad . . . I could feel his eyes on me. But I wouldn't look at him. Out at the fence I had finally seen exactly what he did, how deeply involved he was. And now, had he lied about Ma, too? I crossed my arms and stared at the floor.

After a minute, a door opened and closed.

With a hidden button or a focused thought, a panel in the wall behind the desk lifted away, revealing a mirrored bar.

"Drink?" asked the CEO.

"No," I said.

"Come, now. We're grown men here. This is forty-year-old Lagavulin."

"No. I'm okay."

"Here." The CEO tossed me a bottle; I flinched. "It's fine," he said. "It's water. I'm not poisoning you."

"You already did that, I thought."

The CEO smiled. "Ah, you sound like a Cole."

With his back turned, he poured himself a glass of scotch to replace the one he'd thrown across the room. He rolled it around the glass for a minute, took a long sip. Then he sat down on the edge of the desk nearest to me, crossing his arms and his ankles. His shoes shone like small black stars. His cologne was a musky, choking cloud of richer-than-God.

"Coles. So much stubborn righteousness. Do you think other employees talk to me the way your father does?"

"No?"

"No. Exactly. Would be worse if he didn't always cave in the end."

I didn't say anything. The CEO reached back for his glass and raised it in a toast.

"Congratulations," he said. "From the bottom of my heart. You've earned it. The world is at your feet."

"Sir?"

"True, you have issues. For one thing, though according to your IQ tests, you have your mother's brains, you appear to have inherited your father's inability to wash a shirt. But this is not a sob story. You've got the gift, son. You feel the energies clear as day. Hell, I can't feel them. I can't feel shit. And you can *handle* them, our reports confirm; you'll be able to control and guide them like your father does—or did before he started screwing up. A lot of people can't handle them. They overload. You've seen what happens to those folks, I take it. Best case, we drug them to the gills. Worst case, we drug them to the gills. Medium case, drugs, gills. But that's not you." He held out his hands to me. "Lo. The gift."

I understood. I was seventeen years old, with nary a single life plan and with gritty lake mud in my underwear. The CEO was from another species, one that already had flying cars and real estate on asteroids and drugs that shut down cell death. But he needed my help.

Help making sure that charged-up Sen energy particles didn't send whole schools to the emergency room. Help making sure the night people stayed peacefully in their lane.

That's what he wanted me to do: herd the night people to their power-plant executions, so the hairdryers and coffee-makers of America would keep running.

Lo. The gift.

"Can you not?" I asked him.

The CEO raised an eyebrow. "Hmm?"

"Can you just let it alone?"

"Let what alone?"

"All of it. The energies. My friends at school. All of us."

He looked at me, surprised. "When the Sen tech switches on, it can cause reactions. But that passes. As of tonight, actually, that's all done and gone."

"But we don't want it gone."

"You'd prefer to be at constant risk for hysteria? You'd prefer the world to burn?"

"No. That's not right—that's not what I'm saying. The energies—we need them. They're a part of us. They're trying to—"

"No, son," the CEO interrupted. "They're not part of you. They never belonged to you or your friends. They are side effects of our technology. Hell, you could say they're our intellectual property." He laughed. "I bet we could sue you in the courts, if you tried to keep them. And which side do you think the courts that I paid for will take?" He stopped laughing. "The technology is mine, and those energies are mine. This was the last test run, and tomorrow we're going national, expanding to seven more states. That's where you're going to help."

"Seven states? You're going to do this in seven states?"

"Yes. To start."

I choked back a scream. "I don't want to be a part of this."

"Are you not concerned for the world?"

"Of course I am. But this isn't how you save it."

The CEO shook his head. "Right. I'm not being clear. Let me explain to you exactly how this will go."

"Number one, you will never speak a word to anyone of what we are discussing. Never. Until the day you die. Number two, you will immediately stop behaving like a child. Mouthing off, breaking the law, running around after curfew, taunting my police force."

"Your police force?"

"Mine, yes. And my school board and my county government. My fucking United States Senate. It's the way of the world, son; learn it while you're young. Number three, we start right away. There's a new plant in Minnesota, five times the size of this one. I need you there immediately. In fact, we're flying there tonight. Together. You'll love my jet."

Number four was he told me how much he would pay me. It was a number so large it seemed fake, like a GoFundMe for a border wall. It made me even more nervous. When money was no object, what was? It gave me the chilling feeling of being a character in someone else's movie, lines already written, choices already made.

"That salary is just to start," the CEO added. "We haven't gotten to the bonuses and options yet."

"I don't want it."

He snorted. "Please. Don't be so predictable. You think you're righteous to say no? Better than me? This is what the energies do. This is why it's better without them. They get in your head and make you act like a twelve-year-old girl with her first crush on shirtless *Twilight* vampires. But that's a lie." He opened his hands and showed them to me. "We make a better future with these, understand? Not with daydreams. Not with dancing wood fairies. With our hands, sweat, and blood, we at Jackduke make the future."

"But I don't want that future!"

"You don't want it? Wallace Cole, you have no idea what it is." He picked up his glass and drained it. "Come, it's time for you to learn the truth."

The CEO pushed himself up from the desk. He pressed another secret button, and on the wall behind him a panel lifted up. Behind it was a door. No, an elevator. It slid open, and he motioned for me to join him. My legs, jackhammered for the last hour, took some effort to get moving.

It was a small gray elevator with no buttons. We rode in silence.

What did the CEO want to show me? Did he not understand that destroying quantum energy came at an immeasurable cost? Clean energy wasn't worth this.

And a horrifying thought struck me then: What if he *did* understand this?

And didn't care.

The elevator door opened, and we entered a gray hallway lit by a single exit sign. We walked down it and came to another door. The CEO placed his hand on a touch pad, and the door swung open; inside was a large room filled with machinery, monitors, keyboards, and switch panels. There were no people.

"Behold," said the CEO. "The control room for the energy technology that will change the world. What do you notice?"

"It's empty."

"Exactly. No one here. You know why? Because you were right."

"I was?"

He nodded. "Sen energy is not a good energy source," he said. "The energies simply aren't plentiful enough. It gets used up fast. Even with the strongest levels of stimulation, if you got all of New York City's SE fed to the grid . . . five, six months and it would be gone. It's not going to stop global warming. It's a drop in the bucket compared with what the world needs. Also, the technology goes further than intended. Way further. It's ravenous. It takes everything inside people and out."

"Wait, you know it does this?"

"I do."

"Then shut it down! Don't take it to other states!"

The CEO shook his head.

"What? You have to!"

"No. The alternative is worse."

"The alternative to sucking the souls out of people is worse?"

"Souls? Please, I already explained they're a side effect. And, Wallace, take a look at anyone over thirty. Twenty-five, even. They're already gone. They've already traded the energy inside them for a subsistence paycheck or a mortgage they can't afford or five hours a day on a hi-def porn site. They're stumbling along on what's left, grasping for cheap thrills and hate fumes to feel alive. They're a joke. And not one I made, to be clear. But what happens when this energy is systematically gathered by our technology instead of haphazardly cast away? This, Wallace, is the greatest discovery I've ever made."

"You're asking me?"

"I'm asking you."

"What happens when you take all the Sen energy?"

The school cafeteria this last week, the students like empty fields. The backyards of North Homer, with its vacant technology addicts. The spirit of the lake, disappearing. The dreams of the town in the sky above the plant, burned up forever. My mother . . .

"People hollow out," I said. "They become like zombies, their own ghosts."

"They do what you tell them to do," said the CEO. "They buy what you tell them to buy, watch what you tell them to watch, eat what you tell them to eat. And note that I have

controlling shares in 187 different corporations in the manufacturing, technology, medical, food, and service industries."

I felt nauseated. "This is about money?"

"No!" yelled the CEO. "No! This goes way beyond money!"
He stabbed an arm at the door. "The world out there is fucked!
Every analysis of every indicator says we're past any hope of
sustainability. Fifty fucking years past it! There's going to be a
reckoning really soon, and it's going to be fierce. It's already
here! And you and your teenaged wonder-friends are going to
bear the brunt of it. It will destroy you! Burn you! Flood you!
But wait! Maybe not! Because this is what I figured out: capture
the Sen energies and people are calm. Fear, the fear of life and
death that runs everything, it shrinks to a size easily manageable with technological diversions and third-generation SSRIs.
Hell, a new iPhone and every kid in town will be content for
up to a month. Content, even though the world is literally in
flames! Right now, your friends, their parents—everyone in
North Homer—are about to sit down to Sunday dinner, thinking about their boyfriends and their selfies and Christmas shopping and can the Bills make the playoffs with their atrocious
quarterback play—and what they are *not* going to be thinking
about is the runaway, overheating bus relentlessly accelerating
directly toward them. I give them that. I give that to them!" He
slammed his fist on a table. "And when the time is right, I will
control how much energy everyone uses, what they eat, how
they sleep, what they dream of. Do you understand what that
means? Do you have any idea?"

His face was bright red and throbbing, slick with sweat. His lips shuddered with each breath. His fists were white-knuckle tight.

What did it mean? Money, power—he already had those. *All* the money, *all* the power? Is that what he wanted?

I didn't know. What did it mean?

"Peace," said the CEO.

"Peace?"

"The better world we've all been seeking. I will win the stability and order that human civilization has craved since it was born."

I gasped. My breath was taken away—and boxed and taped and shipped to the middle of the ocean. The CEO was going to eliminate the fears of humanity by making sure they were never felt. He was going to control people by emptying them out. He had a plan to rule the world.

And he was actually most of the way there.

There was genius to his plan. There was even, in a twisted way, compassion. Because the people nominally in charge, in Washington and Geneva and Silicon Valley and other such important places, didn't have the will or the tools to address the world's wounds and instead ignored them or blundered around in them like old-timey surgeons with rusty scalpels, making them worse, making them gangrenous, septic. And I could feel—anyone could feel—how battered people were by the rising apocalyptic tide, how deeply they wanted to just go to sleep and wake up in a better place. They just wanted a lie-down.

The CEO was giving them that. He was giving people a way to lie down. To get through the coming hard years. To get through the terror, all the way to the end of their lives. To sleepwalk to the grave.

He took a handkerchief out of a pocket and wiped his face. "You said you were worried for the world, Wallace? Then let's save it. You're worried for your friends? Save them. It will not be easy. But we can do it. Together."

He held out his hand for a shake. My own hands tightly gripped the edge of a table to stay upright.

"No. I'm out," I said.

The CEO closed his hand in a fist. "You're still misunderstanding me."

"No, I get it. And my answer is no."

It had been fast—ask me a couple of weeks ago, and I would have said sure, why not. But everything had changed since I had arrived in North Homer. I had woken up. All of us—Megan Rose, Stuart, Brad, who knows who else . . . We had woken up. We couldn't sleepwalk anymore. The night people were making sure of it. The future, that future of being awake, was dangerous and uncertain, and it would require that we bear witness for Mother Earth as she burned, as her pain got worse and worse—but it was alive.

I had seen it at the glade, I had seen it in the trees, I had felt it in every cell. Alive. Bright and shining.

So, no, I didn't want to be a part of the future the CEO made.

And I didn't want power or wealth or anything else that he could offer.

And if I couldn't stop him, I could tell him to go to hell.

And when he reacted as I expected, I could wait for him there.

"You're insane," I said. "On levels you don't even realize. Killing the soul of the world to save it? I would never work for you in a thousand lifetimes."

The tremor throbbed under the CEO's eye. "Never speak to me that way again."

"Are you going to kill me? I got nothing to lose. Go for it."

"Your girlfriend, Megan Rose?"

I blanched. "She's not my . . . What about her?"

"Impressive young lady. Such ability, character, goals. Princeton is a fine school. I should know. I donated an Olympic-size pool to the athletic center a few years ago. I can make sure she gets in."

"She doesn't care about that anymore."

"*Tsk.* Throwing away one's future for patchouli. Do understand that her father has seen the error of his ways and has put her under the care of my physicians. Why, tomorrow morning they will determine the next stage of her healing regimen. Perhaps a surgical intervention is needed."

"You wouldn't."

"It's a complicated case. Hysterics is a nebulous psychological condition. Some say it doesn't exist. Some say there is no cure. Dissension gives physicians a lot of leeway. What path will Megan Rose's healing take?"

"You can't do that," I said.

"Will the poor girl need to be institutionalized . . . operated on?"

"You can't do that," I said again.

"Your choice decides what happens."

"You can't."

That's all I could get out.

The CEO shook out his sleeves and straightened his tie. "What do you want to do, Wallace? I had hoped that if I presented the illusion of choice, this would be easier, but yes, as you can see, your future's already been decided."

I was a beaten street dog, cowering under a truck. He put a hand on my shoulder, turning me toward the door.

"Don't be so sad," he said. "The town's calm. The children are no longer afraid. The parents are all getting generous Christmas bonuses." He squeezed. Hard. "We all end up different from the person we planned to be. We all make sacrifices for the ones we love. Just like your father. And your mother, too."

THIRTY-ONE

WE DROVE IN silence for a while. Late afternoon, a seasonal chill at last, the fields that brisk-fall lonesome, trees huddling, clouds a dead gray like they'd overdosed. We stopped at a Subway and Dad grabbed two turkey subs, two bags of chips, two hot coffees. He drank his coffee like he was testing his pain tolerance. There was a clean shirt and jeans in the truck, and I changed into them. Unfamiliar roads—we were headed to the airport, I guessed. Minnesota. Cold there. Lakes. Hockey. People who said "ya." He pulled over at a parking area, a sad place with a picnic table and a kids' play area that contained in its entirety a seesaw and a slide.

He put his hat on the dash and started to eat. I did, too. I was starved.

And sore. I'd never been so sore. Raw, chafed legs from swimming in the lake in jeans. Scratches up and down my arms from creeping through the woods at night. Blisters from wet socks. Older throbs in the ribs and shoulders from philosophical debates at keg parties. A twisted ankle from I'm not sure where. An ache in my head like it had been squeezed in a vise.

And angry. I'd never been so angry.

And sad. And shocked.

I had all the feelings, I'd inhaled them all.

It had been intended. Deep energies had been stimulated so they could be fed to a furnace, and all the North Homer chaos and suffering, the PTA brawling, the ambulances at lunch, the curfews, and the drug regimens—all of it had been intended.

Why? To power lightbulbs. Why? To save the world with a new energy source.

Actually, no. That's not why. The real why? So we would become pliant sheep.

And if, in that process of stimulation, Megan Rose and Stuart and I and even Brad Stone and who knows who else happened to uncover shining inner parts of ourselves . . . well, tough shit. That's all gone now. Forever.

But hey—I could have money! So much money! I could buy stuff! Pimple cream! Buttered coffee! Fish egg sushi! Organic cotton sweaters! They come in colors like plum and tangerine!

And if that wasn't enough? If there was somehow still a feeling that there was more to life? Well, then: here's a football game. Here's Tom Cruise running hard. Here's six beautiful women in a hot-air balloon fighting over a rose.

And that was it. Shop. Watch. Like. Share. Day after day. Day after day after day. Day after day. Day after day. Day after day after day.

What was that word the CEO had for all this? For the world to come?

Oh, yeah.

Peace.

Dad finished his sandwich and turned to me for the first time since we'd gotten in the truck. The ball cap had made a crease right across the center of his forehead, above which his skin was milky white, the white you only see in lifelong farmers or unwanted Tinder photos. He looked as ridiculous as I felt.

"You ready for your flight?" he asked.

"I'm not going," I said. "I'm not going to work for that psychopath."

"I held Hoch off for as long as I could," he said. "Years. It gets a lot harder when you show up at his fence."

"I was trying to get him to stop. Dad, he's lying. It's all a lie. It's not about clean energy."

"I know exactly what it's about."

This next part I yelled. *"Then how could you? How the fuck could you?"*

Before he could answer, an image: Megan Rose in a padded room, belted to a cold bed, a white gown pulled tight over her body, pale, undefended legs sticking out, doctors checking the incision scar on her shaved scalp, nurses with brick-hard faces sticking needles under her skin.

"Goddamn it."

"I get it, Wallace."

"He'll hurt her. He'll hurt her if I don't go. He'll kill her."

"Then go. Just go. Get on the plane."

He lit a cigarette. He cranked down the window. Cold air came in. His hands were opening and closing in that agitated way that had started at the power plant. My own hands wanted to punch the future in the face, but how could they do that? They shook in my lap.

"If we don't continue this program, the world is screwed," he said. "It already is screwed, actually. It's screwed for the next fifty years, minimum; the next thousand, more likely. This is the one chance to unscrew it."

"You sound exactly like Hoch. Why is it that the solutions rich old men have for the world's problems always require immeasurable sacrifices from young people?"

"What would you do? Watch the world burn?"

"Fix it! We'll fix it! Get out of the way and let us have a shot!"

Dad shook his head. "No. I used to believe that once. That every generation deserves its chance. But I don't anymore. Every generation blows it. Every generation is born in hope and dies in greed and adds to the floating garbage patch. Civilization is the record of their failures—and it's a perfect unbroken streak."

Now my hands wanted to punch civilization. "You're wrong," I said. "We're different from you. Growing up with a dying world, we're connected in ways you can't understand. We can feel what you can't."

"It doesn't matter. It's hardwired in human nature to put our own stomachs before the fate of the planet."

"Dad, the plant eats souls."

"Life does! It chews them up. And that word, would you stop with that . . ."

He trailed off, rubbing his face. Put his cap back on. Turned to the window.

"Can you answer one thing honestly for me?" I said. "Just one?"

He nodded, noncommittally.

"What about Ma? I don't get it. I have these memories, and she's one thing. I see her in these visions in the woods, and she's another thing. And Hoch says she's something else. And you never tell me a damn thing."

"We don't have time for this."

"Please. Who was she?"

"Wallace."

"Please."

Dad checked his watch, sighed, took his cap back off and put it on the dash.

"Your mother developed the quantum technology," he said. "It was her life's work. She and her team spent ten years refining it, testing it at plant after plant around the country. It was hard work, such a subtle thing they were going for, and the side effects were so unpredictable. I was a nobody standing behind them, writing down test numbers, tightening screws, and replacing fuses. Valued for doing what I was told and keeping my mouth shut. I was always good at doing what I was told. And then later, valued when I could interact with the energies without breaking down. And I don't know why your mother fell in love with me, but she did. Fourteen years and seven months we were together, and I never quite figured that out. She said things so intelligent it was like a different language. Hell, I never know quite what to say, so I often don't say anything. People think it's intimidating, and I go with that."

"You do come off strong," I agreed.

"You should try it sometime. Talking less."

"So I can be more like you?"

He bowed his head. He'd walked into that.

But hold up: My father, a lowly foot soldier? My mother, the coauthor of this insane story?

"Ma really developed this?" I said.

"A big part of it. Did you ever ask her what she did?"

I hadn't. It had never occurred to me.

"Right," he said.

"Hey, I was ten."

"She was the most brilliant woman I ever met," Dad continued. "Not just brilliant. The best woman I ever met. The best. Have you seen those maps of how global temperature is changing? How blue is cold and red is hot? Except now scientists are out of shades of red to depict overheating, so they use brown. Too much heat for their charts. The Arctic looks like it's wearing a coonskin hat. Your mother knew. That was all she thought about. And she knew that humanity was just too stupid, too shortsighted and selfish, to do anything about it. I hope you see this someday, Wallace! She knew the oil and coal billionaires would never admit their crimes if it cost them more than a dollar. Most people would have given up then and there and figured out how to make a buck. I would have. I did give up, actually, every damn morning. But I never told her. I just followed behind her and believed again.

"And when she got that cancer all of a sudden and died despite Hoch taking over her care, I didn't see the point of continuing. Forget about continuing to work on the project, I mean continuing to live. It hurt too much. At night, after you fell asleep, I would sit here in this truck"—he rubbed the seat—"and think of ways to kill myself. But then Hoch said he had a way forward for me. A way Claire herself had created. A way that could be world-saving. And I took it. I was the first."

He looked over at me. His eyes were rimmed in red, as if tears or smoke had gotten into them, yet still they were as blank as always. Blank dark stones.

And suddenly I understood.

"You're dead inside," I said.

"Not quite how I'd phrase it."

"This isn't about humanity's future. This isn't about saving the world or my generation's greed. You wanted to be dead! You didn't want your soul, so you gave it to Hoch!"

"I couldn't live without her!"

"What about me? Did that enter into the equation at all?"

"That's why I did it! So I wouldn't leave you! I was so afraid I'd leave you!"

"But you did leave me," I said.

A plane banked over us, low and getting lower, seething like a vengeful God. Dad banged open his door and pushed himself out of the truck. He walked away, ending up in the play pit, standing next to the plastic slide.

Who was he?

For so long I had thought his reticence was cool, enviable manhood of the Special Forces, night-goggles, *Mission Impossible* kind or the Clint Eastwood kind—the younger version, before he started talking to empty chairs. I had tried to be like him, past fear and caring.

But it wasn't being cool—it was that he was barely there.

My father was emptied out. My father was a blank space smoking a cigarette.

The sky was darkening rapidly now. Sometimes evening feels final, the beginning of a new forever, like the sun isn't going over to check on China but is sneaking off to Andromeda for good. This evening felt like that.

I got out of the truck. Dad heard me, checked his watch.

"I'm sorry," he said. "But we're out of time. Get back in."

"I can't do that."

"I'm not asking you to agree with my decisions."

"Good, because I don't."

"I know you hate me. But please get in the truck, Wallace."

"I don't hate you," I said.

"It's okay. I would. I would hate me."

"Okay. You could have been a little more honest. A little more . . . here."

He turned to me, raised his hands. "Your mother was my life. I'm honoring her memory in my work for Hoch. I'm taking her project, her world-saving project, all the way to the end."

"Wrong," I said. "This is not what Ma wants."

"How would you know what she wants?"

"She showed me."

"That was a hallucination. Wallace—"

"She showed me in the woods that I'm okay. Just as I am. That what's inside me is good. Bright. That I'm loved. Worthy of love. And that's what matters. More than anything."

"Wallace, that's what every parent—"

"She's gone."

Dad turned and lifted his head to the sky. He stood like that for a minute, his dead eyes going someplace even further away.

He turned back. "Okay, I see it," he said. "It's changed you. It's good. I like it. I'm happy for you. Wallace, I never wanted you to have my life. That's why I tried to keep you away. To keep you in the dark. But it's over. What do you even want to do? Hoch's going national. There's no way to stop him."

"I don't need to stop him," I said. "I just need to do one thing."

"To do what?"

I told him.

He studied my face, deciding something: whether he agreed with what I said or thought we were past agreement, or maybe if the difference even mattered anymore.

"The plant's not the place for that," he said.

"It's not?"

"Get in the truck."

This time I did.

*　*　*

It was dark now. Dad drove fast, taking hard turns that slammed me into the door frame. In fifteen minutes we reached North Homer. Still no cars; curfew must have been ongoing. Meanwhile, Hoch was waiting on a runway to fly me to Minnesota. He expected me to come because he knew my weak spot. He expected my father to deliver me, because he knew how much my father had surrendered. He knew my father did what he was told. And he knew that society, as presently constructed, did whatever he asked and then gave him a tax refund.

But he didn't know everything.

"You're Claire's son," Dad said. "Stubborn as hell. Strong when the odds are stacked against you. Stronger than I ever was. But do you understand how strong Hoch is?" We'd zoomed through the flats of town and were heading uphill. "He's got support in powerful places— No, Hoch *is* the powerful places, and he will come after you with all he can bring to bear."

"I'll run."

"Where would you go?"

"I'll retrace our steps. Kentucky, New Mexico, other places . . . let people know what Jackduke did to them."

"You think they'll support you if you do? Or him?"

I didn't know, to be honest. I knew that billionaires created their own reality, with news channels to back it up. I knew that most people were already pretty checked out.

But I knew what was necessary for me. I was going to start there.

Dad held up his phone. "Four calls. Every police officer in the county will be looking for you soon."

"What about you? You'll go to Minnesota?"

"No."

"Where, then? Which plant?"

He braked the truck to a hard stop, put it in park. "None. I'm finished. I've seen too much. Given away too much. There's too much blood on my hands. Whatever the new world looks like—your vision or Hoch's—I'm not going to be a part of it."

"Dad, that sounds really—"

He pointed across the road. "There," he said.

We were parked on a road with few houses, under a giant maple tree that reached over the road to the other side. The forest crowded right up to the pavement. It was like we had driven into Middle Earth. I recognized it—it was the street behind Megan Rose's house-brick. Up the hill next to it was the glade.

"You knew?" I said.

"That you were out in these woods? Sure. You've always been an open book, Wallace. But more than that, you learn to feel the world. Its soft and hard places. Where it opens. You get a sense." He nodded to the hill. "That's a special place up there." He nodded to me. "You sure about this?"

"Yes."

"You know how you'll do it?"

"Not exactly."

"But you'll do it?"

"Yeah."

"Then go," Dad said.

He pointed to my door handle, and I watched my arm reach

and pull it. Then he awkwardly put his hand out for a shake and we shook hands, up and down, up and down.

Fitting: we had spent our whole lives going right past each other or away from each other, never to each other, never with each other; and now, when we were finally on the same page, we were never going to see each other again.

"Do me a favor?" he said. "Whatever happens, don't make me the villain of your life. I was trying to do what I thought was right for you."

"That what you call it?" I said. And then, "Okay."

"Appearances to the contrary, I'm proud of you."

"Thank you."

"And your mom would have been proud of you."

"I know. I spoke to her."

"Right, yeah. Okay. See you, Wallace."

I opened the door to step out, then pulled it shut.

"Actually," I said. "Could we pick up a couple people?"

THIRTY-TWO

WE ENTERED THE trail-less woods and started up the hill. We moved fast through the dark, cruising around trees and bushes that felt dry and listless, even though there had been plenty of rain. Stuart had grabbed us a couple of sweatshirts before leaving his basement and also a flashlight, which helped quite a bit.

A gunshot went off. We dove to the ground. I reached over and turned off the flashlight, put a finger to my lips. "Is it hunting season?" I asked.

Stuart nodded, wide-eyed. "Started today."

Perfect. "So, explain again why she isn't here," I whispered, after a minute.

"She said she had to do something first."

"Stuart. What could be more important than this?"

"Wallace. I didn't ask! You said we were in a hurry."

"Because the CEO is going to kidnap her!"

"I didn't know that!"

"Shh!" We'd gotten loud.

After tossing the sweatshirts in the truck, Stuart had run across the street to get Megan Rose, because I knew her father wasn't keen on me. It was a good call—Mr. Rose had answered the door holding a shotgun. When Megan Rose came out and shooed her father inside, Stuart had passed along that we were going to go to the glade.

And she had told Stuart she had to do something first.

"You should have told me that," Stuart said. "The kidnapping part."

Good start. Good start.

We hiked to the top of the ridge, walked back and forth until we heard water flowing, located the stream curling down the other side, and, after another five minutes' walking, were at the entrance to the glade.

It had changed. No insects chirped. No birds sang. The tall grass and goldenrod had turned to straw since I'd been there last; the old willow looked sick and brittle. It was like we'd walked into a photograph called *Too Late*. It was cold, too, easily the coldest night since I'd arrived in North Homer.

"This is the place?" Stuart asked.

I nodded, avoiding his disbelief.

"Should we wait for Megan Rose?"

I checked the way we had come. "No. Who knows if she'll make it. Or how much time we have before the police get here."

"The police are coming?"

"Sooner or later."

"You sure? They let me go last night. Chief caught me down by the lake with the mean-ass dog, threw me in the back-seat for ten minutes, and then straight-up let me go. No charges or anything. Why would he do that?"

I saw Hoch adjusting his cufflinks and his tie, sipping forty-year-old scotch.

"They think it's over," I said.

"Is it?"

I didn't answer. I stepped into the glade and walked up to the old willow. The poor tree looked like a pile of dead branches stacked for a bonfire; every branch hung straight down and immobile. I whispered a greeting. No response. Said it louder. Nothing.

I jammed my hands in my pockets and started walking around it.

From the entrance to the glade, Stuart watched me circling; then he tightened his sweatshirt hood over his head so only his eyes were visible, and walked down the slope.

We walked, single file, Stuart a few steps behind me. And though they'd been proficient at it since I was ten or eleven months old, though I had walked in a circle in this very spot just a week earlier, though this was my idea—despite all that, my feet struggled mightily with the activity of lifting themselves up and putting themselves down. My mind raced. The ground heaved. Once I even fell.

"It *is* over, isn't it?" said Stuart. He was scared. "They're gone forever, aren't they? Is this even going to work without Jackduke's weird technology?"

I didn't know. "It'll work," I said.

The clouds thinned slowly, then all at once, and the full moon appeared in the suddenly clear sky. Was this going to work? I counted the ways things could go wrong. There were so many, I lost track. So I ranked them, the ways of wrong-going, the worst of which literally and permanently took my breath away and also took Megan Rose's frontal lobe.

Shit. Where was she?

A siren called out. I fell again. Nothing was happening.

And that's when my brain dove into the darkest place it had ever been.

I mean, no exaggeration. Those new shades of black, the ones they've been developing in labs that are so black they seem like portals to other universes? This made them look like Oompa Loompa lollipops. This was my life itself drowning in an oozing, toxic oil puddle, my own hands on its throat, choking it, pushing it under.

"Wallace?" croaked Stuart.

"Yes?" It took incredible effort to speak.

"I've gone from doubting this will work to doubting if I should be alive."

"You, too?" That's when I got it. "It's the Mega D."

"What? What is that?"

I hadn't known until that moment. Remove all spirit energy and of course you're plunged into complete car-crashing darkness. Hoch thought that killing energies off made everyone numb and pliant, a gift card away from contentment? Wrong. What the hell was he doing to the world?

And how many times had this happened to me?

"Darkness," I said to Stuart. "Mega D is darkness. Don't give in."

Stuart collapsed to the ground and curled himself into a ball, knees tucked up to his chest. "I kind of want to give in," he whimpered.

Mega D backed up and slammed into us again. It chased down our hope and ground it under the wheels. Then it did it again. Again. More sirens called out. There was a rustling sound; I looked over, and the entrance to the glade had filled with dark, sinister shapes.

No. I pulled Stuart out of the fetal position and lay down on top of him in the tall grass. The police stepped into the glade, one at a time. They moved closer, measuring their strides.

But it wasn't the police. They were too small, and their shadows lacked the menacing silhouettes of peacekeeping accessories. And striding in front of them, slender and ruler-straight, in her ninja black sweats and headband, was none other than Megan Rose.

She walked right up to us: Stuart lying on his stomach, whimpering, me lying on top of him.

"Am I interrupting a private moment?" she asked.

Stuart looked up. "Oh, thank God. It was Mega D. It came so hard and deep."

Megan Rose looked very bewildered. I stood quickly.

"Okay . . . ," she said doubtfully.

Relief washed over me. We weren't caught. "Megan Rose. It's so good to see you. It was scary not knowing if you were safe."

"Yes." She crossed her arms. "Imagine how I feel when you disappear into power plants."

"I'm sorry."

"And keep secrets."

"I know, I'm sorry. I'm not used to people caring about me."

"You're an idiot," she said.

"Mega D," moaned Stuart. "I don't like it. I don't like it."

"I brought help." Megan Rose gestured over her shoulder to the people who'd come with her. "I thought things over last night and realized that if the spirit energy can be shared, like we did at the PTA meeting, then the more there are of us, the more powerful the energy will be. All of us, working together, will have a better shot at bringing the night people back. Maybe it will even help others to see them."

There were six newcomers, all girls. I recognized Keely and others from the party, ones who had gang-tackled Megan Rose when she threw her tank top away. Without even trying, I remembered Megan Rose without her tank top.

"Brilliant idea," I said. "It's just that"—I pulled her a few steps away from the others, lowered my voice—"you're in more danger than anyone. Hoch is going to use you as collateral."

"Collateral for what?" said Megan Rose, eyebrows arched.

"For me to work for them."

"You mentioned that. What do they want you to do?"

"They want me to guide spirits to the plant."

She curled her lip, her features getting that warlock look.

"I'm not doing it," I averred. "I can't. Ever. But Hoch threatened to do some bad things to you if I don't."

"Fuck him," Megan Rose said.

"The police work for him. Everyone does."

"Fuck everyone, then."

How could anyone resist such conviction! Her eyes were two fierce diamonds, ethically mined.

"We've got a lot to do," I said to Megan Rose. "But if it's okay, I'd like to kiss you."

She nodded. "We've got a lot to do."

The Sen energy technology had opened the door to a deeper world. Spirit energies had come pouring out of that door, and Jackduke had captured them and fed them to their machines. In a few short weeks, North Homer High School had gone from normal to Burning Man to zombie graveyard.

Hoch was intending to do this all over the country.

But the door was still open.

It *was* open, wasn't it? No one had closed it. We could go inside. We could convince the night people to come back.

Of course, there wasn't *really* a door.

Megan Rose's friends all looked terrified and tired, like old people watching the news. She gathered them close. She touched each of them, one at a time, saying their names.

"It's just us," she said. "Just us, alone at the dark edge. We've all felt it, what they've taken. You trusted me enough to come here. Thank you for that. It means you care. They expect we don't. Or that we're too scared to. They screwed up and then told us we're the ones who are screwed up. That we're hysterical. But we're not. And we're not scared. And what they took . . . This is the place where we get it back."

"How?" Keely asked.

"We wait for it," said Megan Rose. "Keep your eyes and heart open and be as quiet as you can. And pay attention."

"Pay attention to what?" Keely asked.

Megan Rose didn't answer. She looked to me. "The forest," I said. "The sky. What's inside you."

"And then what?"

"Magic," I said.

Keely glared at me like this was a terrible idea and completely my fault. I nodded at her, trying to convey that it was exactly right. She had other questions, but then Stuart made a strangled cry and took off running toward the entrance of the glade. Someone was there. Melvin. Melvin was back.

They met in a deep hug and kissed hard.

"Oh," I said.

From town, a sudden howl of sirens, wolves on the hunt. A dark sphere burst in the sky above the ridge—a helicopter. Its thumping engine sounded like bloodthirst. Its spotlight aggressively snarled through the trees. We all dove to the ground.

"If you want to leave, this is your chance," said Megan Rose.

No one left.

The helicopter moved on, my heart picking up the beat it had put down.

Everyone looked at me. Now what?

I brushed myself off and resumed walking around the tree. Megan Rose's friends watched for a minute, lifted themselves up. Some walked, some sat, some went off to the edges of the glade, some stayed close, one in a far corner either heroically relieved herself or did an extended squatting yoga pose.

Megan Rose came beside me. I extended an arm in invitation, and she fell into step. We walked close together for a while and my heart was thumping still.

"It was during a practice test," she said. "The first time. Ten o'clock at night, I was bombing yet another one, and a voice said to come here. I hadn't been out to this place in years. And when I got here and Susie toddled toward me, I thought I'd lost my mind for sure. God . . ." She rubbed her face with the back of her wrist. "Did you see her at the plant? On that line? How lonely she looked?"

"I saw."

"I want her back. I don't want to go back to what I was. I'd rather die."

Megan Rose: spirit like iron, cheeks glimmering in the starlit air. How I wish we had more time.

"I hope it doesn't come to that," I said.

"One thing I don't get," she said. "Why are we so dangerous?

If this works and the night people return, wouldn't we be making more energy for Jackduke? More fuel for their machines? Shouldn't they be happy about that? We'd be the ultimate renewable resource."

"It's not about energy," I said.

"How is it not about energy?"

"Hoch doesn't care about energy."

The thing about getting the answers to lifelong mysteries, I'd been finding out, is quite often they sucked.

"It's about control," I explained. "When Sen energy is used up, people do what they're told. And when people do what they're told, Lawrence Hoch can rule the world."

"But everyone will be empty inside. They'll be mindless zombies."

"Exactly."

"No," Megan Rose said. "No way. He won't get away with it. No one will let that happen. People will rise up and fight."

"He's rolling out the technology in seven states tomorrow."

Her head fell. She dropped into her deep space, falling down, down into the darkness, and I took hold of her shoulders, whispering her name over and over, until she came back to me.

Round and round we walked.

Wind: faint. Branches: creaking. Sirens: sirening. A hooting owl.

Was that a hum? The hum of them coming closer?

Or that? Was that it?

Was that?

Round and round and round.

Mr. Willow? You there?

Ma?

Anybody?

"Well, this is a surprise. Newb had a stupid idea, and everyone's miserable."

I spun around. Brad Stone stood with his legs wide, arms crossed over a shiny skintight long-sleeve, biceps and triceps and lower lip bulging. He looked from me to Megan Rose. Ten feet away, Stuart, standing next to Melvin, had already grabbed his shoulders so they wouldn't get hit.

"Brad. This isn't the time and place," said Megan Rose.

"I think you're right," he said. "It's four in the morning. Every cop in town is looking for you. And you're doing *Mulan* cosplay?"

"It's not *Mulan*," said Megan Rose.

"Joan Wick?"

"Hey. The little boy gone?" I asked him.

"Yeah."

"Last night?"

Brad nodded. "When I was at the police station, actually. For helping your dumb ass. He was everywhere before that." His dip-filled lip twitched. "I should be happy he's gone, right? I should be thrilled to get back to kicking ass without worrying that I'm kicking my own ass. But I'm not. Your fault, newb."

"How's it my fault?"

"Because your ma—"

"No. No more of that."

Brad Stone waved at the glade. "All right. All right. Explain what we're doing."

I explained how we were holding a calm space for the night people to return. He glanced around, taking in the worn-out willow, Megan Rose and Stuart and Melvin and the others, all of them shaking with cold and exhaustion and bumbling around random corners of the glade like trapped video game characters.

"So, how's that going?" he asked.

"Poorly," I admitted. "It's scary, slow. You have to be so patient, and fear gets in the way. There's so much fear. I'm scared. I'm really, really scared. I'm—" Megan Rose touched my shoulder. I took a breath. "I'm trying to be patient with the fear. The trees feel that patience, I think. That kindness. And then, it's like a door opens. Your heart opens. And you find yourself suddenly unbound, dreaming into being all the love you never received."

Brad stared at me. So did everyone else.

After a minute, I started walking again.

Round and round.

More sirens. Mega D, never that far off, crept back in and tapped my shoulder. *Too late,* it whispered. *Nice speech, but they're all gone forever. The only thing left is to learn how badly you fooled yourself.*

Breathe. Breathe.

One girl burst into tears. Two others, blinded by fatigue, walked right into each other. No one else made a sound, save for Brad Stone, who grunted softly, doing sit-ups and burpees. He always worked out at this time, he said.

Round and round.

A squirrel scurried out from behind the willow. It nervously eyed the shambling figures in the glade.

I stopped short. Paranoid squirrel! Could that mean . . . ?

"Please," I said to it. "Can you tell the old willow we're here?"

It turned and disappeared into the shadows.

"No! Wait!"

Light cracked the edge of the sky.

Dawn? Really? Had the whole night passed, with nothing to show for it?

"I felt something," said Megan Rose.

I'd felt something, too. I'd seen something. Or had I?

A dog barked on the ridge.

"Uh-oh," said Stuart. "I know that bark. I hate that dog. We got to split."

"We can't," I said. "This is our one shot. Hoch will make sure there's never another."

"Why hasn't anything happened? We've been here for hours!"

"I don't know."

"I really hate that dog!"

"Faith, Stuart," said Megan Rose.

Quietly, as he did all things, Melvin placed an elaborately tattooed hand on Stuart's shoulder.

The dog barked again.

Brad stepped over, sweating from a push-up workout.

"Couldn't help overhearing your predicament," he said. "I can buy you some time. The police love my work. My cousin's the deputy. We lift together, though he skips leg day. But are you sure they're coming?"

"They're coming," said Megan Rose. "I felt them."

"Newb?"

I wasn't as confident as Megan Rose. "I think I saw their squirrel."

Brad grunted. "Well, then."

Without another word he charged across the glade and plunged into the woods, directly toward the barking.

Stuart looked at me. "The hell did you do to him?"

"Nothing. He's an interesting guy." I held up a hand. "Listen."

We listened.

I felt it inside my body. Something vibrating. Buzzing. My ribs? My heart? No, the air—the air was vibrating.

Or no, not a vibration. A noise. A hum. Growing louder.

"Anyone else feel that?" I said.

"Holy shit," said Stuart.

"Told you," said Megan Rose.

"They're close," I said.

The helicopter burst into the sky directly above the glade. It banked around, pounding us with wind and noise. A spotlight blasted straight down.

"Holy shit!" Stuart yelled.

"Any second," I said.

"Where? I don't see anything!"

The powerful spotlight pinned Stuart, Melvin, Megan Rose,

and me like dead insects. Dry grass and leaves whipped around our faces. The other students ran under the willow. Then we heard the bullhorn.

"This is. Chief Turnblad! Of the police! We have you. Surrounded! Wallace Cole!"

Goddamn it. "Chief! I need a minute!"

"Give yourself up. If you want to survive! And everyone else. Can. Go home! Tarnation. I will show. No mercy!"

No choice—I took a couple of shaky steps toward the bullhorn. The helicopter spotlight followed me. Megan Rose grabbed my hand.

"Don't," she said.

"I'll stall him. Go under the willow with the others. Wait as long as you can. Then run."

"No."

"Wallace! Your father. Can't save you. Ever again!"

"I'm coming!" I yelled back.

"No!"

"Put your hands up! Hands up!"

"They're up!"

"Negatory! Suck my dangly balls!"

Brad Stone came charging into the glade, shot the chief a double bird with full-arm extension, looked up, gave the helicopter the same triumphant gesture, continued running. He was naked again, save for his socks and shoes. The helicopter lowered its nose and pursued him into the trees.

Megan Rose, Stuart, Melvin, and I ran under the willow, crashing into the others hiding there.

"Why's he naked?" screamed Stuart.

"I don't know!"

"What did you do to him?"

"I didn't do anything! You already asked me that!"

"No! No! Back! Here!" Chief Turnblad was yelling at the sky.

"What do we do?!"

"Everyone hold on!" yelled Megan Rose. "Don't let go! We've got to hold on to each other!"

We held on to each other against the willow, breathless, tight as bark. We were crying, but we couldn't wipe the tears. I closed my eyes. Breathed.

Breathed.

Breathed.

Wind. Thunder. Tears running down faces. Pulses pounding through skin.

Hearts. Hearts beating. Hearts breaking.

Light. Light coming out of the break.

"Look!" yelled Megan Rose.

I opened my eyes: small glimmering lights drifted in the air around us like falling snow.

"Big mistake, Wallace!" Gun drawn, the chief strode out of the woods.

"Hold tight!" yelled Megan Rose. "Don't move!"

"Weapons up! Batons up!" yelled Chief Turnblad. "Assume hostile! Go!"

"Here they come!" said Megan Rose.

"He just said that!" said Stuart.

But Megan Rose wasn't looking at the police. "There."

"Where? What? Oh."

*   *   *

It began with seven blue-and-white pandas floating out of the tall grass. They greeted each other with handshakes and hugs.

Then: a lion the color of water.

A moose with a mane of gold.

A blue horse pawing the air, steam bursting from its nose.

A flock of eagles flapping their wings, silver fireflies pouring from each flap.

A tennis ball walking unsteadily on big feet.

An old lady in a housedress holding a handful of screws. Several older folks, adjusting their suspenders, wiping their glasses, blinking like they'd just emerged from a cave.

A samurai, stretching, rubbing his Fu Manchu, taking stock of the terrain. More samurai behind him, hoisting their swords.

A chubby little boy with a flattop and a runny nose.

A naked green lady, a hundred feet tall.

And then my mother and father, parting branches off a trail so I would not be hurt, each of them holding one of my hands, their eyes astonishingly bright and clear, their smiles as they looked at me as sweet as spring.

Chief Turnblad pointed at me, and his lips moved fiercely, but he didn't make a sound. That I could hear. The police advanced slowly, in a practiced formation, clubs and pistols drawn. But the students under the willow didn't care about the police. They weren't even looking at them. They'd moved clear of the willow and now stared at the sky. Their complete lack of interest confused the advancing officers, and they stopped where they were.

I stepped out from under the willow branches to meet Chief Turnblad.

He nodded to me: at last. He raised his revolver up in two hands, cradling it like a full cup of water, tilting his head to the side, so that he could more comfortably take aim at my face.

"It's over, Wallace," he said. "And you lost."

"No, Chief," I said. "It's just started."

In the sky above us, the night people gathered and balls of light skipped through slow-motion fireworks the color of rivers and fall. And the night people were bowing and smiling in a way that said, This, *this* is what we were trying to tell you, this alone. You and we and the light are the same, and in our embrace the shattered world heals—do you see it? Do you see what's possible now?

I saw.

Then the light parted like a curtain, and Megan Rose was next to me. And she took my head and turned it toward her and kissed me.

And it was everything.

Deputy Sloane grabbed the chief's arm and pointed to the sky. Chief Turnblad lowered his gun, staring. All the police stood motionless, mouths agape, arms slack against their sides, the rules ripped up and thrown away.

Someone was pulling on my hand. Megan Rose. "Come on." She pulled me toward the woods. "Wallace! Let's go!"

Stuart and Melvin were ahead of her, standing in the stream at the entrance to the glade.

I looked up one last time.

In the air above the willow tree, all the night people gathered together with the flakes and balls and jewels of light. The gathering began to swirl. The swirl raced faster and faster, merging, expanding, growing stronger, growing louder, starting to roar.

Then it stopped.

ACKNOWLEDGMENTS

This book would not exist without Dante Paradiso, who read every draft and would not let me stop. Thank you, Dante.

Thank you to my parents who, generous and alive, are nothing like the parents in this book.

Thank you to Ari, Zev, and Sam, my brothers, who inspire me. Thank you, Martha and Mari.

Thank you to the Tompkins County Public Library, and all public libraries.

Thank you to deafness, which taught me resilience.

Chris Boerboom, Glenn Burney, Mark Costa, Matthew Davis, Cameron Garberoglio, and Jeffrey Janger all read drafts, sometimes multiple drafts, and gave me invaluable feedback. Leslie Daniels read drafts and did so much more. Tatiana Maxwell, John Bailey, Shannon Dailey, and David Mulveny also provided deep support. Thank you.

Jim McCarthy, agent extraordinaire, understood the book immediately—even after I put another agent's name on my query email. With reassurance and insight, he worked and worked and found it a home. Karen Greenberg, my remarkable editor, is compassionate, discerning, and flat-out brilliant.

And my boys, Josiah and Asa, this is for you. Please wash your hands. And, Leah, with whom all things are possible, thank you for going to the woods with me.

This book was started in a different era that now seems impossibly distant. But the truth remains the same. Never give up. Honor your light and the world's light. Hold space for grace. My hope is that, in some small way, this book might assist in that. Thank you for reading.